I0663245

Duke of Her Dreams

Olivia Ritch

Published by
Satin Romance
An Imprint of Melange Books, LLC
White Bear Lake, MN 55110
www.satinromance.com

Duke of Her Dreams ~ Copyright © 2011-2016 by Olivia Ritch

978-1-68046-266-1

Names, characters, and incidents depicted in this book are products of the author's imagination or are used fictitiously. Any resemblance to actual events, locales, organizations, or persons, living or dead, is entirely coincidental and beyond the intent of the author or the publisher. No part of this book may be reproduced or transmitted in any form or by any means, electronic or mechanical, including photocopying, recording, or by any information storage and retrieval system, without permission in writing from the publisher.
Published in the United States of America.

Cover Art by Caroline Andrus

Wishing you all your heart's desire.

Chapter One

May 11, 2010

She held an oil painting that had power over dreams, over place and time, but Kathryn Ragland knew nothing of that magic as she dozed off to sleep and to dream of the fascinating images on the canvas.

Wilton, Herefordshire
May 12, 1816
Dawn

Kathryn woke with a start. There was something seriously wrong this morning. It should have been like any other workday. Instead, Kathryn blinked her eyes at the morning light streaming in the lace-covered window and whipped her gaze around the unfamiliar room, registering the conclusion that she was not where she belonged. Surely, she was still dreaming.

Mid-morning

Hours after waking up in a strange bed Kathryn Ragland was still at a loss to understand what had happened to her. Having wracked her brains since dawn for any recollection of what transpired in the night and where she was, Kathryn realized fully that the most bizarre event had occurred and that she was somehow, some way, transported back in time.

After hours of pacing, Kathryn plopped onto the bed, kicked the side rail and let out a frustrated growl. She looked up to find a very large man standing in the doorway of her room.

Surprised, and embarrassed to be dressed so scantily, Kathryn hastily drew the quilt from the bed around her and scrambled to her feet. Not knowing anything about where she was or who *he* was, she asked, "How did you get in?"

"Your door was unlocked and I heard your distress. I apologize for intruding."

Relaxing slightly, Kathryn eyed him warily. The man was her first contact in this strange place and while she did not especially want to divulge the extent of her confusion to him, she was oddly relieved to have another human being with whom to talk. She inquired hopefully, "Is your wife by any chance available? I need a little help."

With an unreadable expression on his face, the man inquired, "My wife?"

"Yes, or your…*companion*?"

"Companion?" With subtle emphasis, Kathryn said the word; the man recognized her allusion to a possibly inappropriate traveling companion. Kathryn was used to watching people. Every day, she used her skills of observation to understand the true nature of her female clients. This man was clearly amused by her state and her question although his rigid bearing kept him from seeming too familiar. She would have bet a dollar he was a military man. Straight shoulders, wide stance, hands folded behind his back.

"Yes, is there a *woman* traveling with you?" It seemed a simple enough question to her.

"Ah, now I understand. No, there is no lady with me. May I fetch someone for you?"

She was so quickly intrigued by the military man's surprisingly warm English accent that Kathryn almost lost the thread of the conversation and her purpose. While she had come grudgingly to realize she was far away from home, England was a bit too far for believability.

"*No!* Sorry, I mean, I don't want anybody else to know I'm here."

"Why ever not?"

"Because I'm pretty sure I'm not supposed to be."

The man smiled fully now at her admission, revealing strong white teeth set in mobile lips and a face lightly tanned and roughened by the outdoors. Tiny lines fanned from his eyes and the cleft in his chin was as deep as her grandfather's had been. "Indeed? And a lady will assist you, how?"

"Something has happened to my clothes," *which is true since they're at home* "...and I need a dress."

"A dress? Do you not have the carriage dress you arrived in?" She watched one of his black brows rise in question, absolutely sure she was amusing him now. *Nope, definitely didn't arrive by carriage.* "No. Well, I don't have anything appropriate for daytime."

He studied her for a full minute and Kathryn grew uncomfortable under his gaze, drawing the quilt higher and shifting her feet like a nervous child. Since she had been studying him equally as avidly just moments earlier, Kathryn felt guilty for being annoyed with his perusal, although she had always fancied her own powers of observation to include stealthy evaluation of her subjects. Having spent the last few hours in frustrated contemplation and pacing while simultaneously salivating over the smell of cooking meat from downstairs, Kathryn was not disposed to be patient nor self-flagellating. She hated feeling vulnerable. When the man finally spoke, it was a wry, "Indeed?"

"It's not what you're thinking. I'm not here in a skimpy ball gown."

He raised an eyebrow. "Ah."

Kathryn struggled to hold her temper in the face of the man's one-word answers. Clearly out of her social element and desperate for a way forward, Kathryn reined in her frustration and asked in a calm voice, "Would you please be willing to help me in getting something to wear?"

Kathryn saw the moment he recognized her plight for the very real problem it was and in that instant he softened. She watched the man's lovely dark eyes shift as he scanned the room for her nonexistent luggage and the changes of his expression from exasperation to confusion and finally concern. While the gentleman, because he surely was that in her humble opinion, concentrated, she studied him in greater detail. At first look, his size, his commanding carriage and the sheer maleness of him had made him seem rather forbidding, but there was intelligence and a gentle sense of humor in his personality that Kathryn found surprising.

On even closer conspicuous inspection, his period attire of tight riding pants molded to huge muscular thighs and what she knew to be a riding jacket that was itself stretched over amazingly broad shoulders marked him as a prosperous man from the 1800s. This man, with his deep drawling English accent and regal bearing, was the real, in-the-flesh confirmation of Kathryn's time travel. Her resolve wavered as the enormity of Kathryn's dilemma became clear. She was, she could not even imagine, in another time and place.

"It has been quite a while since I have been dispatched on a woman's errand. I might not be up to the task," he demurred with a rather charming grin.

Kathryn chuckled at the man's attempt to put her at ease, feeling a little better. "Thank you for accepting my challenge."

"Aye, madam. But, so far giving you a chuckle is all the assistance I have rendered." Even while bantering with her, he had not relaxed his rigid stance, the changes of facial expression the only hints of his amusement.

"It definitely would have been helpful if you had had a five-foot tall wife with a spare size four dress to loan me, she said, gesturing to her still as yet not appropriately clothed form.

"Pardon my thick-headedness. Your sayings are quite unfamiliar to me although I believe I understand you well enough."

"Sorry, I guess I'm not exactly speaking King's English and it has been a totally trying day already. I don't mean to be crass. I'm just…a little stressed."

"Based on your circumstances, I would understand your distress." He smiled at her and moved for the first time to lean against the doorjamb. "Where did you say you were from?"

"America."

"Really?" At that, he crossed one booted leg over another.

"Why do you ask that? Surely I don't sound like I'm from around here?"

"I know several Americans and they don't speak…as you do," he answered with hesitation while crossing his arms over his massive chest.

"Doesn't surprise me." She sighed. "I'm from the…" *South and 2010* "Uhh…newer region in the south. We don't get a lot of Boston accents."

"Ah, I think…" he struggled to reply to that strange description of the modern-day American South.

"Don't try too hard to figure it out." She laughed again now at the absurdity of it all and because of course he wouldn't recognize her accent.

Although Kathryn was really not any nearer to a solution for her lack of dress, she was no longer quite as uneasy as she had been since dawn when she had woken up in the quaint but totally foreign little inn. The bizarre cultural exchange with the large gentleman had lightened her mood and eased her stress somewhat. Before Kathryn could form her next question, the man prompted her.

"Now, would it be improper of me to ask how it is you came to be in this predicament?"

Because he'd been an almost perfect gentleman, and was taking her difficult requests in stride, Kathryn decided the truth would be the best answer. "I awoke here." *Accompanied by an odd assortment of stuff including a totally useless portable phone, wristwatch, one diamond stud earring, and a miniature portrait from the 1800s that now seems to figure somehow in this debacle.*

"I gathered that much. I thought to know *how* you got here, conveyance, companions, route? And how it is you are now stranded without proper clothing?"

"That's just it," Kathryn tried to explain. "Truthfully I don't know. I fell asleep in my own bed in America last night. I'm sure of it and woke up here in this inn. I have *no idea* how I got here and I'm not sure even where 'here' is," she declared peevishly. Kathryn felt frazzled and tired and hungry and was struggling to not let all of that irritation show to the nice stranger.

"As you've deduced, you're not in America. This is Herefordshire, England," he said in monotone. Kathryn realized that her admission had caused a new skepticism in his attitude toward her. Darn it all if he didn't believe her. *What would she do then?*

"Definitely not in Kansas anymore," she muttered to herself. "So, England?"

"The Atlantic passage takes weeks. You could not possibly have made it in one night."

She sighed and adjusted the slipping quilt once more. "You can imagine I am thinking that myself…but here I am."

"There must be some other explanation for your confusion."

Would you believe a time machine or a vortex or a wormhole? Or maybe a little magic painting?

She thought just for an instant about telling him of the odd little painting that so resembled this time period that had been the only thing new in her life in the last twenty-four hours, but since she wasn't sure it was relevant yet herself, there was no reason to convince him she was nuts right on the spot. The warmth had already gone completely out of his dark eyes and it was clear he was no longer really sure what to make of her. "I'd welcome it if you could tell me how I got here overnight but I'll settle for you not tossing me out on my ear."

"I must admit I have no idea what to say."

Having confided in him, she was well aware he could have easily been a jerk rather than a gentleman. "It sounds crazy I know. It's not like you have any reason to believe me."

"I would believe that you are in a predicament. How *are* you going to travel home?"

"Getting home is another story altogether, but right now I'm just working on the immediate problem of the clothing." Kathryn gestured to her quilt-covered form.

"If I might, I will venture out into the street and see if there are any …stores."

"Oh you will, you'll do that for me?"

"I will."

Suddenly being stranded in this bizarre dream world didn't seem quite so bad. "I'll have to figure out a way to pay you back, but if you would find me something, I'd be so grateful."

"Let us worry about payment only if I succeed in the mission."

"Right. Thank you. Do you need my size?"

"I believe I have a very good idea of your size."

"Oh." She felt the heat seep into her cheeks at his obvious reference to having seen more than she meant to show. The night gown she had worn to bed the night before was almost transparent and she was wearing blue satin low-rise panties under it that must have been visible as she struggled to cover herself in the heavy and awkward quilt.

"*Indeed.*"

He bowed to her and because she was suddenly trying to keep herself hidden as much as possible, she waved in response. She enjoyed the smile that lifted the corners of his mouth and lit his entire face. It was a nice face now that she thought about it with tanned shadowed cheekbones and the dark sparkling eyes that had been all shades of warm and cold throughout their exchange.

As the gentleman turned to go Kathryn recalled him. "Sir, what's your name?"

The man obviously hesitated before he answered. "Asterleigh." With that interesting pronouncement, he turned and disappeared down the stairs. As Asterleigh's footsteps faded, Kathryn had her first real sense that things might be okay.

Since her borrowed room was at the front of the inn, she'd have a perfect view of the man as he made his way down the street. After locking the door so no other visitors could barge in on her, Kathryn crossed the chilled wood floor to the window, drew back the lace, and idly scanned the quaint street. Her window afforded her a sweeping vision of a cobbled street clogged with horses bearing riders, and carts loaded with goods maneuvered by nondescript men. The women sported drab-colored street-length dresses with billowing skirts, large awkward looking bonnets, baskets slung over their arms and some even had small processions of dully-dressed children. The shop signs creaked in the light breeze and the humanity was moving as if nothing was at all unusual. But of course, nothing was unusual for *them*. Kathryn had to admit the street was charming. Just like in a Regency romance novel.

She watched Asterleigh emerge from one shop as quickly as he had entered, striding toward the next. She saw that he had not yet acquired any bags but thought the determined look on his face was a very good sign. He disappeared into a shop with a millinery sign. *Wasn't that a hat maker?* That store probably wouldn't have dresses either. As if on cue, the gentleman reappeared and made for a third shop. As interesting as it was to watch his long, graceful strides, and study the activity on the churned road below, Kathryn knew she should probably be doing something productive like developing a Plan B for getting some clothes.

She turned from the window and the very pleasant image of the gentleman vanished in an almost literal puff as the most disturbing thought of the day asserted itself. Kathryn's younger sister Christine would be frantic, worried sick, their early morning emails having gone unanswered, their routine of sharing important news and sisterly gossip disturbed.

Kathryn had always been able to predict Christine's reactions to stress and the question of her sister's safety. Christy would indeed be very worried. Probably enough to take off and drive over to check on her which, of course, would tell her nothing but that her big sister had disappeared into thin air. There would probably be police and an investigation and all the uproar over a missing young woman and Christine would never have an answer if Kathryn didn't get home some day. Thinking about the entire scenario made her nauseous. Kathryn vowed she would find a way, somehow, to get word to Christy that she was okay.

The loud stomach rumble that accompanied these thoughts added to her poor physical state. Devoting her troubled mind to determining a way to get a message to Christy at least distracted her thoughts temporarily from her very empty belly. That dinner of fat free yogurt and crunchy peanut butter had not gone far.

Temporary distractions lasted only a few minutes, and while Kathryn's stomach was still growling, she started shivering and was pretty sure it wasn't just from the cold. She hoped this episode would pass and she would in a short time feel normal, rational and sane again—to the extent she could under the circumstances.

The initial shock of waking up in a strange bed, in a strange town, in a foreign land, in what she now knew to be a totally different century from her own was indeed fading. Kathryn could and would manage. There was really no choice. Kathryn had taken care of herself her entire life. At least she no longer felt completely, utterly alone since the sexy guy named Asterleigh was supposedly out getting her some clothes.

Kathryn was grateful.

After all the years of being on her own with only her sister Christy to care for and no man to rely on, here she was in such a foreign place, with a stranger acting the hero for her, like her very own knight in shining armor.

If he failed her it wouldn't really matter because this was only a dream anyway, wasn't it? Kathryn thought once again she might wake up and soon. A little self-delusion wasn't going to hurt, not if it made things easier for now.

The rattling of the door handle, startled Kathryn from her self-pitying and she plunged under the bed in case the person on the other side had a key. When the rattling stopped, she realized the person must not have expected the room to be locked. Probably a maid had come to freshen up the room.

She obviously needed to get out of it. "Come on legs, move. Breathe, Kat, you can do this." She grabbed up the now useless pile of junk that had made this odd journey with her, slipped the case off the pillow and stuffed it all in. She peeked into the hall and made a mad dash for the room next door praying it belonged to her new friend and he had left the door unlocked.

Chapter Two

Captain Michael Stafford, lately of His Majesty's Army, contemplated the petite woman with her swirling rainbow of hair and warm drawly voice. Thoughts of her brought an involuntary smile to Michael's face and his body reacted uncomfortably to the image of warmly expressive green-gold eyes, an elusive but captivating smile, and dark peach skin. Michael had been particularly mesmerized by the woman's perfectly formed pink painted toes she had not even tried to cover.

She had hidden under the bed quilt but it had done little to conceal her charms because she was radiant. It was all there in her openness and candor, the vibrancy of her skin, the way her words rolled off her tongue as if she was confident, even in such a distressing situation. Good grief, he had clearly been without any proper distractions for far too long if he was thinking of the tiny American's charms in such a hopeful manner.

Indeed, what could possess him? She surely was altogether not respectable. What proper lady travels alone? There's no maid, no coachman, no footman? Why was no one watching her? And while he had not met many Americans, of the ones he had, none had talked like she had. As he descended the stairs, Michael decided the woman was definitely not a lady, at least not in the way the English meant the description. Surely doing the bidding of an improper woman was not a foreshadowing of what this new life was going to be like. Although his life had been rather dull before the Army, the American was no doubt going to cause him any number of hours of distraction.

It was apparent to Michael almost immediately that he would find no ladies gowns to purchase on the street and worse, that if he did it would cause him a scandal he would rather avoid. He hadn't planned this campaign well at all. In fact, looking back at the inn, he half expected and feared seeing any minute the woman being thrown out the front door. Why was the dammed woman, that particular one of all people, commanding his thoughts to the exclusion of all else? It was just *her* and her exquisite shape and her eyes, into which he could drown.

"Pardon me, Your Grace?" The slight man stopped short in his path, fingering his hat in his hands and bowed stiffly.

Damn. Caught, distracted. "Yes, sir. What can I do for you?" The vicar's collar was a giveaway but Michael did not know this one and had not really expected to be recognized just yet. He had been gone a long time and his departure had been as a uniformed officer with close-cropped hair.

"Ahh, it *is* you. Your Grace, we are relieved to see you returned hale and whole...but I forget my manners. I am Stogwell, the Vicar. We hope you will join us for services. Your mother ..." he lowered his eyes reverently.

"Yes, I know. She was a generous patron. I intend to honor her memory. Perhaps you and your wife will call on me after I have settled in and you will share with me how I can assist you." The foray into the streets had been necessary, but now he realized too late the error. Several of the townspeople were regarding them with curiosity and a few with outright awe. His coat of blue superfine and elegant cravat stood out among the drab of the villagers. Smiling at the closest onlookers, Michael returned his attention to the vicar.

"Your Grace, we would be honored. Mrs. Stogwell will be delighted."

"I trust you will bring me news of the festival?"

"Oh yes, and well the ladies of the committee will want to include you."

Michael realized the gentleman in front of him might save him more traipsing. "Mr. Stogwell, have we developed any seamstress shops since I've been gone? I am in earnest for a gift for my sister."

"Alas no, Your Grace. Gloves or bonnets will be your only choices."

"My mistake. I should have gotten a present in London. I must be off. My staff will be expecting me."

"Oh yes, Your Grace. Very well."

Olivia Ritch

Michael nodded and parted from the still-bowing clergyman who he
hoped he had not offended with his curt dismissal.

~ * ~

Determined to have the question of the woman's situation settled,
Michael's quick step gained him the inn's porch in a few short strides. The
tap's few patrons were busy with their morning plates. The sausages had
been quite good and the coffee strong to his liking and he suddenly
realized the woman had probably not enjoyed the hearty breakfast he had
if she had no clothes. Concerned, Michael charged on.

The shabby innkeeper was not at his post. Gut churning at the
possibility that they might have discovered the green-eyed minx, Michael
took the stairs two at a time. He fingered his key and slipped it into the
lock but the door eased open with no effort. Had he forgotten to lock it in
his distraction?

He knew instantly on gaining his room that *she* had been there. The
woman had left a faint smell of woman musk, salt and something oddly
tropical. He had never smelled a woman like her. Hers must be *essence of
America* he thought with a wry smile.

And damn it all she had slipped past him while he had been detained
by the vicar. The muscles in his chest tightened as he caught sight of a
single sheet lying on his bed on top of a puddle of pink fabric.

Dear Sir,

*Someone tried the door to my room and since I did not have a way
to pay, I slipped into your room to get away. I'm really sorry to
run off, but I figured you would not want to come back and be
discovered in your room with a woman wearing only a nightgown.
I borrowed a pair of your pants and a shirt and have left you my
nightie in exchange. I hope someday to repay you, since I am sure
your riding pants are worth far more than what I left you. Thank
you for your kindness. I wish you safe continued travels home.*

Sincerely,
Kathryn

A frustrated growl boiled from his gut, but Michael resisted the urge to reduce her missive to ashes. *Kathryn*. Her name was Kathryn.

Michael slumped against the bedpost. His deceased wife had been Catherine and it somehow seemed fitting that he was once again embroiled in a sure scandal with this Kathryn. Right now, she was walking the street dressed as a lad in likely ill-fitting shirt and breeches. If he didn't find her soon, this Kathryn would be ruined if she wasn't already.

The garish garment she had been wearing was pooled on his bed. The moment he touched it, his pulse raced from the texture, from its surprising softness. He buried his face in the delicate bundle and Michael breathed in the earthy, provocative smell of vital, alive woman. He'd barely been home in the last eight years but the force driving him at this moment had nothing to do with getting home but everything to do with finding one improperly dressed female. Stuffing the garment into his coat pocket, Michael quit the room on a frustrated groan.

"Your Grace?" Michael's mousy man Minton caught him at the bottom of the steps.

"Ah, just the man I was looking for. Can you and John Coachman see to the carriage and take my valise up with you? I have a bit of business here."

"You want us to go on *without you,* Your Grace?" Minton spluttered.

"Yes, don't be so surprised. Surely, you are ready to be at the end of your travels. You need no longer delay here with me."

"Oh, I am ready, Your Grace, but I thought, I mean…"

"They'll welcome you. Don't worry, man, Hallthorpe is expecting you. Go!" The commanding tone left no more room for the servant's excuses.

"Yes, Your Grace." Minton had no choice but to obey the command.

Ridding himself of his all too worldly valet had been imperative so Michael could concentrate on his search for Kathryn. The inn's stables had excellent prospects for hiding a wayward lady wearing ill-fitting men's clothing. Looking as she must, quite enchanting and out of place, the lads would surely take pity on her. Once he ran Kathryn to ground, Michael could solve the mystery of her plight and see the woman settled and on her way to wherever she belonged—out of his life.

"Kathryn, are you in here?" Avoiding the lads working in the far

13

stalls, Michael called her name in a low whisper. She did not answer. Fists clenched, nerves taut, Michael meticulously checked the loft and each unoccupied stall but no minx was in the stables. He stalked through the village and after hunting in all the obvious hiding spots for well nigh an hour, Michael was gravely concerned for Kathryn's safety and completely out of sorts.

After surreptitious glances into the storefronts along the street, to no avail, Michael stepped into the Climbing Vine Inn to inquire of the barman at the tavern. "A pint if you please."

"Yes, milord." The barman filled a tankard and plopped it in front of Michael on the bar. Michael placed a guinea next to the mug and the man's eyes glinted at the largesse. "What can I do for ye?"

"I am looking for a lady who is dressed as a lad."

"Nay. Haven't seen anyone like that through here today. Had some visitors but I'd say they're all in their right clothes."

"Thank you my good man." Michael tipped the mug and took another long drag, but ale was not what he needed right now. He needed a titian-haired houri. Ah, yes, houri was the perfect description, she was truly an exotic temptress.

Michael calculated that Kathryn must have headed directly out of town but how and in what conveyance? Hadn't she had told him she had no money? There were not many ways to leave a town like Wilton when someone was without means to pay. But she had something any number of men would have accepted as payment. He cursed loudly since no one could hear.

The woman had been coy and quite lovely, but she had not propositioned *him*. She had asked for help and he had freely given it. But what if the next man she approached was not a gentleman? That thought was enough to make an old soldier groan.

Cursing her possible fate wasn't going to find the woman so Michael turned his steps back down the street, lengthened his stride and began planning the next move in his campaign.

There were only two roads leading into and away from Wilton and he doubted she'd choose any of the narrow bridle paths. So for departing, Kathryn could make for London or take the split that led to Hawthorne. Unbidden, images of Kathryn carted off by ruffians or set upon by highwaymen flashed before him. His protective instincts surged and he said a quick prayer that she had chosen the Hawthorne track, where she would be safe. She would also get a nice surprise when she landed on the doorstep of the man she had asked to help her then deserted. Michael rather liked the idea that Kathryn would get the opportunity to pay him back in his chosen currency for the clothing she had pilfered.

The satisfaction of that thought was fleeting as he stalked back into the Blue Bell, settled his account, and summoned for his horse to be brought around. Michael could not shake the tightness in his chest he felt at the woman's effective disappearance. He had to beat a swift and steady pace toward the missing woman and to intercept her before she arrived at Hawthorne. As much as he wanted her to be heading there, he didn't want her to precede him. His staff would be in a spate if she arrived at the door dressed...or only partially dressed, as a man in clothes that Minton or his all-too-perceptive butler Hallthorpe might even recognize as Michael's own. That would be unacceptable.

Fury's hooves ate up the distance while Michael scanned the open fields for any sign of her. He remembered every copse of trees, the hedge, and hiding places that had been the site of childhood adventures. Today his land was alive with the smell of earth, sheep, cows, horses and hay, and fresh grass and he breathed it in deeply, letting the familiarity and the constant pounding of the hooves calm his fraying nerves.

As the road drew to its familiar end, Michael's concern for Kathryn mounted. He should have overtaken her by now and since he had not, he knew she had not headed in this direction after all. He contemplated turning around, but his mount would not be able to ride that distance. Michael was too close to home and the possibility of gaining a fresh horse to risk it. He would go back but not yet.

Slowing Fury to a walk, Michael scrubbed his hand over his face and tried to clear his mind from his pursuit of the missing woman to prepare for what lay ahead. He was coming home for the first time since losing his father and brother. He had for thirty years been the second son, the spare after all, the one destined to be a soldier. Now he was riding toward a completely new destiny. Surveying the familiar land spread out before him on all sides, Michael was indeed quite keen on taking the reins of his family's vast holdings and becoming the Duke of Asterleigh.

He kicked his heels and spurred on his horse.

Excitement building, his heart welled as the façade of Hawthorne came into view. Nothing had prepared Michael for the emotion he would feel, the possessiveness of being master of this…of Hawthorne. *Home*.

He reined in. A lad rushed from the stable for Fury and stopped short when he realized who the rider was. The boy was not alone in his wonder, and curtains flickered throughout the building, curious eyes peering out in awe at the lone rider.

"Milord, welcome home," the boy murmured.

"Thank you, lad. He should cooperate for you as he's been ridden hard."

"Yes, milord." Michael saw acceptance in Fury's huge eyes as he gave himself to the lad, as if he too realized the weight of responsibility that fell on his master's shoulders and deigned to acquiesce to the ministrations of an underling just this once. The horse also likely recognized a dab hand. Michael expected the boy would become a fine stableman.

Taking in the view on all sides, Michael admired the long row of stately trees marching alongside the drive that culminated in the wide circular graveled forecourt, then glanced at the lane leading to the stables where the lad had started off with Fury. He could see the stable down below and smell the faint scent of manure and constantly churned dirt. He had been up this drive too many times to count, but now he studied his home, its gardens and buildings anew, appreciating how impressive it all was. And, it was *his*. Michael's chest swelled with pride and he couldn't help but smile.

But he would dally another day and time to enjoy the sights. For now, he had a mission. His long stride gained him the steps quickly and Michael watched the great doors swing wide, spilling servants out into the courtyard while their stately leader Hallthorpe stood at attention on the top step. "Welcome home, milord."

"Welcome!"

"Huzzah!"

"Good show, milord." The hearty greetings came from throughout the line of servants that had formed down the steps and extended back into the great hall. His maids curtsied and the footmen bowed and from all around him he felt the genuine warmth of their welcome that was evident in their wide and glowing smiles.

"Your Grace." He heard affection in Hallthorpe's deep baritone.

"Hallthorpe, I see you have kept the household in order." He clasped the elder man by the shoulder and gripped his hand firmly.

"Your Grace, we have been preparing for your return. The staff is heartened to see you returned hale and whole."

"I have heard that more than once today. I am as relieved as you. Thank you." In a louder voice, he repeated, "Thank you all for your kind welcome. Be dismissed back to your posts." On his words, the greetings died away and servants melted back into the house and the gardens.

"Hallthorpe, will you please not 'Your Grace' me just yet? My investiture is not for another ten days and I'd be quite happy being Lord Stafford or Captain Stafford until then."

"As you wish, My Lord." He did not miss his proper butler's reproving gaze.

Michael took a deep breath and found the light scent of Jasmine floated on the air in the hall since the doors were still open. He had spotted the vine creeping up the arbor marking the entrance to the garden. It had been his mother's favorite place on the property and he had ensured it was well tended in his absence. Like the stables, Michael had paid the garden particular attention in his directives. Bright blooms registered that indeed the gardeners had followed his instructions.

With the hall empty save for his trusty retainer, Michael turned his attention to his butler. "Thorpe, I need a dress."

"A dress, My Lord?"

"I know where. I can get it myself." While he had not originally expected his first action upon returning home would be a visit to his deceased wife's bedchamber, Michael's very real and growing concern for small, bold Kathryn compelled him forward. His legs leaden, he forced himself to mount the stairs. He was completely unsurprised at the scene that met him in Catherine's room. Her closet, untouched for years but for the maids' infrequent attention, was largely empty. As it turned out, there were only two dresses hanging. He selected the brown muslin day dress, leaving an evening dress for a change of clothes. Michael found a valise and stuffed in the only pair of shoes left in the bare expanse of dressing room.

Fumbling through half-empty drawers, he found two unmatched garters, old limp stockings and heaven forbid, a bodice that looked and felt like it could stop a speeding shot. The thought of his earthy American cinched up in that armor… *Had he just thought of her as "his" American? Arrgh.*

Demmit. "Hallthorpe?" he bellowed.

"Yes, My Lord."

"Er…yes…how did you get here so fast? Were you lurking after me?"

"Yes, My Lord."

"Why?"

"I thought you might…need me," the man replied softly.

"Thank you, no. I have much greater concerns at the moment. I need a fresh mount. I have to return to Wilton."

"Yes, My Lord," he answered but did not move. Michael could tell that Hallthorpe was expecting some form of explanation. They did have a more personal relationship beyond that of a Master and his butler.

"There is a woman…a lady…"

"*I see.*"

"It's *not* like you see, Thorpe." Michael resorted to the name he had called the butler since the time he was in short coats. "I came across a woman traveling alone, far from home and without proper clothing. She is lost. There seemed no one to help her but she slipped off while I went to find her appropriate attire. I mean to see her safe."

His repeated "I see" was infused with far more perception than Michael welcomed.

~ * ~

Thunder ate up the return distance much as Fury had on bringing him home. As the buildings of Wilton came back into view, Michael's thoughts returned to their obsession with the wayward American. Where would she be hiding? *What if she had taken the afternoon coach?*

"No, My Lord, no young ladies or lads on the coach today. Only two men and an older woman." The Innkeeper at the Blue Bell shook his head. Michael was grateful this one was not the same scraggly youth who had been unaware of Kathryn earlier that morning.

"Have you by chance seen a gentle lad dressed shabbily in his Father's clothes?"

"Well, yes, now you mention…odd fellow, excuse me, odd woman in truth asked for the road to London. Had no shoes on. I noticed special cause when he, umm she, quit the door, the taproom men stopped their yapping and stared. She was a piece, mind you. Hard to miss. No mistakin' her for a man even though she was in breeches. Small hands, and feet and well, she hadn't been able to disguise everything. She didn't stop at the door even with all those eyes trained her way, just walked right out into the street with no shoes." He clucked his tongue, clearly puzzled.

Yes, that would be her, someone who drew eyes not even realizing she was causing heads to turn. "How long ago?"

"Been a while. An hour, maybe two. I was worried she would walk out onto that road and be first target for some highwayman. Man or woman can't look right dressed as that."

Michael tossed a coin onto the counter tipped his hat and strode briskly for the door signaling the lad who had led Thunder away. If she had been walking an hour, it would take him but a matter of minutes to overtake her. As long as she was on the road and not stopping or worse… He pushed the unwelcome thought from his mind. Hauling the sack of ladies clothes up onto Thunder's broad back, Michael mounted in one fluid motion and raced from the inn yard toward the errant American.

Once the Blue Bell's door had banged shut and Michaels' footfalls retreated from the porch, a gentleman slipped from the shadows of a corner alcove where he had witnessed the exchange with the barkeep from behind his half-empty pint and a discarded newssheet. He strode to the window and watched Stafford's departing back. He was fascinated to learn of Michael's interesting quest. He had always been so stuffy and staid, completely too righteous for his own good. Surely now that he was the Duke-presumptive, Michael was not involved in anything scandalous? But if he was, life would be so much sweeter. If he found the woman first, what fun that would be. His plan suddenly taking shape, the gentleman quit the tap and made for his horse, a satisfied smile curving his lips.

Chapter Three

Kathryn's feet were no match for the dirt road pocked with stones. The fields had seemed better for running, but soon it was clear that she had to constantly keep watch for the greater dangers of horse droppings, cow patties, and sheep pooh. Coupled with the occasional small shrub, pricker bush, or hole, the excrement made running on the grass just as difficult as running on the road. She finally resolved to walk and realized just how far away from her destination she was. She would not cry though. She would *not*.

The innkeeper had said London was a two-day trip by coach. And she was on foot. Would that make it a ten-day trip? It had seemed like the only thing to do to just to start out and go forward since she didn't have any money, anyway, or friends or food. What would a small town do for her when she couldn't very well show her face? She couldn't get caught in the gentleman's bedroom and she certainly didn't like hanging out in the bar with the way the men had ogled her as she passed by. She shuddered to think about that group.

She was, she thought, usually better at planning than this little exercise suggested. Kathryn needed to think through where she would spend the night, how she would get food, how she might make a little money and possibly even how to get a horse. The most logical solution was to get a waitress job at an inn where she might stay in a staff room and eat and be given a real dress.

Her chest tightened at the thought that she would not see the gentleman Asterleigh from the inn again. It would have been nice to get to know him. Kathryn was sure those dark eyes would twinkle with mischief. His voice had been commanding and soothing at the same time. And he had been funny. There was something about him, something familiar and welcoming and tempting. Asterleigh had been terribly appealing.

Now she was walking all alone on a road with who knows what dangers. If Kathryn had just figured out how to become inconspicuous, she could have waited on the man and learned whether or not he had indeed acquired a dress. She could only imagine how aggravated he must be having gone to the trouble for nothing. Or would he be just as glad to be *rid* of the aggravation of dealing with her?

Lost in thought, Kathryn had walked quite a distance without paying any attention to the countryside. So for the first time since she had started down the road, Kathryn took in her surroundings and realized just how absolutely breathtaking the land was. Having been distracted by the hard dusty roads and animal droppings, she had missed the sheer beauty of it all. Now she looked, she saw the lushest, greenest grass she had ever seen for as far as the eye could see, dotted by white blobs that upon inspection were sheep lolling on the distant gently rolling hills.

She also passed a group of lazy cows that looked familiar, like ones she remembered from a farm near her home. Big brown cows with white heads. Had they come to America from this region?

Kathryn had just passed a cottage but had paid little heed. Now that she was paying attention Kathryn noticed heaving window boxes, a gray stacked stone foundation and low white picket fence dipping in spots where earth and time had given way. The house reminded her of the Tudor style homes near her own with gables and heavy wood doors, sinking foundations, bracketed shutters, ancient plantings, and beveled glass windows. Truly, if this was not such a wrong century and she was not penniless, shoeless, in constant discomfort from rubbing ill-fitting clothes, carrying a bag of odd assorted personal possessions, and without a passport or any transportation, Kathryn would surely have thought this to be one of the most amazing and glorious places she had ever been.

The low rumble, a steady thudding coming from behind, triggered Kathryn's survival instincts into high gear. She searched the landscape for a hiding place and though there was not much cover near the road, she opted for a low bush and flattened herself in the grass. The earth

21

thrummed, her heart matching its beats to the pounding. With her gaze focused in the direction of the approaching horseman, she watched as a powerful beast came into view, ridden hard by a man hunched low over the horse's neck, coattails flowing behind. The rider slowed his horse and she got a sudden sense that he was scanning the area looking for someone or something. Her heart now pounding faster than the hoof-beats that had slowed to a walk, she plastered herself to the ground and prayed he would start riding again. Otherwise, he would discover her and she would be out here in the middle of almost nowhere alone with a man on a horse.

As the horseman approached her position, Kathryn took a chance by tilting her head in his direction. From her view on the ground, Kathryn recognized a familiar blue coat, one she had studied at length while talking to the gentleman in the hall. Not quite ready to reveal herself until she was absolutely sure it was the man she had met at the inn whose clothes she had "borrowed," Kathryn ducked once again behind the bush to catch a clear view of his face.

"Hello?"

His "aye" was comfortingly familiar. Scrambling from her hiding spot, Kathryn slapped at the litter on *his pants* she wore as he slowed to a halt in front of her.

"Well, what have we here?"

Kathryn stretched to her full diminutive height then hurriedly explained. "I was walking, then I was running, then walking again, but when I heard you I hid behind that bush."

"Do you find me frightening, then?"

"No, not you. But I didn't know who it was." Now that she could see his face, Asterleigh was wearing a broad grin and did indeed have the twinkle that she knew would be in his eyes when he was laughing.

"Ahh, so you had the sense to be frightened by an approaching rider, yet you are walking down a public road dressed as a lad with no shoes on?"

"I guess I deserved that." She half-smiled at him. "Are you on this road for a particular reason sir?"

"Indeed. I was riding to fetch you," Asterleigh announced.

"Me?" Her experience with foreign, slightly-arrogant-sounding men was severely limited, but her woman's intuition served her well enough.

She stayed quiet and just smiled at him beatifically.

"Yes, I realized you would have no shoes or ready funds and you would certainly not have the good sense to stay put and secure proper conveyance." His smiled vanished during the little speech and she heard irritation in his tone and felt a little like she had just been scolded by a parent.

"Wow, you rode out here to what...sling me up onto your horse, which by the way is quite magnificent, scold me for disappearing, and carry me back to town?" She said that last with as much playful anticipation as she thought might pique him since he had just treated her like a kid.

"No, not exactly, but I am going to 'sling you' as you say onto my horse, and ride you to my home where you will be properly gowned, *shoed* and fed."

"All of that sounds really nice of you. I *am* in trouble and I *do* need a ride. I'm just not quite sure that I should ride off with *you*. Is that even allowed here? You know, woman with man thing."

The glint was back in the black orbs. "It is not typical, but I daresay your situation is not. We shall have to make do."

"That's an understatement. Have you ever encountered a woman wearing your clothes who needed rescuing?"

"Rescuing yes, wearing my clothes, definitely not. I will say you did a remarkable job of disguising yourself. The innkeeper *almost* mistook you for a boy."

"Almost?" She smiled at him impishly.

"Yes, he said that you were too feminine to get away with hiding your charms."

Kathryn did not completely cover her pleased expression and could feel a blush rising on her cheeks. "You, my dear, are blushing and it makes your lovely peach skin a quite orangey hue."

"That doesn't sound pretty." Kathryn knew she had always been an awkward blusher, pink and peach blending oddly to make her look frightening.

"I can assure you it is quite charming."

"Thanks."

"Now may we address the matter of your situation? My horse is growing restless standing here as we exchange pleasantries."

"I'm sorry. You've been so nice to me. I don't know why I'm hesitating."

"I will ease your suspicions with a proper introduction. I am Captain Michael Stafford or was until recently. My family's estate is Hawthorne in Wilton, Herefordshire. Our lands begin at the split in the road just past the inn. I stayed the night in town in order to arrive in the daylight hours and not stir the staff after dark. They would have wanted to provide me a proper greeting as I am also Lord of the house now that I have recently returned. They are now as we speak, expecting me to arrive with a guest."

Kathryn did not have much choice. There was the matter of not having any money…and being virtually starved. And she was sure her feet were not going to take much more walking. "Lord Stafford, your offer is very generous. I'll agree to come with you if you will agree to allow me to repay your kindness." She would not be beholden to an English Lord for anything, certainly not for basic necessities—clothes, food or shelter. Accepting charity seemed a little too cozy for her.

"That arrangement is acceptable." With that, her rescuer reached for Kathryn's hand and hoisted her effortlessly into the saddle at his pommel. Lord Michael Stafford turned the horse and Kathryn found herself heading back in the direction from which she had come.

~ * ~

Hallthorpe dispatched the footman to retrieve Eleanor Primble from the village upon Michael's orders. The girl would make an excellent ladies maid for an unconventional Duchess-to-be. As the young woman entered through the kitchen, Hallthorpe congratulated himself on his selection. He gestured for her to follow him out of the way of so many interested ears into the servant's hallway that was currently deserted. "I have asked you to join the staff as ladies maid to a most special guest." Eyes wide as saucers, Eleanor just listened and nodded.

"She is arriving with the master but will not be expecting to find you in attendance. She will most likely be dressed as a lad, so do not gawk. I know you have spent many years running your father's house and caring for your sisters. This lady will likely need that same kind of attention. You are to talk to her, soothe her, and help ease her into the household. Do you understand?"

"Oh yes, sir." Miss Primble, Ellie as she had asked to be called, had apparently gathered her wits by this time and was able to comprehend what Hallthorpe was telling her. He imagined that indeed, standing in the hall of this great house, she had dreamed for years of a position such as this. Ladies maids traveled with their mistresses all over the country to house parties in elegant country homes and he suspected she thrilled at the prospect of coach rides, shopping and the sights of London.

"One more thing, Eleanor?"

"Yes sir?"

"We want her to catch the master's eye. I am counting on your expertise. Of course, she will not want to know we…" his words trailed as Eleanor nodded her head enthusiastically. He did not need to explain further. Hallthorpe had chosen well.

~ * ~

"This ride is relaxing…it's making me sleepy. Do you find yourself relaxing, Lord Stafford?"

No! Having her on his saddle had the opposite effect on him. Every nerve prickled, his senses were all fully engaged. Indeed, they had been from the moment he had laid eyes on her in that gauzy chemise she thought she had been hiding from him. He ached for a closer look at the dark strip of lace she had worn under it to conceal the apex of her thighs. No, he was definitely not sleepy.

Now, with every one of the horse's steps, her bottom pressed firmly to his groin, Michael was aching. He hoped she could not feel his arousal since he had barely just convinced her to trust him. He didn't want her to fear being ravished on this road. "No, I am not sleepy," he ground out.

"I was thinking about the rocking. It's comforting…almost lulling me…"

"I don't find myself desiring to fall asleep on my mount. I fear it's the surest way to find yourself falling somewhere else."

"I guess you really can't get sleepy since you're… what do you call it when you're riding with a passenger?"

He rolled his eyes. "Riding." Being out of her line of vision did have some advantages. "You may leave the managing of the horse to me, but you must maintain your position. It becomes difficult to manage a limp or

25

lifeless 'passenger.'"

"I can imagine. But it's still very hard for me to not be drawn into the motion."

Ahhh…if she did not stop talking about rocking and motion and lulling she might find herself learning just how useful the rocking of a horse's gait could be! Michael tried to shake off the unnerving notion, but it planted itself in his head and he imagined all methods of showing her.

Kathryn smelled so enticing, her pungent aroma now wafting to his nose. With his face just inches from her hair, Michael thought she had a wonderfully tropical smell like citrus and bananas and there was a touch of baby softness he could not place. It was an odd but entirely sensual mix.

Michael's gaze fixed unbidden on a single bead of sweat trickling slowly from Kathryn's temple down her sculpted cheek. As he watched the droplet disappear under the mat that had become her hair, he found himself wanting very much to taste her, it, the sweat and her skin.

"So how far is it until we get to your home?"

Her words jerked him back from his fantasies with a start. "We'll just miss the village and this path will connect soon with the lane to Hawthorne. Not long until you will see the towers."

"Towers? Like a castle?" She was breathless and turned her face disconcertingly close to his.

His lungs seized when she looked at him like that. "It's not exactly a castle," he choked out.

Michael considered telling her the truth of his home's origin as a fortress ordered by William himself in preparation for an 11th century Welsh uprising but decided on a more circumspect answer. She was an American. Would she even know of William, of Normans or earlier, Viking, Celts… "Hawthorne was originally built for protection, but in the last one hundred years, so many changes have been made that it looks much more like a large manor home than a castle. I confess, it might seem imposing if you are unused to six-story sandstone towers as part of your house."

"So when was it built—the Norman period or later?"

What? "The Norman period. You know some history then?"

"Yes, they do teach us a little English history in American schools but actually I know it because my family's part English. My grandfather traced our family all the way back to the Vikings. Does that surprise you?"

"Yes." *More than you know*.

"It's true, and my mother has some Welsh blood. She told me I look English, got the cleft chin and the cheekbones. Probably have to remove the hair highlights for me to look really authentic though."

Michael recalled in vivid detail the cleft of her chin again and the very high cheekbones he had just been admiring and wondered how he had missed it. She *was* English. There was a tell-tale aristocratic tilt to her chin, leanly muscled limbs, the gorgeous hazel eyes, and the altogether stubborn profile. Then, in contrast, there was the oddly striped auburn hair, and glowing freckles and well the bronzed all over complexion. She could easily grace the pages of a picture book on Viking women or Valkyries. Her smile brought out the laugh lines at her eyes. He knew Vikings were bold and adventurous. She was surely that. He could not decide which described her better though because Kathryn was also a petite package.

"I've surprised you. You thought that the silly American girl could not possibly know anything. Well, I know who I am and I think you agree based on that intense look on your face." She laughed loudly startling him from his closer than proper examination of her physical features.

"You do look rather…familiar," Michael admitted.

"I think that might have been another compliment?"

"Two in one day. What would my staff think?" He regarded her wryly and shook his head at his own relaxed manner.

"Yeah, what will they think? Or more to the point, do you have any family who will freak out with you showing up with a strange woman?"

"I've not much family left. My brother, the first-born, died last year and my Father has recently died. That's how I came to be heading home just now." His voice was resigned.

"I'm really sorry for your losses. My mother dying just about killed us."

"I too am sorry for your loss." He hesitated. "My Father's and brother's deaths were…part and parcel of their lifestyles."

"Lifestyles? Tell me about them." Her counselor's instincts were pricking at this intriguing admission about his male relatives.

"My elder brother Charles spent summers here at Hawthorne with our cousin Harold Stafford. They were six years older, inseparable and left me

27

largely to myself. I was much too young for them to even bother with teasing me, which suited me fine. My earliest memories were that the two of them were much like my father—arrogant, taking their due as lords of the land. Lord Charles was heir to a Dukedom of course."

"They don't sound particularly nice. You obviously didn't approve of their attitudes and behavior?"

"No," he agreed but amended, "Not that I meant them any harm but I wasn't like them."

"So...?"

"You want more of the story?" He sighed. "I suppose you want to know how they died."

"If you want to tell me." She was quite sure he did want to keep talking.

"Charles' accident had happened just as Wellington was amassing our forces in Belgium before Waterloo. I could not leave the continent for the funeral since I was intimately involved in the planning and execution of what ultimately became the defeat of Napoleon. I have only learned there was a fall from a horse. He died of a bleed. My presence in Wilton would have done nothing to assuage Father's grief over losing his favored son so I didn't leave Wellington. My brother's death made me the only son however, thus my return to a home that now belongs to me."

"As a Duke?

"A Duke, yes."

He remained quiet while she digested his story. Charles had been gone for almost a year; it was their Father's death in January that had finally pulled him home, to the duties and responsibilities of their family—so that he could assume the title. The fortress he had never expected to inherit beckoned, calling him to the land, his new destiny. He was vaguely aware the woman on his horse figured somewhere in that destiny.

~ * ~

Her rescuer had gone quiet and Kathryn recognized someone who had been drawn into the past. It suited her to remain silent as well. As they ascended the grand drive lined with trees, she became extremely aware of the magnificent castle coming into view. "Phew, Wow." He didn't respond and she just drank in the sheer size and grandeur of it.

Kathryn's seat was all but numb while the flesh that had been rocked slowly back and forth had been rubbed raw and was now throbbing painfully. She was eternally grateful the horse had stopped moving, but as the hulking presence that had overcome her senses slid from behind her, she felt oddly alone and empty in his saddle.

She had been acutely aware of the large male form pressed to her back. With each step of the horse, she had eased back and forth into the Captain and every time she brushed him, fascinating smells reached her. He was wearing musky cologne that covered a slight smell of sweaty man. There was the tangy odor of an old-fashioned soap but none of the soaps or colognes could cover the distinctly earthy smells of leather and wool and coffee and something like sausage, as if every smell he had encountered today clung to him. He had had an erection. She was sure of it. It was oddly flattering to think that she had had that kind of effect on him.

Kathryn had dismounted horses, on two previous occasions, so swinging her leg over was, while not as impressive as his smooth motion, not altogether embarrassing. Before she reached the ground, his hands closed about her waist and she found herself gripped by arms of steel sliding down a startling wall of muscle and bone that was his expansive chest. Their gazes locked. She watched him battle his own instincts to finally release her.

~ * ~

The same lad who had retrieved Fury from Michael earlier ran for Thunder only to nearly trip over his own feet upon coming face to face with the new arrival. This was probably more excitement in one day than had occurred in his whole life as a servant here. Eyes pasted to the ground, he towed the great beast away.

Michael watched the lad's reaction with amusement. Kathryn's introduction to his household promised to be entirely eventful and possibly pleasurable. Forcing the smirk from his face, Michael plastered on his mask of country ease as he reached for Kathryn's hand and was jerked to a stop when she recoiled from his touch. "Miss Kathryn, it is customary for a gentleman to escort a lady. You need not fear I am stealing your hand." It had come so easy to call her by her Christian name.

"Oh, yes, oh, I'm so sorry. I knew that. I feel stupid."

"No, I apologize for startling you."

"I admit, I'm a little nervous. This house is so huge and you're Lord of all this?"

"This is my home and I hope you will not feel intimidated. I know it is imposing on first glance. You do get used to it."

"I'll have to take your word for that. Now, I'm ready." She extended her right hand to him.

"I almost forgot…the staff will expect to address you formally. May I have your surname."

She blinked, and he watched her register his question. "It's Ragland, but I am perfectly happy with everyone calling me Kathryn."

"Kathryn, I can assure you *they* will not be fine with calling you that." He hesitated to allow Kathryn to take in her surroundings.

Ragland, well she was also part Welsh. He had to shake off the sensation that she was not as foreign and unfamiliar as he had assumed.

He watched her face while she considered the towers, wonder, excitement, awe. So many emotions were there. "When I was a child, I imagined the watching guard with his suit of armor and a telescope scanning for invaders."

"Yes, and there would be colored flags flying poles all around the top," she said her voice trilling higher.

"I think you are right. And probably an archer always at the ready," Michael warmed to the game.

"And don't you think there would have been a bugler?"

"Miss Ragland, I do believe you have a wonderful imagination for medieval make-believe."

"I am counting on a tour up there sometime and we'll see what other characters we can conjure." She cried delightedly. "Oh, but that was totally presumptuous of me."

"Not at all. I will be delighted to show them to you."

She smiled that glorious smile that made the green-gold eyes sparkle. She was truly dazzlingly lovely. Then, he felt her wince as they took their first steps on the gravel and he heard the groan she tried to suppress. "Miss Ragland, your feet. Are they injured?"

"Just sore. I don't think I can…" She shrieked when he lifted her smoothly from the ground, towing her at his side a few inches above the sharp stones then placing her firmly at the foot of the wide stone steps. His erstwhile butler emerged wearing an inscrutable expression.

"Miss Ragland, let me present Hallthorpe."

"Hello, Mr. Hallthorpe. It's nice to meet you," she said breathlessly.

"The pleasure is mine I assure you, Miss Ragland. Let me show you to your room. I am sure you will want to make yourself comfortable. Ellie will attend you. Luncheon will be served at noon."

"Luncheon? Wow, that sounds…formal. I'll be fine with something simple. Don't go to any trouble for me. I don't want to impose on you."

"Miss Ragland, I will see you at luncheon. Hallthorpe will see you settled." Michael stepped back, reluctantly releasing her into Hallthorpe's more-than-capable hands.

"Thank you, Lord Stafford. For everything."

"It was my pleasure Miss Ragland."

The butler was climbing the stairs briskly and she struggled on her sore feet to keep up with his long strides while also gawking distractedly by the house. It reminded her of a particular Bed and Breakfast she had stayed in during her one and only trip to England as a teenager with her family. It was all there—a collection of swords on the walls, beveled glass windows, and the suit of armor on the first landing of the majestic staircase. Candelabra sconces were everywhere, obviously for lighting. It was a prominently displayed tapestry with what she assumed to be the family crest that made Kathryn realize what an amazing privilege she was being afforded to be in a castle, in England, built in 1100! It was an enviable position and she would make every effort to appreciate it even though she had not landed here intentionally.

"Miss, your room?" Hallthorpe stepped back, allowing her to enter. "Ellie is here to help you settle in and find some suitable clothes from among our meager offerings. I fear we have not had many ladies in the house in some time so our spare garments are well, spare."

Chuckling at the very proper butler's pun, Kathryn was struck all over again by the opulence of the feminine bedroom. She hesitated just inside the door of the massive chamber that was graced by a four-poster bed with billowy curtains and a virtual cloud of pillows with soft pink covers that were so inviting she could have curled up in them immediately. She

31

couldn't believe she was being shown into this room, and that she was going to sleep here tonight.

Kathryn was so awed by the splendor of the furniture and accessories and the history of the castle she forgot momentarily about its lack of modern conveniences like electricity and running water. She almost reached for the switch at the door but recalled that there would not be light switches or hairdryers or electric toothbrushes. *Would there even be toothbrushes at all...and tampons? Oh no, no* tampons *in eighteen hundred—something*! That ranked right up there with not having any money and even higher than being without shoes as one of the unfortunate drawbacks of being back in time. This *was* still a fabulous room though, and an amazing highlight to cap a bizarre morning's adventure.

She noticed Hallthorpe waiting patiently while her mind worked. "This was the Dowager's room, miss. We hope you will find it to your liking." He passed Ellie the bag of clothes Michael had scrounged earlier that included the day gown they had packed that would be squashed.

"Mr. Hallthorpe? This is an incredibly beautiful room but I'm just passing through and, I wouldn't want to mess up a perfectly good room. I'd feel so much better not putting you out by staying somewhere less nice. I've got to get going tomorrow or I'll never find my way home. I may never find my way anyway, but I've got to make a start. Do you have something less...?"

He did not answer, but waited for her to finish her question. "I just can't take so many favors from you all."

"Miss, this is the country and it is our distinct pleasure to welcome travelers. We do it as a courtesy and for me, for the entire staff, it's an honor to have such a lovely lady from so far away. You do us the pleasure of your company and we benefit from new experiences. It's quite the thing here."

"I just feel like such a..." *moocher.* "What's the word for someone who takes advantage?"

"Miss, in your case, it would simply be, *guest.*"

Ellie the maid was still waiting attentively and Kathryn had no idea what she was supposed to do next. The romance novel heroines let their maids dress them and fix their hair but since Kathryn had no intention of asking the girl to dress her, or undress her as the case would be, there wasn't much point in her lingering.

"I will leave you in Ellie's care."

"Thank you again." She followed him to the door but left it open.

Turning to the expectant young woman, Kathryn smiled and pointed toward the door. "You can go now. I really just plan to rest."

"Oh miss, you'll need to change for lunch."

"You're right. I'll probably wash my face as well."

"I'll just help you…"

She stilled Ellie's hands.

"I'm good. I can get ready by myself. You're excused."

"But miss, I do really think you will need me," Ellie pressed.

"I promise if I need you I'll call you. Is that what this cord's for?"

"Yes, miss. You pull the bell cord and I'll come right away," Kathryn recognized the maid's distress but wasn't going to change her mind.

"Deal. Now you can go. Really." Ellie frowned but she didn't argue further.

Kathryn was not in the mood for a battle. She was exhausted. The maid left reluctantly.

Kathryn slipped off the riding pants wincing at her chafed thighs and flopped back on the luscious silk counterpane. In the quiet of the lovely room, Kathryn took the opportunity to think back to exactly how it was she had come to be in this place and time.

She had left work the evening before and rather than going home, Kathryn had stopped at Tilly's Treasures. That's where this adventure had begun.

The memories and thoughts flooded in, crowding together to remind her of just how she had achieved this transformation. Since moving into her loft, she had meant to stop at the little antique shop on her way home so many times. Its window boxes and lace curtains were so charming that she craned her neck as she drove past every day to see if there was anything of interest visible from that view. So yesterday afternoon, she had slowed and turned in. She had no money to spend on covering the bare wall space in her new place. This visit was to be just for checking out the shop, not actually buying anything.

~ * ~

Olivia Ritch

The shopkeeper had been a lovely older woman with soft silver hair swept up in a knot. She was bent deeply over a large roll-top desk peering through glasses perched on her nose. When the bells stopped jingling and Kathryn stepped fully into the store, the lady inclined her head toward her customer. "Young lady, you hunt through my treasures and then if I can answer any questions, I'll try to." She waved and bent back to her papers.

"Thank you. Your shop's been calling to me. It looks so inviting," Kathryn acknowledged, moving deeper into the crowded space.

"You'll find something special you'll want to take home with you. I am sure of it." Her voice trailed Kathryn as she moved farther into the store.

"I am sure I will find many things I like." *And I won't be able to afford any of them on a counselor's salary.*

Tilly's Treasure Chest was as charming and inviting on the inside as it was from the outside and stuffed literally to the rafters with treasures. Knickknacks littered every surface. Kathryn made her way through room after room filled with all manner of items from gorgeous baubles to unrecognizable discards.

In a small low-ceilinged space at the back of the shop, Kathryn was drawn to a grouping of four small paintings lying on a dining room table. While the woman probably had plans to hang them, for now they lay flat and in no apparent order. She reached for the closest one and found herself studying the form of a dashing military officer on horseback. She read the elegantly scripted notation on the back of the price tag and immediately knew the antique oil was indeed far out of her price range.

Each of the four miniature oils was from the early 1800s; all framed differently, as if they were not actually a set but were just surprisingly similar in size and composition. She imagined the gentleman on horseback, looking so dashing in his red coat had most likely been a soldier at Waterloo, and wondered if he had survived the battle. What had become of the war hero? Of the others? Had they all been soldiers? Had they all faced the carnage of the battle? Had they all survived?

She hoped they had, and suddenly felt an intense affection for long-dead men who most likely had fought in that war and had made the world a better place for it. She had a special affection for soldiers. They sacrificed. They deserved respect.

But the cavalry man's image was not the picture that intrigued her the most. Of the four miniatures, only one featured a man and woman together. On the back in beautiful faded script was *Wilton c.1810*. Kathryn wondered if Wilton was an Earl or a Duke or someone as dashing as the mounted officer. The woman was pretty in a plain sort of way, much as all the women she had ever seen in old paintings—no cheekbones or color to her face at all and puffy light piled high curls. Neither of them was smiling. In fact, they looked sour. The price, as high as the first, had her setting the painting aside.

With one last glance over the long gone faces, Kathryn quit the overstuffed room and turned back toward the front of the store. "You liked the paintings, did you not?" The woman had seen her looking at the paintings and Kathryn recognized a faint British accent. The lady must be Tilly herself.

"Yes, ma'am. The one with the couple was intriguing…they seemed unhappy, like they were not glad to be painted together."

"My dear, that's exactly what I thought. When I bought that set from a dealer in Herefordshire, England, I had the distinct impression that theirs had been an arranged marriage," Tilly elaborated.

Humph. "Yes, most likely. I'm so glad we've outgrown that tradition. If it were still acceptable today, I'd probably be married off to one of my great aunt's bridge group member's sons." Kathryn pulled a face at the thought, which was not too much of an exaggeration.

"That's an idea. I will have to take another look at the boys available to my granddaughter. She's not as young or quite as pretty as you." Then, she thought somewhat wistfully as she inclined her head. "You want the painting? The sour couple?"

"You know, I think they're fascinating, but I can't spend that kind of money just to take them home and rejoice that I'm not in their shoes."

"I will give you a deal you can't refuse." And with those fateful words, Kathryn had become the owner of the Wilton picture.

As Kathryn's thoughts returned to the present, it seemed she had gotten much more than she had bargained for.

~ * ~

Michael met his butler in the hall. "Thorpe, is she settling in?"

35

"Yes, My Lord, but she is also insisting we are making too much of a fuss over her and that she is leaving first thing tomorrow." Michael recognized the tone intended to get the master's attention. "She is determined to leave."

"We can't hold her against her will, but we can insist she be better prepared for a journey. Has she yet said where she is headed?"

"No, My Lord."

"Send Smithers to the study. We will spend a few minutes on business before our guest joins us for luncheon. Also, she will need slippers. Please see to that too."

"As you say, sir." He spoke with deference but Michael caught the censure in Hallthorpe's tone, that his Master was altogether too blasé about Miss Ragland's plans...to leave. His henchman was wrong.

Chapter Four

From somewhere in the house, a gong sounded and Kathryn looked up from her mirror wondering if this was the luncheon bell she had read about in Regency romance novels. Having dismissed the maid so thoroughly, Kathryn had found out quickly just why maids were so necessary. She hadn't been able to get her dress together by herself and finally succumbed to the need to pull the rope in her room that would summon help. When Ellie arrived just seconds later, Kathryn was feeling extremely contrite.

Ellie went right to work lacing up the gown without being asked. "Miss, will you let me help with your hair, too? I have a house full of sisters and I've lots of practice with styles," she said. "Besides, the Master will expect it. Ladies wear their hair up." *The master would expect her to look more respectable than the ramshackle way she had arrived. Men's breeches and loose hair no less!*

"Might as well. I've already been a pretty big failure at putting on the dress. Clearly I need a little help," Kathryn acknowledged graciously.

"As you say, miss."

"How many sisters do you have?" Kathryn watched the girl in the mirror work wonders with her hair.

"There are five in all, miss."

"Wow, I just have one sister. I guess there's always a line for the bathroom?"

"Line for the bathroom, miss?"

"Uh, umm…line to use the mirror and the hair styling tools?" Kathryn realized her mistake; no point in bringing up a subject that didn't even

37

exist.

"So, have you worked here long?" Kathryn thought to try a different conversation stream.

"No miss, I've arrived today," Ellie announced proudly.

"Today? Let me guess, your arrival coincided with mine," Kathryn pressed.

"Yes, miss. Isn't proper for a lady not to have a maid," Ellie fussed.

Kathryn was quiet and Ellie prompted, "Miss?"

"Sorry. I was thinking about something else." *Someone* else. Someone who had ordered up a maid for her in the short time since they had split? Had she thought him just a bit arrogant and controlling? He was definitely masterful.

"I—I…like it here. This job, it's my chance to help my family. So if it's all the same to you…"

"So you do *want* this work?" Kathryn had interrupted her then realized too late as she heard her own embarrassingly condescending tone that this was probably a very good job for a girl from the village. Ellie's eyes were downcast but her strong fingers continued moving in Kathryn's hair. It did feel wonderful for someone to be working her hair like that. It had truly been a long time since her last cut and color and there was no question her hair was ragged looking. Kathryn was shamed by her prejudices. Ellie was obviously a strong competent woman who knew what she wanted. This job was her way "out." "I'm sorry, that didn't come out right. I'll try to behave."

Ellie's inelegant snort suggested she knew exactly what Kathryn meant.

Ellie had turned Kathryn from the mirror and she figured the maid had done so before her mistress had an opportunity to complain. "There, you can turn around now."

Kathryn faced the mirror and wondered at the woman's reflection. She knew she was looking at herself but this person was so different, with piled high curls, some of the bouncing tendrils dancing down to touch her cheek, her ear and her neck, and one long curl even wound its way down her back. Absently, she reached her hand to touch and Ellie jumped, obviously fearful she would tear down the cascading waterfall of hair. "It's amazing. You did this all with just some bobby pins and, oh my gosh, it's got ribbons woven through it. It's...stunning." Kathryn turned to bless Ellie with a smile that lit her entire face causing the girl in turn to blush profusely. Ellie hurriedly set about returning all the implements to their rightful places.

For the first time since waking up in the alternate dream universe, Kathryn felt like—not that she fit in—but that at least she wasn't any longer a total embarrassment. It was a start.

Recalling that the luncheon gong had pealed some time ago and surely, she was late by now, Kathryn rushed from the room into a wall of hard human flesh. Huge hands grabbed her upper arms, squeezed tight, and steadied her. She was not sure if it was the impact that had stolen her breath or if it had been the faint smell of man's cologne and earthy cleanliness that teased her senses or the tightness of his grip, for all of those had enveloped her as she raised her gaze to Michael Stafford's eyes.

"Well, Miss Ragland. You look...presentable."

"Presentable? That's certainly not a compliment."

"No. I guess not. In the army, had an officer said..."

"I'm not in the army and I'll have you know that it took me probably thirty minutes to get into this dress and Ellie more time to lace it and then this hair..."

"Miss Ragland, you look lovely." He interrupted her tirade and gifted her with a smile. "I have come to fetch you for luncheon and am most pleasantly surprised to find you ready." He paused. "Have I now been properly appreciative of your efforts?"

"And Ellie's..." she teased. "You know. I didn't mean to be fishing for compliments. It's just that..."

"Fishing for compliments? An interesting past-time fishing?" A dark brow rose, his eyes teased her.

"It's a figure of speech...baiting you to tell me I look nice. Surely you recognize it from the young ladies at balls when they flutter their fans at you and look expectantly up at you to make some kind of comment about their gowns and tell them they look *lovely*?"

"Indeed?" He gave her a look of mock innocence.

"Oh you, you're looking at me like I am a dummy. You knew that all along."

"Yes, Miss Ragland, I think there has been compliment fishing since

39

the beginning of time or the beginning of real fishing at least. But, as you say, I guess the 'misses' rather do *fish* a lot." He laughed at the vision because he was certain she was right. It was a lovely image, especially if one considered a hook in the mouth of some of the more simpering misses. He of course was fully aware of the expression; he just loved to make her explain it to him as if her education and experience were superior to his. She was a wonderful sparring partner for his simple jests. "And here I thought it only a man's past-time."

"Fishing is most definitely a practiced art form. But, you know, I like the real kind with hooks too."

"You fish?" He could not be sure he had accurately heard this latest figure of speech. He had also not quite calmed from the overwhelming sensation of her small form slamming into his body, pressing her charms into his chest, the charms that were so amply revealed by the low cut neckline and supportive bodice of the simple muslin.

"Oh yes, the old fashioned kind that's done with a bamboo pole and crickets or worms where you sit on the side of the family cow pond in the hour just before sunset. I could actually fish almost anywhere with any kind of gear…for hours. It is so relaxing and one of the few times I really am able to be quiet and patient and whoever I'm with has to be quiet too."

He had been guiding her down the stairs and now that they were walking abreast with her hand resting on his arm, Michael regarded her hair piled in ringlets as the image of a pot of gold at the end of the rainbow. His guest's freckles glinted ever so slightly, less he was sure than before, and the most radiant smile had softened her face. Michael knew he could bask for hours in her warm glow. Michael drew a breath and found once again that scent of earthy woman but could no longer make out the tropical flavor from before. It must have been bathed away and he was oddly saddened by the cleanliness of his family's regular soap that had diminished some of the flavors of her tantalizing smell.

How had she described it? *The hour before sunset and the cow pond?* He could not even register that this vexing *American* stranger knew his most favorite spot. The smell of cow, raw and dirty, dark descending, anticipation, then capture. Exhilaration, relaxation. She knew what it meant to fish. Michael could imagine Kathryn sitting on the bank of the quiet river with a pole lazily dropped into the depths, her fine legs encased in men's breeches while her burnished skin freckled further in the sun. Heat stirred in his belly at the thought of joining her there, of her utter perfection at that moment, for what man could resist a woman who adored fishing? The vitality and life of the woman on his arm gripped him and she was in *his* house, under *his* roof. Immediately, he recognized the latest wrinkle in his rescue plans.

"Miss Ragland, as you undoubtedly know, English society is very strict about ladies staying as guests in the homes of gentlemen. Fortunately, our current circumstance is being remedied as we speak. I have sent a note to my Aunt Agatha asking her to join us immediately. For the short term, you will be chaperoned by my sister."

"Chaperoned by your sister? Interesting phrasing but oh, wonderful. Then I *am* looking forward to meeting her. Will she be at lunch?"

"No, she eats in her rooms." As they approached the dining room and he reached for the knob, he turned to her. "My sister has been ill for some time…since her husband died. She rarely leaves her rooms."

"I'm so sorry. Is there…"

"No. No one can force help on her, not until she wants it."

He was unable to hide the note of sadness in his tone. Kathryn elected to stay quiet, and he left that last sentence hanging in the air.

Kathryn's place was set to his right, intimately rather than at the end of the table as had been the custom when his parents dined in this room. Today was his first meal at the head of the table and he contemplated the significance of that change as the footman set the soup bowl in front of him with Hallthorpe supervising.

"My lord, I hope the meal meets with your approval. Cook has made some of your favorites. This is…"

"Yes, I can smell the lamb. I know it will be excellent. Thank you."

"Miss Ragland, I am afraid you will have to endure the machinations of my staff with the seating and the menu. It appears that they have taken it upon themselves to see to my every need."

"I think they're glad to see you." Her lips turned up and she graced him with a warm smile. As their eyes met, and he returned her regard, she seemed to him to become all of a sudden quite self-conscious. Their close seating arrangements must not have been lost on her either.

As she dedicated herself to her food, Michael wondered how she must feel wearing a stranger's clothes with her hair styled as it was. Probably very uncomfortable. She had been in breeches and wearing her mane of red-gold hair wildly long and loose about her. But now she looked astonishingly...perfect. He shook his head and attempted to bring her out of her brown study.

"You're obviously correct, but I believe my staff is quite as glad to meet you as they are to see me."

"And why is that?" She took a dainty spoonful of the delicious tasting soup.

"I am a stuffy old soldier. You are a fascinating traveler from America."

"Actually I'm a lost, shoeless commoner who was lucky enough to meet a nice man, who felt sorry for me and brought me to his palatial home," she catalogued.

"Lost and shoeless, yes. Common, no."

"You are absolutely blowing your compliment quota out of the water. I believe that was another one." She gave him a flirtatious grin.

"I will set about rectifying that by plying you with insults. I believe you are using the wrong fork for your figs, Miss Ragland." She began to laugh and he watched her glance back and forth from her plate to the remaining silverware.

"What is funny, Miss Ragland? Am I now dripping my wine?"

"Oh no, Captain. That was pretty lame as insults go and I was just thinking about how, umm...*proper* I looked."

"Please enlighten me on how that is funny."

"Well, just yesterday I was wearing shorts, with my hair pulled into a pony tail and presenting a picture about as unfeminine and improper as well, as opposite as this."

Shorts! He was visualizing men's smalls! "Tell me, what are shorts and a pony tail? It sounds intriguing."

"Shorts are short pants, cut off above the knees. Shorter than your riding pants...I believe your society matrons would call them *positively scandalous.*"

He laughed out loud at her very successful imitation of those feared ladies.

"A pony tail is the way of wearing hair pulled back into a rubber band so that it has the effect of looking like a horse's tail."

"You choose to look like a horse's tail?" he asked with a low rumble barely concealing his enjoyment at her expense.

"No, not look like a horse's tail. Just the hair part—the tail—not the… Ahhh, it makes doing strenuous activity easy, gets your hair out of your face," she chided.

"Your hair is now out of your face." He could not wait to see how she would answer his challenge. With a sigh, she put down her spoon and recognized he was once again, teasing her.

"Okay, this…" she swirled her finger over her head "…is not a hairstyle conducive to any activity except sitting demurely and looking pretty. For fishing or almost any physical activity, a pony tail is much preferred."

"Well, I must say, you wear the sitting-pretty-and-demure-style rather well. I shall take you fishing so I can also see the pony tail style."

"Captain, you and your staff are being so gracious but I don't think I'll be here long enough for fishing or pony tails. I've got to try to get on the road to London in the morning." At that moment that he was looking at her with his eyes glassed over and there was a muscle twitching at his jaw. Was he angry? He sure looked like he might explode.

Then he did that eyebrow raise thing he did and the footmen in the room disappeared. He used that look very well. She could imagine the privates in his units shaking in their boots and wondered how many of them had actually wet themselves when he called them out for doing something wrong. She was certainly shaking in her shoes under the enormous pressure of being in this house, thinking of the distance she had to travel and the absolute absurdity that she had landed in this dream.

"Miss Ragland, I believe it is time you told me where you are from and how you got to Wilton. The *truth* would help."

That stung but she wasn't surprised he still didn't believe her. "I know it sounds nuts, but the honest truth is I went to bed in my own house and woke up here. I have no idea how I got here. I don't expect you to believe it or understand it because I don't either. I just know that I need to make my way back to London so I can figure this thing out. Maybe catch a ship leaving for America."

"You're going to 'catch a ship' and that will get you home?"

"That sarcasm is not particularly flattering on you, Captain. It makes you look severe and sound well…mean. But to answer your question, I'm not sure. But staying here…" *unless falling asleep with the picture again works…* "I truly have no idea how to get home."

"Where is home?"

"The US. I told you that and I'm not lying. Surely you can tell by talking to me and looking at me that I am an American?"

"Actually, your accent is quite unfamiliar as I believe I mentioned earlier. You sound like no one I have ever heard. As to your circumstances, I was now ready for more specifics. *Where* in America?"

"Okay, so if you thought the part about my being beamed over here was a doozie, well, I am from the state of Alabama which I don't really think was even a state in your era. It's in the South."

Michael shook his head and tried to fathom just how he had landed with such a woman who was a best described as a conundrum. Bright, charming, an honest face and smile, with looks that had grown on him considerably but yet, clinging to a bizarre lack of trust in him.

"Miss Ragland? If I concede that you are far from home and don't know how to get back, will you concede that there is not indeed any reason for your precipitous departure tomorrow?"

"Yes."

"Yes. *That's it*?"

"Yes. I can't really fault your logic. Since I don't know how to get there, I might as well organize my travel plans better first."

As the last dish was cleared, Michael wanted to prolong their time together. Being with Kathryn was the most fun he'd had in years. He had thoroughly enjoyed this verbal contest with her. "Would you care to take a ride with me? I had thought to make my return known to the farmers whose cottages lie along the western boundary of my lands."

"I would absolutely love to ride with you but I'm saying up front I'll only do it if I can ride with my legs on different sides of the horse like we did coming here."

"Astride?"

"Yes, that's it. I can ride that way but I'm not about to get on a horse holding my legs on one side. Whoever invented the sidesaddle was not a woman!"

His fingers clenched and released as he all but blurted out the *reason* for women to ride sidesaddle. She was clearly unconcerned with that particular consequence. Her strident declaration just made it all the more deliciously scandalous. A woman, on one of his prized beasts, riding astride down to the cottages of his tenants…Michael shook off the image. "You shall ride astride as you wish."

"Awesome…I mean, oh thank you. That's wonderful. Maybe as we ride you can show me how to really ride. All I've ever done is ride in circles at summer camp."

"*Summer camp?*"

"Look at you raising those brows at me. You wield those things like weapons!" she teased.

"I guess I do. It's a habit that I am too old to break. It worked very well with my soldiers. But, tell me of summer camp."

"Summer camp…when city girls go off for a week in the country and live in tents, ride horses, fight off bugs, cook over open flames, go days without showering or shaving, swim in murky lakes, drink spring water, take long hikes…you know?"

"Yes, I just spent the last several years doing that. It was called war."

"Are you always so on?"

"On?"

"Funny."

"No." *It's something about* you *that makes everything funnier, brighter, more.* When she appeared at the stables in the same dress, Michael wondered what happened to the proficiency of the maid who had done such a remarkable job with the hair but this…

"Why are you looking at me like that?"

"Because you can't ride astride in a dress with your legs…"

"With my legs showing? Don't worry. I've got that part taken care of. I borrowed another pair of your riding pants. See?" And she lifted the hem of her dress enough to reveal a pair of buckskins that molded to her sculpted calves. The sight of her dressed so provocatively sent his blood thrumming. His mind dimly registered that the fabric of his pants was caressing her most private parts. Shaking his head to clear his unhelpful wayward thoughts, he moved away from her lest she see how she disturbed him.

45

Catherine's mare was the obvious choice for her but he was not enamored of having to explain just whose horse she had been. True enough she was now his horse and had become the one that inexperienced young ladies rode when visiting the estate, but she had been Catherine's and a wedding gift to boot. Michael knew women well enough to know she would be offended later if he did not tell her now who the horse had originally belonged to, but he weighed the threat and decided he did not want to break he pleasant mood. "Her name is Jasmine."

"Beautiful. It fits her." He watched as Kathryn ran her hand down the velvet head of the gentle horse. "My memory is that jasmine is a delicate, creeping vine with small white scented blooms. This horse seems delicate."

"She is that," Michael assented absently. He would not tell her that Jasmine had been named for his late wife's favorite fragrance, not because it was delicate but because it was her favorite. He didn't believe she had actually been thinking of the horse when she named it.

He much preferred this woman's description of the mare. He had thought her delicate and a safe mount, which was indeed why he had bought her for his wife and any girls they might have. As he watched the tantalizing picture of Kathryn Ragland whispering to the mild animal, he was struck with the realization that his first wife had not ridden Jasmine even once. Jasmine had been waiting all these years to meet her mistress.

Her mistress? Bloody hell and damnation.

He made the mistake of stealing a glance at her as they departed the drive for the bridle path leading to the cottages. The picture she cut with leanly muscled legs encased in his breeches, her small booted feet clinging desperately to stirrups while the breeze tugged at straying strands of spun-gold hair stole his breath as surely as if he had run headlong into an immovable object. Worse yet, as he watched her settle on Jasmine, he remembered Kathryn's heavy-tongued words as she had talked about the rocking motion of his horse's gait. Pressed up against her as he had been, the words had echoed the sensations his body had been feeling. Watching her again this afternoon, he was flooded with that new sense of anticipation, eroticism, and longing

"You said you might teach me a little about riding. I know when you're just walking, sitting is okay, but what should I do when we start

46

going faster?"

"Rise just off the seat with your thighs supporting your weight," he said as he showed her the correct position.

"Okay, this is like riding a bicycle so that when you go over the bumps your skin isn't slapped silly."

"Exactly. Shall we try a faster speed?"

Michael eased Fury into a trot and Kathryn naturally assumed the position on Jasmine. The delicate horse stepped properly into Fury's wake and as both horses responded to his pressure to increase their speed, they began eating up ground. He hadn't told her he was going to make them gallop so that she would not have time to be afraid. She had made it clear she had not really ever ridden, but for an American female with no particular riding experience, she was taking to it rather naturally, her strong thighs showing remarkable stamina in holding the position. While she was so much smaller than he was, her lithe form was perfectly suited to riding.

When it was clear Kathryn was straining and unable to hold herself off the saddle any longer, Michael slowed and turned. "I must compliment you on your lesson."

Rather than answer him, Kathryn nodded, likely because she held a mouthful of ribbons since hair had come loose entirely from her delicately spun coiffure. With the mass getting more unruly, she had gathered it into her hands then began winding the ribbon about the length. With her hands working her hair thus, it was at that moment that the Viking warrior goddess came to life. Michael drank in Kathryn's flushed cheeks, barely restrained mane, wildly sparkling eyes and the upturned corners of her mouth. The sun loved her, made the bronze skin and honey hair fairly glow. The woman was a stunning vision.

"That was amazing. I feel so good. Don't get me wrong, it totally exhausted me and my quads are burning but oh my gosh, I now know why people love riding horses. The power, the freedom. Ahhh..."

It was almost as if she had been made to order just for him.

Chapter Five

The tenant visits were, in a word, instructive. Each and every female he encountered regarded Kathryn Ragland with awe and the deference he would expect to be afforded his presumptive Duchess. It had not occurred to him how specifically she would be viewed by literally everyone they encountered; he had merely been seeking the excuse to spend the afternoon with her.

"Have we just passed another apple orchard?"

Her question shook him from his reverie. "They're not apples. We have pears, too."

"I love pears. We had those pickled figs at lunch. What do you do with the pears?"

"Probably anything you can imagine. Stewed is my favorite."

"That doesn't sound quite as good as fresh off the tree," she mused.

"Then you will have to try one when they ripen."

She looked at him then glanced away. He realized she was probably going to say she wouldn't be around that long, but had caught herself. He was sure she would be wrong.

He let the silence stretch. "Do you like cider?"

"I appreciate cider but I don't much drink it. I don't really drink any juices. I just prefer to avoid all the sugar calories."

"Is that why you are so trim?" He couldn't help himself.

"That and a fortunate combination of genes from remarkably well built people and a lot of exercise."

They arrived at a small residence with well-trimmed shrubbery growing against the high, small windows.

"Here we are."

As he lifted her down, Michael heard her in-drawn breath and felt the shiver that ran down Kathryn's spine. She was not unaffected by him. He released her reluctantly and she stepped quickly to the side. They moved toward the first home side by side, not touching. At the blacksmith's home, the third they had visited, the man's young wife and his three children were in awe of his companion just as the others had been. Kathryn stepped up to the woman with her now familiar self-assurance. "Your daughter is gorgeous. She looks like my sister did when she was little. What is her name?"

"H—Her name is Te-ess," the woman stammered and Michael realized she was searching for a title to call the exquisite lady in front of her. Kathryn with her striped golden tresses, surprisingly well fit gown, glowing eyes and genuine smile looked positively expensive and yet she compared this woman's small lowborn girl with her *own sister*. Mrs. Smith's face was glowing with pride.

"Captain Stafford, I don't believe I have seen a prettier little girl."

She turned to him, beaming, and his soldier's heart fluttered. He had not realized until these moments what message he had been sending to his tenants by presenting the lady. He might need to deal with the notions at some point but right now, with her conquests, she was making his life so much easier. This lady was charming his tenants and building exactly the kinds of relationships with their wives that would make their loyalty absolute. He reminded himself to thank her properly when they were on the way back.

In hindsight, he decided that it was not a mistake to allow the supposition to grow in strength. From what little he already knew of her, Kathryn Ragland would be a formidable partner to help him rebuild the strained relationships with the tenants and villagers that had festered due to his Father's inattention.

"My sister's name is Christine but we call her Christy," Kathryn explained. "She has thick brown hair just like yours and pure green eyes. You are a little beauty." The small child could only stare wide eyed at the lady until she finally reached out and touched Kathryn's shoulder. It was at that moment that he saw Kathryn recognize too what was happening. These were poor people, commoners, and laborers, and now she must

49

realize they thought she was a noble. Did she also realize that they thought she was soon to be their Duchess? She seemed to take the moment at face value and then with ease pulled the child toward her into a motherly embrace.

Michael almost reached for her because he knew, just knew, the family would be petrified but he should not have worried about Kathryn for as he moved he could see the girl sink into the embrace.

Mrs. Smith's in-drawn breath caught his attention. Her eyes were huge and filled with horror as her daughter embraced what Mrs. Smith surely thought was nobility. But Miss Kathryn Ragland, enigmatic beauty personified, was not finished. She hugged the child and he watched a tear run down her cheek as she squeezed little Tess.

"Thank you, Tess for that wonderful hug. I very much miss my sister. I think you just made me feel better."

And little Tess twisted some of Kathryn's hair about her hand and laid her head on Kathryn's shoulder once again slipping her stained thumb into her mouth.

"Gold," she lisped. The two of them embraced rocking slowly back and forth, and his soldier's heart melted a little more.

This was also the first time he had heard Kathryn mention a sister and really understood she was indeed far away from her family and her home. He had not believed the first word of her story at the inn or her insistence at luncheon that she was magically transported here, but her genuine expression of loneliness while cuddling the child, well it had been telling.

~ * ~

"I wanted to thank you, Kathryn. May I call you Kathryn?" He hesitated until he was sure he had her attention since she seemed to be fumbling with the reins and trying unsuccessfully to pull the skirts of her gown out from under her bottom. When she finally looked at him, there were questions in her eyes that shone honey in the bright afternoon light. "I've not been the landlord. I mean, I was manor born but never inclined to visit the tenants. You…you positively charmed them. That is important and I am grateful."

She regarded him, her eyes narrowing, and he realized that she had just decided that it was a very heavy admission from someone such as he.

"Would you say that I earned my keep today?"

He wanted to say that it was so much more, but he was dealing with the proud, headstrong woman who had been walking to London without shoes and so he was inclined to let her believe she had done only a day's turn. If he told her the truth—that she was helping him warm badly-strained relations with his people, she would think him to be exaggerating.

"You did. If I fed you an evening meal and provided some mild entertainment, we could call today even. Is that fair?"

"Fair," she said. And suddenly he no longer wanted her in his debt; he wanted so much more.

They traveled the remainder of the trip in a comfortable silence. He had seen a woman today who knew how to talk to people, women especially, to smooth his way, and ease his burden. Talking with women, especially uneducated ones, was naturally a great deficiency of his. For the first time since he had assumed the mantle, he saw how a woman could be a partner rather than just a person to be attached to and yet he had only known this one for only part of one day.

The few relationships with women in his life were mostly poor. He had struggled to find a way to talk to his sad mother. He and his Aunt Agatha probably got on the best. There was his beloved sister Cassandra who he desperately wanted to reconnect with, but the abject failure had been his relationship with his unwanted wife. Not being able to talk to her and, in reality, only barely tolerating her had made for a difficult marriage. Thankfully, he had been away for most of it. She had mostly been miserable and he found that he was not sorry that they were no longer married.

He wondered how to reach Cassandra, whom he loved with all his heart, but she suffered and he could offer her no solace. He wanted so much for her to heal, to be made whole, to have a new husband and children if she wanted, but at least to have some kind of life. Michael realized it was time to make Kathryn known to his fragile sister.

He'd had few sexual liaisons as well. Not being inclined to casually bed women, although he'd had ample opportunity being an officer possessed of enough fortune and passable looks to attract any number of followers, he had preferred abstinence to promiscuity. His lack of partners would probably surprise most of his friends. He had bedded one woman on the Continent several times but stopped when it became clear to him that the perils of risking getting her with child outweighed any pleasure he had found.

And he had never paid for sex, not with money, jewels or even simply opera tickets. He had never had his first wife Catherine either for she was already with the child that his cousin would not acknowledge when they married and he had not wanted her. Truly, no one he had bedded had meant anything to him and that above all had been the reason his partners had been so few.

He had been comfortable being celibate because he knew absolutely that he had not contracted pox and left behind no by-blows. If he did marry again, it would be a lot easier without any of *that* baggage. Now that he had to think about choosing a bride, he knew he could never be interested in simpering London chits. He was more Puritanical at heart than he would admit publicly, but his lack of interest had manifested itself in a strong desire to ultimately choose a Duchess who was not necessarily a gently bred virgin but also was not prone to dalliance. He would not tolerate his wife's infidelity and he would make clear that they were to keep their vows, even if theirs was not a love match.

He had seen far too many marriages in which one of the partners suffered at the hands of the other just for trying to be faithful, or worse because the mistresses or lovers were flaunted in society so that they knew they were being cuckolded. Even when they were not all flaunted as his Father's had not been, they still caused such pain. His Father was so arrogant to think that his mother and children had not known of or been affected by his widely known relationship with Clarice Moorecombe and the ones before her.

Then there was the question of issue. When neither partner was faithful, how was the man to even know a child was his? Or if the affair was ongoing, that he would not stumble upon his wife in a compromising position? Surely a marriage should be based on mutual respect. He really was so much more provincial than most of the gentlemen of his acquaintance whom he knew partook of the affections of willing married women. There were a few notable exceptions like his friend Matthew Drake who was also rather staid.

He glanced over at the woman riding beside him and, without

hesitation, determined *this* Kathryn would indeed make a fine Duchess. He didn't have to love her. He just needed her to be in his life. She had nothing really to recommend her other than what he saw as quite stunning physical features, an ability to share feelings openly, a warm disposition and charming wit. There was no dowry, no family, no connections. He did not need any of that, thankfully. He just needed her to make his life easier, warm his bed, and provide an heir or two. She would do that nicely, and she was already here. Simple. He had not expected to be drawn so strongly to a female who possessed the qualities he might want in a wife. He could very well imagine bedding Kathryn Ragland and being very satisfied with her for his remaining years.

He had traveled the entire distance lost in thought, uninterrupted by the woman riding beside him. Upon gaining the forecourt, Michael watched the enamored stable lad run for Kathryn's horse. When she blessed him with a gracious smile, the boy flushed from his head clear down his shirt. He could not be more than eleven or twelve and thankfully, the lad's look was worshipful rather than lustful. But when Kathryn leaned down and whispered something to the boy, Michael felt a ridiculous pang of jealousy run down his spine. He knew better than to ask her what she had said but he could imagine she was giving loving, supportive thanks to the boy in that incredibly warm way she had of endearing people to her. *Bloody hell.*

She caught his eye at that moment. Michael realized that his social mask must have slipped and she saw something he did not want her to recognize. He knew jealousy well and it was unattractive, he certainly did not want her to see it in him. Stiffening, he announced, "My lady, now that you have charmed the tenants and the staff, it is time for you to retire for a well-earned rest. We shall dine at seven o'clock and I will in the meantime see to that entertainment I promised."

"Would it be horribly unsporting of me to ask what kind of entertainment?"

He hid a smile at her attempt to sound like him. "Your accent is coming along, but no, dear lady, it must be a surprise. Do you like them? Surprises I mean?"

"Very much. I also like parties and birthdays and Christmas. I'm a very festive person."

"Well, then you shall not be disappointed." He brought her diminutive hand to his lips letting them linger just a moment longer than proper as he stroked her palm with his thumb. She smelled of saddle leather, people, and life.

~ * ~

Kathryn forced herself to take the stairs one at a time. In truth, she was probably tired enough to crawl after her miles of walking, then riding behind Michael on his horse, then the hours riding on her own mount, and endless conversations with so many different people, but she was too excited to give in to her growing list of aches and pains. This had been one of the most interesting days of her life. The tenants, their problems, and how Michael fairly beamed at her success with them pumped her up. This afternoon she finally felt like she had done something worthy of all the effort he and his staff had gone to on her behalf.

She had not spent any time on her own very real problem though, a wave of guilt roiling up in her stomach at the thought. *How the heck was she going to get home from this dream world?* Lost in thoughts of missing Christine and her job and all of those who would be frantic over her disappearance, Kathryn missed the landing for her room and ended up one floor above her own. Not realizing her mistake, she reached for the knob and opened the door into what was clearly not the Dowager's bedroom she had been assigned. This was a sitting room, shrouded in darkness, with old-fashioned furniture and smelling oddly of mold. Kathryn began to back out the door when she heard the voice. "I saw you."

Who? His sister? "Hello, I'm Kathryn."

"I've heard." The voice was almost a whisper but heavy, sad.

"Are you Michael's sister? Cassandra?"

"Yes." One word answers. Great. Kathryn thought and moved into the room.

"May I come in? I'd be thrilled to meet you." She couldn't however say that she had heard so much about her since Michael had said almost nothing but that she was ill and an unqualified chaperone.

"Please." The word was resigned and as heavy and sad as the first she had spoken. Then she said nothing more. Kathryn decided that she would go forward with Cassandra as she had with the tenants, naturally and unassuming. "I apologize for not coming to visit you upon first arriving at the house. I seem to barely find my way around and am constantly having to be shuffled back to wherever I am supposed to be. I have to admit that I actually found you by accident today."

"Rarely anyone finds me. My footman and my maid know where I am, but everyone else leaves me alone."

"Why is that?" It was the bold frontal approach that her instincts and training told Kathryn would have the best chance of success with this delicate bird.

"They think I am crazy and are afraid to upset me."

"Why do they think that? You being crazy I mean?"

"Probably because after my husband's death, I tried to kill myself."

"Kill yourself? Wow. That probably would make me concerned for your safety too."

Cassandra was regarding her through eyes blacker than her brother's, her pale skin almost translucent, the bones of her face evident. She clearly never got any sun or exercise, probably hadn't been outside in days. Only her hair shone healthy. Its blackness glowed almost blue in the dim light.

There was a saying Kathryn recalled about being killed or judged or something like that for a sheep as a wolf or some such so she went forward boldly again. "I can imagine that losing your husband was terribly difficult but killing yourself would not bring him back."

"No, but I did not want to do it because I missed him. I did it to try to punish him, or at least his family."

"What did he do to you?" Kathryn whispered. She could see those obsidian eyes lighting and warming to her subject now that she had gotten her admission off her chest. "I'd be very comfortable listening."

"He humiliated me in the most disgusting of ways that a husband could humiliate a wife." She paused and Kathryn wondered if she would continue. "He actually fought with another man over his mistress and got himself shot in the process."

"Was it in a duel?"

"Of sorts. It seems that Edward was not ready to give her up even though another unmarried protector was nosing around. She had hopes of choosing a protector that would one day flout society and marry her as she was and when Edward married me, she wanted to move on." She paused thoughtfully and regarded Kathryn's expression. "I can see you're probably wondering how I know this."

"Yes. I had gotten the feeling that men around here are very private, especially I imagine about mistress dealings."

"After he died, *she* told me. She thought it might be easier on me to really hate him rather than grieve over him. In a rather twisted way, it probably was a blessing, because from that moment on I was determined to have some sort of revenge for what he'd done."

"Did you know he had the mistress when you married?"

"No. I was nineteen and naïve. I was a highly sought after prize and my father pushed me toward Edward as first son of an Earl with vast holdings. I recall at the time that I was sure he would love me and come to that conclusion very quickly. Why would he not?"

"Of course." Why *would* he not?

When she did not continue right away, Kathryn saw for the first time, the wistful look of a young woman who had believed in the dream of a happy marriage only to find betrayal at such a young age. She could not be any older than Kathryn herself. "I believe he loved his mistress. She told me that he had professed his love but had married me anyway. She had tried to convince him to marry her, that because he was the only son, his father wouldn't disown him. We agreed he must have been too cowardly. So instead, he married brilliantly—a woman of means who would allow him to continue his adultery after marriage."

"Did you have sex with him?" The provocative questions kept her talking so this one just seemed natural.

"On our wedding night, he came to my room and took my virginity, but it was rough and callous and I hurt for days. I woke to his being gone in the night. I believe he went to *her* for satisfaction. We never had… sex again."

"Wasn't he even concerned with an heir?" Kathryn tried not to sound as surprised a she felt.

"I suppose he would have got back to that eventually, but he was so busy trying to keep his mistress that he didn't have much time for me."

"How long had you been married when he was killed?"

"Just over a year. It was the loneliest, most despairing time in my life. I didn't know why he was rejecting me, just that he was. Gone all hours but keeping me almost captive in the house by refusing invitations. It was as if he wanted to be sure I never got out and discovered what he was doing." Cassandra trailed off.

"So what happened?"

"Since you seem to be able to handle all of this talk of mistresses without swooning, I shall tell you exactly what happened. There was a gun battle in her townhouse. I believe she finally wanted to rid herself of him and his possessiveness so she invited her new protector over to send him on his way. Words ensued and finally they drew pistols and shot. He must have been drunk or too outraged to aim properly and his bullet hit no one but did leave a hole in her plaster. The other man was deadly accurate."

"And she *told* you all of this? I mean, I don't doubt you, it's just that it would seem like her new man would have gotten into trouble."

"She knew no one would believe me, and her new protector had taken great pains to make it appear that it had been an accident. It sounds like quite an outrageous story now that I am repeating it to another human being."

"It's hard to believe someone thought that two men with guns in one woman's apartment with one ending up dead had been an accident but I know from what I've read, the English male aristocrats seem to let each other get away with a lot." Kathryn shook her head, digesting this tale.

"That is an understatement," Cassandra said dryly. For this first time during their interview, her lips curved in what might have been thought to be a smile.

"So, mistress comes to unburden herself to you out of a sense of guilt or was it female compassion?"

"When she said she wanted me to hate him it was because she knew I would find out enough about his death to wonder, but not enough to be angry. She thought I deserved to be let out of the agony of grieving for such a scoundrel. It was oddly kind of her, but she probably also got some sick revenge too. *I* had married him after all."

"So. No one tells publicly that your husband was fighting over a whore, no one is punished, and you're supposed to be the grieving widow? I'll bet you were pissed. Oh sorry, I didn't mean to cuss."

"No matter. That's exactly how I felt and I was also at the mercy of his family. His father was not at all pleased to be stuck with caring for me

57

since I had not bothered to bear him an heir in the whole year I was married to his son."

"So, that guy was definitely an ass!" Kathryn cringed at her own cursing.

"I told him everything." Her eyes and skin glowed as Cassandra made her triumphant announcement.

"What did he do?"

"He slapped me and told me to never utter one word against his son again," she said scornfully.

"Oh, my gosh. So when you went to his father hoping they would admit what he had done he hit you. Then you tried to take your own life to punish him?

"Yes!"

"Brilliant but tragic solution, awfully Shakesperean for me," Kathryn offered.

"Just so, I made sure to leave notes in several places but alas, my brother intercepted me before I could complete my task." She turned longingly toward an outside window that must have reminded her of him. "He had come back from the Continent for the funeral and came to visit me just as I was completing my letter to him. He was always able to read me very well and he could see something in my eyes that told him there was a different problem. I tried to hide it but he saw it. He pulled the letter from my hands and then carried me bodily from the room."

Kathryn could see the pride in Cassandra's eyes as she recounted her brother's heroic rescue. "So now I am on the edge of my seat. What did he do?"

"He called a footman to come attend me and gave him instructions that I was very ill and he was not to let me out of his sight, then he marched down to the Earl's study and beat him silly. I heard him yelling words like 'whore' and 'honor' and 'trash' and oh yes, I heard one whole phrase 'bloody well that he is already dead,' then he rejoined me in the hall looking perfectly put together but his eyes burning in fury, and dragged me through the door.

"Did you attempt to kill yourself after that?" Kathryn asked now sure that she would not offend.

"No. I had Michael and he brought me here and I was free." Cassandra

58

shrugged.

"So you never actually tried the act, just planned it, and wrote about it?"

"Correct. I never did anything to hurt myself except maybe shut myself up in this room."

Kathryn wondered how Cassandra had worked through her grief and anger and fear. "Were you alone out here, after he went back, I mean?"

"No, his wife was here until she died. But I did not cry terribly long over her either."

"I'll look forward to hearing that story soon." Kathryn gave her a conspiratorial grin. "But, for now, I promised Michael I would rest before dinner. It was a long ride out to the tenants and there was a lot of greeting and talking and well, Michael has promised entertainment."

"Entertainment? Has he given any clue?" Her pitch dark eyes danced with this revelation.

"No. He just asked me if I liked surprises. I told him yes, then he sent me on my way. Well, actually he kissed my hand first. What am I supposed to make of that?"

Cassandra's sparkling eyes lit up the delicate features of her stunning face. She might be tiny and frail and fragile but she had a natural beauty to rival any New York fashion model. In fact, she was just right for the cover of a haute couture designer's brochure. "You should wear green," she offered.

"What do you mean by that?" Kathryn asked, immediately noticing the twinkle had turned thoughtful.

"The color will set off your hazel eyes."

"Oh."

"Indeed."

Kathryn was feeling especially successful after breaking the ice with Cassandra. The woman had been hard to reach at first, but she warmed immediately after a few probing questions. *Has no one ever tried it with her before?* Her training as a counselor and her particular experience in women's issues made it easy for Kathryn to recognize the symptoms and to attack them.

Cassandra was hurt and angry. Seeing that was easy. What was harder to cure was the self-flagellation she had endured by shutting herself off from the world due to the betrayal at the hands of her husband—someone who was supposed to love and honor her. Sadly, Cassandra had felt like an idiot for being so naive as to not realize that she had never been important to her husband. Feeling that stupid was probably the most difficult of her problems to overcome, but she had made a huge leap in telling Kathryn today. There were signs during the conversation that Cassandra was turning an important corner even as they talked.

Five years is a long time for self-loathing. Indeed, when women no longer felt stupid and taken advantage of and helpless, they usually began coming out of their self-imposed exiles. It was time for Cassandra Stafford Penthoven to start living, again.

~ * ~

"Miss Primble, I have asked you to attend me here with a challenge."

"Yes, My Lord," she whispered. He could tell that she was quaking with fear to be facing the master in his lair. There was nothing for it but to do this business in secret.

"My guest, your mistress, is in need of more gowns. She cannot continue to wear the same gown over again and men's clothes." He paused.

"Yes, My Lord."

"I am going to retrieve some of Lady Cassandra's gowns and ask you to alter them to fit Miss Ragland...without her participation. I would not wish to argue with her over old, hand-me-downs which we all know she needs."

"Yes, My Lord."

He lifted a box off the desk and handed it to the maid. "And these slippers are for her evening wear. I believe they are her size. Please tell her they are a gift but make as little of it as possible. Also, can you have a fresh habit altered for a morning ride? She will wear breeches again of course underneath."

"Yes, My Lord." The maid held the box against her chest as if it were a treasure.

"I will have a gown delivered to your quarters. Thank you. You are dismissed." She slid from the room with her gaze glued to the floor.

Thorpe came up behind him as the maid left the room. "If I may suggest, My Lord…"

"Yes, Thorpe?"

"Miss Primble has four more sisters at home and I daresay her father could spare her third or fourth sister to come join her here to act as seamstress."

"Yes, make it so," Michael agreed quickly.

Hallthorpe breathed a most contented sign as he left his master distracted and starry-eyed. *This* is what he had always wanted for this house…someone vibrant and full of life that cared about the people in it enough to make it a home.

Chapter Six

Ellie responded immediately to the pull of the cord. "Yes, my lady. We have your bath coming shortly." She bustled around the room working at drawers and gathering as if her very life depended on how fast she got Kathryn into a bath.

"A bath. Wow, that sounds really nice, but since there's no bathtub, I don't exactly see what I am going to sit in."

"Ah it will be along shortly. Water was already warming for you, miss."

"Water was warming? How do they do it?"

"Buckets by the kitchen fire and strong footmen. It's all right easy after all. We've been cleaning gentle-ladies for many years this way."

"Well, I won't argue since I can smell myself, but it still sounds like a lot of work."

"If I may be so bold, miss. You mentioned smelling. Would you like some smelling soap?"

"Would that be to hide the stink or keep the stink from getting bad again once it's washed off?"

"My Lady, everyone starts to smell as the day wears on. S'why ladies change their clothes for each meal I figure, and probably to show off."

She suddenly realized her mistake and gasped, bringing a hand to her mouth, ready to apologize.

"No need to apologize," Kathryn murmured. "I am sure you are absolutely correct. I don't find any need to change clothes all through the day, unless of course I really do smell bad. No question I want to smell better right now. What scents do you have?" *And if you say powder fresh*

Sure deodorant I'll kiss your hand!

"Jasmine, lemon, vanilla, and rosewater."

"Vanilla tonight. I think it's the most comfortable smell. I want to be comfortable."

"As you wish. It is a very lovely fragrance."

Ellie took extra care washing the mistress's hair. It had such an array of color but it looked so much brighter when it was clean. The gold and bronze streaks were just glorious when not weighed down with the day's dust and wear. She had warmed the curling tongs and secured all the pins she could find from the Dowager's room and the former mistresses' and found lovely strands of beads that would adorn the tresses.

Ellie's sister had finished with the alterations to the first of Lady Cassandra's dresses so she was screwing up her courage to tell the mistress that they had a new dress for dinner when the door creaked just a little. Ellie suppressed a squeak and then the door moved further ajar. She slid behind the large armoire because somehow she knew that she should.

Ellie did not yet know all the back workings of the manor house but this quiet invasion unnerved her. She backed behind the cabinet door and watched a maid's feet step over the threshold. Miss Ragland splashed water over the tub and squealed at the slip of the soap and the maid's steps stopped. When Miss Ragland quieted, the maid continued into the room.

Ellie studied the feet. They were well shod but she did not recognize them although she really had not had time to learn everyone in the household's feet. Nonetheless, there was no one, not in the household of a Duke, that was allowed in the mistress's chamber but her own ladies maid and the housekeeper and well, those were not the feet of Mrs. Staggs, whose boots she remembered right away.

Ellie watched the feet and skirt, turn toward the bedside table and peeked around the armoire door. A woman, dressed in all the black and white of a house maid, deposited a tea tray for one onto the table by Miss Ragland's bedside.

No one. *No one*, was to bring Miss Ragland tea without Ellie's knowledge. This was highly irregular and she immediately felt a spike of fear race down her spine. Ellie was one and twenty, old enough to know what's done and not. Miss Ragland was destined to be the new mistress of this house and someone, *someone* was invading her private bedchamber and bringing her unordered tea.

The unknown maid, as she was with plain brown hair in a severe knot and no special color to her skin, surveyed the room and then she did exactly what Ellie expected, she poured something into the teapot. Ellie gasped but thankfully, at that exact moment Miss Ragland squealed. She must have squirted her soap free again and with that exclamation, the imposter maid made for the door and was gone.

"Ellie, are you there?"

"Yes, Miss Ragland, I am here," she choked out, trying not to let her mistress hear her distress. Her mistress was especially astute to people's feelings, uncanny like her knowing what's what.

"I forgot to put my towel close enough to the tub. Do you mind bringing it to me so I don't make a mess dripping everywhere?"

"Yes miss," she whispered and crossed to her Lady's side. Ellie hoped and prayed Miss Ragland did not ask for tea. She was not yet ready with an answer about the mysterious pot, but she knew she needed to get it out of there right away.

~ * ~

Sometime later that night, in the Master's study, the poison-laced tea was being examined by his Grace of Asterleigh and his close friend Julian Thornton, Earl of Weatherford, recently of the Guards and His Majesty's Secret Service. The house had been scoured from the basement to the rafters and there was no sign of the well-shod house maid. "Arsenic?" Michael asked Jules.

"Concentrated and deadly, but I am not sure what, although arsenic makes the most sense. This is something very sinister, expensive, to be executed by a hireling. And why, Michael? It's very deliberate if Miss Primble is to be believed."

"You don't believe her?'

"Yes, I do."

"I knew you did. Don't tease me, Jules. What the hell is it?" He forced through clenched teeth.

"Something lethal and clean. Is that really what you wanted to hear?"

"Yes. *Dammit, no!* Do I want to hear that a guest in my home is the deliberate target of an assassin? What the hell?"

"I have been in this line for a number of years and I need to know. *Is* she just a guest in your home?" Jules was deadly serious. "It makes a difference."

Michael knew it was true, but he stiffened at the implication reflexively. He had not laid a demmed hand on the woman and no one could accuse him of any impropriety. "What the hell, I say?"

"Michael. Is she more to you than a guest? It may explain things."

Michael hesitated before he answered because truly, he had only known this woman for half a day. What did he know of her at all? "She's just a guest. Really, though, she is better described as a wayward traveler, a rescue of sorts. I spent the night at the Blue Bell and she was there alone." He relayed her strange circumstances including the shoeless walk in his breeches, which elicited an evil grin from his friend, leaving out any mention of his utterly unexplainable sensibilities toward the woman.

"So she could have enemies? She could be lying about her lack of circumstances and trying to hide, right here in your house?" Jules suggested it and Michael was forced to answer.

"I had been considering that this evening but she is so open, nothing is false with her. She is either a brilliant liar or she is who she says she is." Michael had seen her, truly *seen* her and she was not a liar.

"I won't ask for an introduction this evening while we sort this out but, we must consider that she is here because someone wants her dead. You'll want to take precautions."

Protectiveness was Michael's most ungovernable emotion. Any woman in his realm was subject to its strictures and this woman, who had already breached so many of his usual defenses, drew out the most violent of tendencies in him to keep her safe. "I will see to it," he growled low.

"I think we should also consider another scenario. You are the one who has recently returned and everyone knows you have been the heir since January. This assassin may have been following you and your lady friend had the unfortunate luck of being a target by association or simply accident."

"Any of those scenarios fit Julian. I don't need to tell you that strange deaths of the males in my family recently give me pause."

"Yes, they may have been the accidents that the witnesses claimed but..."

"…there is a Dukedom to consider."

"Indeed."

~ * ~

Kathryn had been looking out the window when the mysterious, dark-haired visitor had arrived on horseback. He had stayed for more than an hour and when she heard his horse being brought around, she watched him again from her perch in the window. Even in the deep shadows of the night, with the angles of his face hidden, he looked familiar.

She had seen the man somewhere before.

But how was that possible? She had only been here in this place for less than twenty-four hours and at Michael's for twelve hours. Though it did seem more like several days since this very first one had been so full. But that man was very familiar. He reminded her in dress and carriage of a dark looking, slimmer Michael, but he was also Mediterranean with olive skin and wavy silk hair black as night. Like someone who had a French parent or parents. She could imagine the visitor as a spy, sleek, dark, dangerous, and maybe even a little wicked.

But none of that made him familiar. It was something she had actually seen before with her own eyes. She thought of the painting. Maybe it was him. The period would be correct. She retrieved the painting from the spot she had hidden it in the desk and was struck literally with the force of recognition.

Michael.

Kathryn's brain began working in overdrive putting the pieces together. Michael and his first wife Catherine had been unhappily married in approximately 1810 or 1811 so she thought based on the snippets from her conversation with Cassandra. Here she was in what she now knew to be an estate near Wilton in the year 1816. Kathryn's breath caught and she looked closer at the image of the man while her mind's eye added definition, angles, and texture and light and a raised brow to the plain painted face. She added color to his skin and a slight curl of the lips and she saw him clearly for the first time.

The painting was of Michael.

How had she not realized it before? It had not been until she saw the dashing French spy look-alike in person that she had revisited the people in the picture. Now that she could recall all four of the paintings, there had indeed been a dark-haired stunner who very much resembled the man who had just ridden off. There was also her favorite of the mounted Cavalry officer, the sour couple she had purchased and a fourth. It was of a man with hounds, a more jovial looking blonder version of the other three. The Frenchman had stood, posed on his hearth with a sword.

As all of the confusion and frustration and unanswered questions of the morning coalesced into one unbelievable theory, she concluded that her presence here must be due to the painting. It was a most bizarre, unrealistic, crazy, insane…could she keep on going…theory but it was the only one that explained why she had been found and rescued by the man whose picture she had bought. Had he needed her? Did someone need her help and had she somehow been brought here by magic or conjuring. Did he have powers or was it just the power of one little magic painting?

And were the other paintings magic and were they here? Hope, thrill, and excitement grew, meshing with determination until she fairly burst from her room to search out the other artwork. This time, she didn't crash into her tall, firmly built host as she hurried out into the hall, but Kathryn was equally as distracted as she realized something about Michael that had been different from the Regency Romance characters she so loved. He wasn't lean and narrow-waisted as they usually were. He was solid muscle and much more so than he had been in the painting. No, he was more like GI Joe with bulging biceps and rock hard thighs, totally flat belly from the looks but not thin at the waist, probably able to bench press a woman. Michael looked like a big muscular soldier—like an Army Ranger—who had probably lugged, toted, slogged, fought hand-to-hand, and maybe even carried a wounded comrade or two on his back. His was the body of a workhorse who had done other equally manly activities every day for the last five years.

When she reached the foot of the stairs, Kathryn slowed her pace, ready to face the man into whose life she had somehow fallen. *Should she tell him about the portrait?* There were consequences and rewards on both sides of that argument. If she did tell him, then maybe he would believe her and offer her assistance in getting home or maybe he would think the opposite, that she was a stalker come to find herself an eligible rich widower. The possibility that showing him the picture would lend credibility to her story was very tempting.

She took a calming breath and pushed open the study door, fully expecting him to be standing like a statue with his hands behind his back. Instead, he was lounging casually in the chair by the hearth, a book open on his lap. He stood immediately upon seeing her.

~ * ~

"M'dear Miss Ragland, you have joined me. I was beginning to wonder if you had forsaken our entertainments?" He inflected the words playfully and she wondered if he had been suggesting an illicit hidden meaning.

"I'm so sorry. I noticed you had a visitor so I took my time. Was that wrong?"

He bowed over her hand, released her, and motioned to the chair adjacent to the fire arranged opposite his. "No, you were quite right. That business was unexpected and I appreciate your forbearance." She noted the brittleness in his voice. He seemed like he was trying really hard to sound nonchalant and she was very good at recognizing dissembling.

"Was there a problem, something wrong? You seem stressed out a little," she prodded him.

"Stressed out? No let me guess, anxious, worried, concerned. American slang you told me earlier, correct?"

"Very good, Captain, you are a fast study."

"Fast is not a compliment."

"Oh? Where I come from it means quick-witted. What does it mean to you?"

"Of loose morals," he said blandly.

"Oh. Not a compliment. Very well, Captain, then you are quick witted. There?"

"Unwieldy but much more appropriate."

The unexpected laugh lit her face and sent golden rays of light dancing from her honeyed hair and earthy eyes. She was really truly exquisitely gorgeous. Not in a portrait artist, perfect chit of the *ton* way, but in a dazzling, goddess, Valkyrie-like unusual natural way. He really could not believe how susceptible he had become to her beguiling face in such a short time.

"So, can I be nosy and ask about the visitor?"

"Nosy, *you*, Miss Ragland?" he intoned, his voice dripping with sarcasm. Michael hoped to vex her, somehow distract her into not asking why Jules had called. He didn't know what to tell her yet as he was not one to lie, but he just wasn't ready to share any of his suspicions. He certainly did not know her well enough to suppose how she would respond to 'someone tried to kill you in your room with poison laced tea'. Yet, she still managed to surprise.

"I—I need to know who he is. I've…seen…him before."

All of Michael's senses focused on her words. She had been in the inn, on the street, in Michael's own house with him and nowhere else, or so she had said. None of those were places where Jules could possibly have been so she must have seen him before coming to Hawthorne. That realization unnerved Michael and that recurring pang of jealousy was unwelcome. Very real and potent, but unwelcome nonetheless.

"Do you know my friend, the Earl of Weatherford?"

"No." She hesitated and he thought she might not answer. "Is he French?"

"Miss Ragland. I cannot follow your mind. What makes you think the Earl is French?" *Bloody hell, she had seen him or known him to be French. What was she about?*

"He looks like…" *all the English spies that I've read about who blend in so well behind Napoleon's own lines because of their gorgeous French features* "…he's got Mediterranean blood. Does he?"

"Yes, you are very perceptive. Julian Thornton's mother was a French émigré who married the Earl of Weatherford and settled happily here in the English countryside in the 1780s, long before Napoleon fully destroyed the Bourbons and made himself Emperor. She was reputed to be the most sought-after beauty of her time but was quite happy to settle here with the reclusive Earl."

"Did the French Countess love her English Earl?"

"I understand…with a passion…" he answered wistfully.

"Her son must look very much like her."

Demmit to hell, he was a dark Lucifer. Of course, he looked like the former beautiful Lady Weatherford. What was Kathryn about noticing Jules' good looks? A pang of jealousy spiked swift and sharp through

Michael. He had never in his life been jealous. His brother had been a jealous fool, and his cousin Harold and his Father some of the time, but he had never been jealous. He was the second son. Second sons were notoriously *not* jealous people. Now, he was jealous because this woman had noticed his friend.

Kathryn Ragland was a wanton *houri* to be asking him about another man, a beautiful one was she not? No. In fairness, she was flesh and blood, susceptible to Julian like so many were and he *was* envious, plain and simple. "Her beauty was widely regarded and Julian…he is well-received by the ladies."

"I am sure he is. Thankfully, I've never been a fallen-angel type myself."

Surprised, he asked, "What, you are not enamored of the Earl?"

"Well, your friend, who looks very French, is amazingly gorgeous from what I could see but in a very threatening, unapproachable way. My tastes run to earthy and wholesome."

He stood looking at her, body turned half from her toward the fire, and she tilted her head in question. His jealousy had receded only a little but with her, for some inexplicable reason, he had to know. He just couldn't help himself. "What of me, Kathryn? What do you see?" Even as the words came from his mouth, Michael could not believe the impulses that had brought him so low. No matter, he still had to know.

Kathryn regarded him for a long while knowing her answer would reveal much more than he was probably interested in hearing but she realized on some primal level her complimenting his friend had possibly wounded his pride. She would tell him the absolute truth.

Taking a deep breath to gird her loins and calm her skittering nerves, she watched him take his seat once and spoke. "You, Captain, are maybe the sexiest man I have ever met, maybe ever seen." She stepped back, kept her hand to herself and the smile from her eyes so he could not misconstrue her compliments for making a pass at him. "You have…please don't think I am trying to flatter you, but rather am just being honest …the most…hottest body I've ever seen. Captain, you're well …you're…melting hot. There, all that's the truth."

Michael had let his head fall back against the seat at her candid words about his being sexy. He wasn't sure sexy and hot and melting were words he would ascribe to himself but they were all very flattering, warming, words of desire that made his pulse race, and his heart pound in his breast as he watched her totally comfortable recitation of his charms. Never in his life had any woman looked him in the eye and told him he was 'the most' anything. They had flattered, cajoled and hungered greedily for him, but no one had ever unmanned him with the kind of genuine direct assessment that Kathryn had.

That she sat across from him completely comfortable with what she had done fascinated him even more. She was just being honest she said, or was it candid. She complimented Julian for his Byronic beauty but in the same breath said …

"Captain, I have just paid you a compliment and I realize that we are now well past the hour in which you promised me entertainment. What's it going to be? Are you singing, doing a two-step, a monologue, maybe miming, piano, dueling with swords? Out with it!"

"Kathryn Ragland," he said as he stood, then bowed with a ridiculous flourish, "be treated to a poetry reading."

Kathryn bit back a look of surprise. "Poetry? You? Who are you reading?"

"Me."

"You? You write poetry?" She was incredulous; it made him laugh.

"I assure you, you will recognize this as my work.

There once was a lady so fair
With golden streaks in her hair
She showed up in town
Without even a gown
And he whisked her off to his lair!"

"No way!" She laughed so hard tears began streaming down her face and he joined her because, well, her joy was infectious. "I always knew you were a predator…is this your lair? Do I need to worry?"

Michael regarded her almost stoically and replied.

"There was a lady fleet of feet

71

Olivia Ritch

He picked her up from nearby street
She questioned where he might lead
He answered that she wouldn't bleed
She fought her aches to stay astride
He fought his welling desire to hide"

"Did you write that one down or just come up with it right now off the top of your head?" She was staring at him and he tilted his head and shrugged. Right now with her he was somehow acting the ridiculous romantic. He rose from his seat, crossed the space separating them and she stood to meet him. Kathryn reached for his face and Michael turned his check to accept her palm. A lance of desire raced through the contact. He put his hands on her shoulders to bind her but in reality to steady himself from the wave of physical need that was roiling up into his breast. "I am going to kiss you very hard," he growled, his burning eyes pinning her gaze.

"Yes," she whispered. "You do that...and I will respond very urgently."

He crushed his lips against hers and she melted instantly into his chest, parting for him instinctively, reaching for his nape while pulling one knee to his hip as if she was going to crawl up his front. He was stunned. Hers was the reaction of an experienced woman. She was no virgin. He pulled back from her to search her eyes.

"Michael, where I come from...this is not so foreign," she said, her voice a low seductive whisper. "I am not going to ravish you or demand you marry me."

"I admit I am surprised at your..." He had pulled away from her further but did not release a loose hold on her lower back.

"Interest? Response? It's okay. You don't offend me. I realize it was too much for you. Can I just go ahead and tell you the truth?"

"You seem to always tell the truth, Kathryn. Please." He could not actually step away from her or relinquish her touch even though he was taken aback by her blatant sexuality, absently rubbing the length of the long muscles of her back with his hands.

"I'm not a virgin and...I like some of the activities that men and women do together, the pleasures we can give each other. But I want to make clear, if I do anything with you it's because I want to and it feels good, not because you are the master here or that I expect anything in return. Is that *clear*?"

Using his catlike reflexes, he grabbed her waist and pulled her to him. "Kathryn, you are so much more…than any…than any…" he could not finish. *Than any woman who has been in my life, in my home, part of me.*

"It's okay, Michael. I'm sorry I freaked you out. You are really hot you know and your poetry turned me on."

"You are turned on? I think I like that and I do know what it means. You want more pleasure."

"Yes, touch me, Michael. Here." She took his hand and spread it across her belly. She moved his hand on her breasts, then around her back, and then he took over and ranged down to cup her bottom. He learned her body with his hands and he could sense she was already far gone with passion from the kiss and the caressing. He traced across her midsection to her most sensitive place and her ragged breathing was too much for him.

Kathryn's small hands had played over his back but since she had overwhelmed him, she had pulled back, obviously trying not to surprise him again. He needed more, to feel more. Michael grabbed Kathryn's hand and pressed it to his erection. "Touch me," he growled.

"Michael, you are so…hard.

She pressed her hand again and he rolled into her in response. It had been so long and she was…she was loving him so efficiently, her mouth, and those firm breasts under his palms. Trying to pull away only made her more vigorous and before he could disengage, the sensation bloomed beyond reason. He cried out and convulsed like a green lad.

"Michael?" He didn't answer her and tried to turn away.

"Are you okay?"

"Kathryn, I—I… am so sorry." Surely she could see the look on his face was of abject misery mixed with distinct pleasure.

"I want to hear you say you enjoyed that," she whispered against his cheek. "I wanted to make you feel that way, Michael." He pressed her close in a fierce hug kissing the loose curls on the top of her head and breathing deeply to recover from the heady pleasure she had given him. "Did you enjoy it?"

"Kathryn, Kathryn, you cannot imagine."

They held each other for some time standing in his study in front of the low fire, then she slipped from his grasp and walked to the door. She turned to look at him, smiled simply and headed for her room.

Kathryn dreamed that night of riding free with Michael, thundering over the rolling hills, making love out of doors, lying splayed over his large rock-hard body and for the first time, she belonged in the picture. She awoke the next morning with an amazing sense of calm and an annoying ache in her own most tender places.

Chapter Seven

Michael was reading the news sheet when the door opened, having risen early to assure himself last night was no dream. What had happened had been the most pleasurable, and simultaneously lowering interlude of his life. Michael was expecting Kathryn. What he saw stopped him cold. Cassandra's footman Jem was holding the door while his sister glided into the room gowned in a lovely blue morning gown, hair perfectly styled with a sunny smile on her gaunt face. Jem hesitated, clearly unsure where to seat her. Michael suspected that not once in the last five years had Cassandra eaten in this room. Certainly, she had never done so any time he had been here.

He jumped up rather quickly, shoving his chair and motioned for Jem to seat her at the other end. Once Cassandra was seated, Jem, who was well paid to anticipate his mistress's needs reached for a piece of toast for her plate when she spoke. "I believe I will have eggs and sausages today, Jem."

Stunned, thrilled, and altogether taken by surprise, Michael stared with wonder at the sight of Cassandra at the table, as if it was a normal occurrence. It might have been for anyone else, just not for her.

Jem placed a perfectly organized plate in front of Cassandra and retreated. With a glance from Michael, he quit the room. "I met your guest Kathryn yesterday." He couldn't take his eyes off her; he was basking in the glow that was his baby sister, here at his table. "She has asked me to show her how to tend roses."

"Roses?" He had yet to truly accept she was here and talking about the mundane subject of gardening.

"Yes, she says hers are skinny and weak and twisted while ours are …I believe her word was 'glorious'."

It would be just like her to use a word such as glorious to describe his roses. His mother had tended them during his childhood but as her despair grew over his father's failings and his complete abandonment of her, she had allowed the gardeners to take over. They were as immaculately kept as ever during her time but there was something missing to him. Kathryn would still find their natural beauty glorious. That was like her wasn't it? Positive, optimistic, seeing beauty everywhere.

"I do not believe I have ever met as charming a woman as Kathryn. She fairly bursts with life. I could not wait to join her this morning for breakfast. *Is* she joining us?"

"I am expecting her although she may be running late. I kept her up rather later than she is accustomed." Her brows rose. He realized the implication. "Not that! I was entertaining her." As her brows remained lifted, he was forced to explain. "After yesterday, when she went with me to visit the tenants, I was determined to show her a good time last evening."

"And?"

"Of course, the only thing an old soldier can do well is tell stories so I spun her merry tales and she joined me. I believe we laughed until very late." *And then she pleasured me beyond my comprehension, and I struggled to return to earth afterward.*

He was grateful she let him off with that feeble explanation because they could hear footsteps approaching. Kathryn was rushing. He might ask Cassandra to tell her later that hurrying was unladylike, in the most subtle of ways of course. He wouldn't want to hurt her feelings or curb her natural joy with life. Kathryn fairly burst in. "I'm so sorry I'm late. I overslept. Midnight is late for me and well my room is so dark and cozy. And of course, no one came and woke me up."

When she finally stopped talking, Kathryn took in for the first time the tableau. Cassandra. At breakfast. And Michael grinning like a Cheshire cat. As well he should.

"Cassandra tells me you have an interest in roses. Do you garden?"

"Well, Captain, I work at gardening although I'm not sure I actually garden. I mostly buy things that are already blooming and plant them and then work to keep them alive. My track record's spotty, though."

"And you have roses." It was a blank statement but he recognized it for what it was. Cassandra offered it helpfully knowing Michael's special passion for the roses his mother had loved so much.

"Yes, but they're scraggly and yours are glorious. I almost can smell them from here."

Michael's heart had begun racing the moment her footsteps had neared. He could not stop feeling over again the rush of passion she elicited from him last night in his study. No one had ever brought him to climax in such an exciting and openly uninhibited fashion and fortunately learning that she was not a virgin had not unnerved him as it might have. He did not believe she was a loose woman, but she definitely was comfortable with showing affection. He could cultivate her passion, or maybe more likely she would cultivate his and they could have a very fulfilling time in the marriage bed.

"Are you to going to withdraw to the gardens then?" he asked his sister.

"I believe we shall, big brother. Kathryn can ask all of her questions and I will try to answer with reasonable intelligence. It has been several years since I worked in the garden."

"Then maybe the two of you will be quite companionable."

~ * ~

Kathryn had watched for any sign that things between Michael and her had changed and she saw nothing. The fact he showed no recognition seemed quite odd to her, but maybe he was just very good at hiding behind his mask in front of others. He had smiled welcomingly as always. Certainly in front of Cassandra was not the time to discuss last night. "Shall we, Lady Cassandra?"

"Brother, you will excuse us?" she asked rising.

"Ladies."

When they stepped onto the flags from the French doors in the parlor, Kathryn turned to survey the windows that overlooked the gardens. She thought she saw the one that was Michael's study and realized he'd be sitting at his desk just feet from where they walked. She would be sure to move further into the garden if she touched on the subject of the elder

Stafford sibling. "So I wanted to ask you a mistress question. Can I just jump into that?"

"Yes, although I am certainly not an expert on mistresses, just my own personal mistress experience mind you." She grimaced and Kathryn had the courtesy to be chagrined.

"No, but this is general knowledge building. What the heck do men need so much sex for that they actually pay the living expenses of a woman to have her at their beck and call...when they have the urge?"

"It's just the done thing. I guess their animal natures have to rut around every day, and the only way to accomplish it is with a...whore."

"But why is it okay? I mean, most of those men go on to marry and their wives what...just marry them anyway?"

"What do you mean exactly?" Cassandra asked Kathryn.

"I mean I cannot imagine marrying a man who had kept a mistress. It just shows such a lack of self-control and it's infidelity, Cassandra. It just does not seem like it should be acceptable and there are so many reasons I couldn't tolerate it. First, I would wonder whether I was ever enough for him or if he was going to fall right back into that life style. Second, I would never know if he had had a child with her or loved her and third, oh my gosh...how do you walk around in polite society not knowing if you're going to run into her?"

"Well, you've obviously touched on all of the subjects most dear to my heart when discussing mistresses. I think you must actually have a relationship with a man before marrying him, know he is not the type to keep a mistress and assure yourself that you have engaged his affections. It's not the way of our society, but since you're so passionate about it, I think you would want to limit yourself to someone who you could trust, who hadn't kept anyone."

"I might as well ask since I'm here and we're on the subject. Has your brother had mistresses?"

"Kathryn, I am so glad you asked me that. I'm just going to tell you that I hope you have engaged my brother's affections. I haven't seen you together except just now at breakfast and he could not keep his eyes off of you. And, no, I don't think he's ever had a mistress. He's spent too much time away in the army. I think...well..."

"You think he saw the men in your family set a bad example?"

"Yes, exactly. You're perceptive. I think just to not be like them—our father and our brother—who were notorious womanizers and my husband as well. Michael is better than that."

"It's good to know. Not that it means anything, I was just…wondering."

"He did not love her, you know." Kathryn's pensive mood had clearly not been lost on Cassandra. She was finding her new friend to be quite direct and rather readable. "He did it out of duty and honor because she was ruined."

"You are speaking about your brother's late wife?"

"I am. I think he would have been glad to have the baby and very likely he figured he might not live to be married long. He made her respectable and if he died, she would go on with her life."

"Do you really think he thought about maybe not living so marrying her wouldn't be any sort of sacrifice?" Kathryn asked incredulously.

"Yes, I do. Michael is very serious and he never went off thinking he was a happy warrior. He went off knowing soldiers die. It was duty and service and death was a part of it."

"He sounded…noble."

"He was. He is."

All of this personal talk was making Kathryn uncomfortable. "Let's change the subject from mistresses and dying and talk about more fun things. If you don't teach me something about roses, we'll have to admit we sneaked out here to talk about your brother."

"Yes, well roses…"

~ * ~

"Where is this paragon of…?"

Aunt Agatha was as formidable a matron as any on the *ton* but she was his favorite relation—nay the only relation Michael liked—on his father's side. She had been widowed in her 40s, too old to secure another well-placed marriage but too young to hide away in widow's weeds. So she had been a regular visitor with his mother when he was growing up and she and Cassandra had always been close until Cassandra's marriage. He thought there may have been a lover at one time but now she was simply Aunt Agatha, matron of the *ton*.

Olivia Ritch

When he stepped aside from the window, her words trailed off. "My Cassandra," she whispered. As she moved closer to the window, he watched her gaze lovingly on her favorite niece who was *laughing* and walking in the garden on the arm of the attractive *stranger* he had found quite by chance.

"She's laughing." She turned toward him with awe and an unusual hush in her voice he did not recognize.

"Yes. They've been out there for over an hour strolling and then sitting on the bench. I think Miss Ragland is regaling Cassandra with stories because there has been much laughter and gesturing and even some tears. They were supposed to be discussing the roses, but I don't think there's been much of that." He tried to disguise it but when her eyes flared, he knew Agatha had heard the fondness in his voice.

Well, well, we might have discovered our new Duchess. "You have gotten her a suitable maid, I see," Agatha commented pointedly.

"Yes, her maid has done wonders with her hair. Now I am working on dresses and shoes." Her eyebrows shot up and she looked her question. "Calm down. Not me personally, the staff. We are having to do it all clandestinely as she seems unwilling to accept any generosity. All of the sneaking feels much like those years avoiding Boney and his minions." He watched Agatha look back out the window as Kathryn turned toward it.

"She is *bronze*, Michael!"

"She calls it a tan."

"That is no color of tan I have ever seen. She's out there without out a bonnet. She'll freckle something awful."

"She already has freckles. A lot of them."

A look of horror bloomed on Agatha's face. "But don't worry, the maid covered them last night for dinner," he said with a chuckle. Her expression relaxed into a pinched grin as she watched the two women continue their exchange.

"She's rather expressive and her smile seems to be quite…"

"What, Aunt? You have never minced words."

"*Infectious*. There, are you happy?" She snorted but he knew she was giving her approval. It was high praise from Aggie.

"Did you expect horns, a snout, or fire-breathing maybe?" When she

80

didn't answer immediately... "You did. You expected her to be an uncouth freak or an antidote. Surely you know me better than that."

"You married that horrible Catherine what's-her-name."

"That was a mistake."

"Yes. You will get it right this time. I will help," she said with relish.

With that it was settled. Kathryn Ragland was well and approved by one of the *ton's* highest sticklers. Now all he had to do was convince Kathryn herself she was capable of running his households. He would also help her find her family, train her without her knowledge for introduction to the *ton*, convince her to accept a new wardrobe and then avoid his own temper that he knew would erupt as soon as she graced her first ballroom when his peers got one good look at her. It was enough to bring on a headache. She would be an original, intelligent, charming, sparkling, and refreshing; men would fall at her feet. Of that there was no doubt.

But she was his. Of that there was no question.

Chapter Eight

Michael struggled to concentrate on the small mountain of paperwork on his desk. His steward, Smithers, had faithfully sorted the bills, invitations, letters, and complaints into four ordered stacks. And then he had prepared the dreaded "all others" stack. Michael hated that particular pile of paper with a vengeance because it always held something to take hours of his time. Today he didn't have any to spare; he wanted to take Kathryn on a late afternoon ride just before tea.

He could still hear the low murmur of the voices of his two favorite ladies enjoying his gardens as he contemplated stealing one of them away. They giggled some but seemed to be trying genuinely to concentrate on roses; at least he thought so when he stole another glance. Returning to the dreaded stack, he found the first letter to be bearing some well-anticipated good news from his man of business.

Just as he suspected, it contained a letter noting the purchase of a 2,000 pound note from one Lord Sebastian Drake, Baron of Worley, dated April 26, 1814 to one of London's notorious gamesters. Matthew Drake's brother had gambled heavily and run the estate into near destitution while the younger Drake was off making a name for himself in the cavalry and routing Napoleon Bonaparte from Belgium.

Indeed, because of his drunken, slovenly, wastrel brother, Matthew was now up the River Tick with nary a way to rescue his estate. Knowing that the house had been stripped of all its valuables and that there was but one horse in the stable, Michael had been inquiring from those in business circles who knew as to the status of the estate and found it to be heavily leveraged. Indeed, if one person were to buy up the vowels and hold them, he would own the land. Michael intended to be that landowner, with the express purpose of helping Matthew come about and regain his family's status.

Of course, he could not easily get away with buying all of Matthew's spendthrift's brother's debt without someone alerting Matthew, so he enlisted Julian Thornton's and Colin Hamilton's help. Among the three of them, they would purchase the debt so that no one other individual could own a large enough share to take away Worley from Matthew. He had estimated the debts to be about 50,000 pounds and he was prepared to invest 20,000 or more if needed and the other two would do the same.

In exchange, because Matthew would surely figure out their charity, they would help him set up a stud. Matthew's dream from the time they had all been in short coats had been to breed horses and he had the most beautiful land for it. Matthew had few tenants so there was no one to kick off of a farm in place of the track and truly, there was no one more enamored or more competent with horses than Matthew. Even Michael was itching to get his hands on some gorgeous horseflesh closer to home. After he and the others received a few more notices like the one he got today, they would propose the idea of the stud partnership to Matthew.

Michael was prepared for him to rail at them, but he had an argument that not even the redoubtable hero of Waterloo could argue…they all wanted a stud and they were doing this to purchase the few acres of his farm that would allow it. He could run the stud or not and if he did, he could pay off the debt. Michael was convinced that Matthew would agree with them in the end. He loved Worley enough that his pride could be overcome.

The other stack that held the mildest interest to him was the pile of invitations from some of London's most illustrious hostesses. One day soon, Michael would have to take Kathryn to town and let her make her bow but he also needed to provide for her protection. Unleashing the wolves on her now was unacceptable.

"You are a wonderful teacher, Cassandra." Kathryn's voice drifted to him from the hallway and pulled him from his planning. He heard his sister laugh and slip off upstairs.

He joined her in the hall. "Kathryn, I was wondering if you would be interested in another riding lesson this afternoon," Michael asked expectantly.

She turned her lovely flushed face to him, gave that heart-melting smile, and then winked at him. The bloody minx winked! "Actually, Captain, I was wondering if I could go for a run. It's been too many days for me and I need to pump my legs. Would you accompany me so I don't get lost?"

"A run, Kathryn?"

"You know, speedier than a walk, done on two legs, by a human?"

He raised one eyebrow at her. "I know what running is, but what do you mean by it?"

"I mean to put on some comfortable shoes and start running down the lane until we've gone a couple of miles then turn around. It's very good for me. It's how I stay in shape."

Ahhh, there's the explanation for the sleekly muscled thighs and calves. "While I understand your request, it is not done to go running around the countryside," Michael stated flatly.

Kathryn was undeterred. "Is this not your land? Can we stay within your property? Certainly your staff would not question your judgment."

"You are no doubt correct that they will not question me, but that does not mean they will approve."

"Please," she asked simply.

As a soldier, Michael knew when he was beaten. "Certainly. Shall we meet back here in thirty minutes? I just have a few more things to wrap up." In fact, he had dozens more items to wrap up. There were still the multiple well-organized piles that he had attacked at 4:00 a.m. before the household awoke, still sitting only partially attended. But getting the early start on business had left precious daylight hours for a much anticipated afternoon adventure with Kathryn. Michael had no idea what to expect from running with her, but he very much wanted to be able to accept Kathryn's challenge.

~ * ~

When Kathryn gained the hall, she saw Michael standing by the banister dressed as the most charming country gentleman wearing a loose linen shirt that sported untied pull strings tucked into some type of knee length breeches that were not as tight fitting as his riding pants. He was terribly appealing. "Your ankle boots don't look as well-worn as mine. I hope you will not be miserable very soon."

Kathryn had borrowed a pair of ladies work shoes from Ellie that were just big enough that she could wear the socks Ellie had produced, with some searching, to protect her feet from rubbing. The two of them together had been quite ingenious she thought. It helped having the benefit of two hundred years of sports technology advancements to draw on, but what she wouldn't give right now for her well-worn pair of running shoes and a tight fitting jogbra. "But Kathryn, this is to be running on the hard packed ground so I shall be well protected from offending stones or turning my ankle in rabbit holes."

"Okay, I can't argue with that but are your socks thick enough to protect your feet from blistering?"

"My stockings should suit admirably. As for my poor feet, I have spent the better part of the last five years traipsing all over the Continent. I suspect my feet are far past the sensibilities for a short run."

"So let's walk outside and you can tell me which way we are going while we stretch a little."

"I would like to see what type of stretching you have in mind." He said it with an almost seductive purr in his voice.

"So, you'll get a really good view of my *bottom* because stretching the legs involves lots of leaning over at the waist."

"Then by all means, lead on!" She saw the wicked gleam and wondered if he realized he was flirting.

The day was warm, but the sun was not high. It was perfect May weather this afternoon to work up a sweat. "Lean over at the waist and touch your toes. Count one Mississippi and two Mississippi to twenty," Kathryn ordered.

"What's Mississippi?"

"A really fun word to count seconds with. We could say one Herefordshire, two Herefordshire if that would work better for you. You're not stretching," she chided.

"I think I like your fun word better." Michael was not bent as far as she.

"Now, lunge with the left and stay in the deep bend for the same count of twenty, then we'll do the other leg." Kathryn was struggling not to laugh

85

at his attempts to stretch. Michael was a large man.

"I am enjoying this stretching. It gives a great full view of your rather perfectly shaped bottom as we indicated it might."

"Thank you. I'll take that compliment. I work hard to keep everything in shape and where it's supposed to be." Kathryn wondered when she had ever turned stretching into a sexual discussion.

"Kathryn I can assure you, everything of yours is exactly where it should be."

"You sure are being playful. So much less stuffy than when I met you."

"Stuffy? Why I am most offended." They laughed together as he notched slightly lower.

The mock smile he gave her made him seem almost boyish and Kathryn was reminded that not only was he enjoying their time together, he was bucking convention for her and making this little scene for any and all of his staff to see. Surely no-ot," she exaggerated.

He stopped being playful and looked at her directly before dropping his gaze. "I am a little ashamed to admit it but I have been able to think of almost nothing else since...well...since...demmit, oh sorry... you. Just you. You turned my brain to mush and I have not yet recovered my senses."

"So, maybe today, you can pay me back for that?"

He regarded her with what she thought was a gleam of respect for her forthrightness and definitely a flash of desire. A hot streak shot straight to the juncture of her thighs and she had no choice but to pull her knee up in an impromptu stretch. His eyes hadn't left her and she realized he was sensing her physical reaction to his look. Another pain that definitely required more stretching.

"Can we go now," she squeaked.

"By all means, we will start toward the stables and take the bridle path toward Worley's land." Michael had never jogged simply for the health and fresh air of it and he immediately felt himself relaxing into the pounding of their feet and the rhythm of their breathing. The vixen next to him kept her tiny legs well-paced with his longer strides and he knew she was probably working half as hard again as he was to keep up with him. "Shall we set a slower pace?"

"Heck no, this is perfect for me. I can keep any pace we set. Since it's been about five days since my last run, I've got tons of pent up energy."

"May I ask you to save a little of that energy so I can repay that debt we spoke of just a while ago?"

"You know, if we were racing, I'd accuse you of cheating just for bringing it up. You saw what your challenge did to me. It shoots straight to…"

"Yes, it gave me infinite pleasure to cheat…in just that way. In fact…I am…thinking of pleasuring…"

"Michael! Stop it!" she squealed. "You are making me totally tight and it's starting to hurt with each step."

They were several hundred yards past the stables when he grabbed her arm, stopping her progress and spinning her into his heaving chest. His lips slammed hard onto her mouth but her surrender was complete and absolute the moment he tasted her, the ragged breathing from their exertion sending him sinking wildly into her.

Kathryn Ragland was like no woman he had ever known. The sweet, sweaty taste of her lips and the soft skin just under her chin where he steadied her was intoxicating, better than his best brandy. Her perfect breasts were rising and falling in rhythm with his fast beating heart and they pebbled just from brushing against the linen of his shirt.

She wove one of her sinewy arms over his shoulder into his hair sending tiny sensations over his scalp, down his neck and spine. The other hand grabbed his shoulder and found purchase in his muscles, nails rasping his flesh. He pressed her hips to his erection that was throbbing in time with their hearts. He wanted her here and now.

"Kathryn…I need to touch you."

"Yesss."

Before the word was out of her mouth, his hand brushed the front of her breeches. He slipped the buttons with one hand and slid the tight fabric past her hips, the fabric easily pooling at her feet. When he slipped his finger under the tiny tight piece of silk at the apex of her thighs, his mind whirled and he sunk to his knees to view his discovery.

"They're… bikini panties…Michael. They're my only pair. Do you…like …ahhhhhh…them?" He was circling with his thumb just on top of the see-through fabric, buckling her knees. He braced her with his other arm.

"I don't know what bikini panties are…but I want to taste them like I want to taste… you. Don't touch *me* though or I will explode, my darling." He bent to her. "I think I like…the taste."

And he showed her just how much.

Later, when she collapsed into his shoulders, sated and spent from fighting his ministrations, he slid himself up her body so that her slumped form was molded to him. She did not open her eyes. "Kathryn, darling, I can carry you if you need me to," he said with a low rumble of satisfaction in his deep drawl.

"Not a…chance. I just…need to get my legs back and we'll continue on."

"Continue on the run? Are you sure?"

"Abso…lutely. I just need…" she continued to pant.

"You need a chair and a brandy, my dear," he cajoled.

"No…now more than ever I need a run. In about five minutes, I'll feel better than I have in days. You've had me so tied up in knots and now all that pressure has been released. I feel soooo good."

"You've been knotted up?" he asked not sure he was supposed to be thrilled or concerned.

"I am sure you can imagine. That encounter after the poetry in your study. I was wound tight. Even thought about…"

"What, Kathryn?"

"Helping…myself."

"You know you needn't have resorted to that drastic measure. I would have gladly taken care of your needs." His deep passionate drawl and scandalous repartee' surprised him anew.

"You have now and I feel exceedingly good for it. I'm also about recovered enough to run again. Can we start at a slow jog?"

Quite satisfied that he had indeed released the tension that had been building in her for the last two days, Michael started off down the path, Kathryn falling into step a few seconds later. Just as she moved, a whizzing sound flew past her ear and Kathryn reacted with a start. At the same moment, a loud crack sounded in the distance.

Michael knew those two sounds and turned to throw his large body onto Kathryn's. He caught her in the chest and landed squarely on her in the bridle path. He held her down with one arm and took the quick chance to look around for the shooter, for that had been the crack of a pistol. The shooter was not terribly far away.

With the lower half of his body on the ground, he felt the hoof beat vibrations and knew he would never catch their assailant. Since the villain was fleeing, he took the opportunity to rise to his full height and look in the direction the shot originated. His well-honed senses caught the flank view of a midnight black horse. The rider was cloaked and from this distance undistinguishable.

He turned to see Kathryn lying on the ground on her back, breathing shallowly. "What the heck was all that?" Her rasping voice had him back to her side instantly.

"A stray shot. I am sorry to have been so rough with you. I expect I knocked the wind out of you landing on you that way."

"Yes, I'm ...well...I think my shoulder..."

"Oh, my god, Kathryn, are you injured?" It had not occurred to him that his weight and the force of his shove might have hurt her or a rock or...

"Not...bad...just..." She winced, and he saw the very real pain in her eyes. "I think my shoulder is... a little out of joint."

"Your shoulder? Let me see." Michael was familiar with all type of war injuries but dislocated bones were rarer battlefield occurrences than bloody wounds on which he was expert. He had known someone once to be thrown from a horse and the remedy for the dislocation was to put the bone back into place.

"Owww...that hurts. Don't pull."

"Darling, you'll have to let me see. I promise I won't do anything until we agree."

"No tricks. It hurts like the Dickens," she hissed.

"You and your phrases. I am sure you could teach me a pronouncement for any occasion." His intent was to keep her talking while he examined the shoulder. Distraction worked wonders with treating injuries in the field. "What would you say to me if I said I was going to beat you in a running race?"

"That's easy...like heck you aren't."

"How about if I suggested a wager on it?" He had found the separation and was just ready to surprise her by yanking it back into place.

"I would say you're on. How much....!!" She screamed.

He released his hold. "There you are all back in place. How does it feel?"

"You bastard. You tricked me."

"While I do admit to tricking you. I can assure you I am not a bastard."

"Where I come from bastard has nothing to do really with your parentage, it's more of how you act…like jerk or idiot, something like that. You just pulled my arm back into place with no warning."

"And yet you are even now rolling your shoulder as if you are healed while scolding me with the most vulgar language. I do hope your tirade has helped you get over the worst of your discomfort."

"So the trick was to distract me?" She looked at him sideways.

"Yes."

"Well, it does feel better." She was rolling her shoulder. "I guess you didn't mean to lie to me. Thanks. I'm sorry. Now I'm really embarrassed at my language. You'll think I'm a regular trash-mouth."

"Kathryn, I think nothing like that. You are wonderfully strong and amazingly bullheaded and I do not blame you for being angry with me. Shall we start back?"

"Are you kidding? I've had a mind-blowing orgasm, been shot at, thrown jarringly to the ground, had a shoulder dislocated and then re-located all in a span of less than one mile. I wouldn't miss the end of this run for the world!"

"When you put it like that, how I can possibly do anything but challenge you to beat me to the cottage on the other side of that rise?"

"You're on. Go…loser owes the next debt."

"It's a deal. You will regret that wager because I will not be so…easy on you."

"Leaving you in my dust, old man…see if you can keep up." She bolted, yelling at him over her shoulder.

Kathryn was beginning to outpace him and a spine tingling terror marched its way into his brain. What if the shooter had ridden further on the path but had not departed the scene and was waiting in ambush for them? Kathryn hadn't even mentioned the shot again or what it might mean since he so effectively distracted her with the shoulder repair, but he was well aware that the long-barreled pistol was a favorite of gentleman—those who practiced at Manton's for example or collected dueling pistols. That was not the stray shot of a poacher. He didn't have poachers. They knew well enough to stay away from his lands now that he had returned. He was among those reputed to be a crack shot. His reputation was an effective deterrent.

No. That shooting had been deliberate and the villain had been aiming for Kathryn. The step forward at the right moment had saved her. Michael realized the bullet must have missed her heart by inches so he was now running faster than he ever had in his life. Not after any battle on the Continent and not since childhood in races that at the time seemed ever so important had he run as fast as he was now. He had to draw up even with her, put his body close enough to her that he would take any shots that came again.

"You still back there? I can't hear your breathing. I must be opening up a gap."

"My lady, your mouth will out run your feet yet. I am overtaking you as we speak." That was obviously all the challenge she needed.

Michael watched in horror as her muscles rippled, her stride lengthened and Kathryn's form began pulling away. With burning lungs, screaming legs and a terror filled heart that was pumping so fast it was meeting itself coming and going, Michael did all he could do to keep her in sight. She was going to most definitely reach the cabin before him, but what drove him the last hundred feet was the absolute fear that there was danger awaiting there at the cabin.

Her scream pierced him like a knife.

"Kathryn!" His fear was palpable as he raced that last few feet toward her. "What's wrong?"

"I win. I win!" she yelled. "I know it's not at all sportsmanlike to gloat, but your mouth was running faster than your feet, to quote a pious Englishman I know. Well, I knew I had you when you said it. I haven't raced like that in years, not since college cross-country and then it was exhilarating. Now, wow…I knew just how much I had to beat you."

His heart would not steady. He thought something had happened but her scream was of joy. The gunshot had obviously affected him more than he could even have imagined and the race had taken a huge amount of energy. He was becoming lightheaded, and when Kathryn pulled him by the hand down the path, he realized he was grateful for her ministrations.

"Don't you know that after that kind of run you have to keep moving, keep the blood flowing."

"I…I…"

"Yeah, big boy. I know you are one solid wall of muscle but you don't do a lot of aerobic exercise. Endurance is different from muscle and brute force."

"Somewhere… in there, there was…a…compliment. Something about muscles…"

"Yes, you have them and if you don't mind me saying so, they are quite impressive."

"You find my muscles impressive?" Michael was beginning to catch his breath, and his wits.

She stopped and turned to face him, his hand still clasped in hers. "I think I told you once before what I think about your body, but I will tell you something else if you promise not to accuse me of flattery or flirtation."

"Kathryn, your assessments of me don't…"

"I know, they don't make me a flirt. So here goes. I've not seen a guy with your muscles and your size run like that…ever. Most runners are sleek and slim, long lean muscles. You are powerfully muscled. You must be in amazing shape to have made that run carrying all those muscles with you."

"Again, somehow I think that was a compliment although it was wrapped in an awfully odd assessment of my physical abilities."

She laughed and released his hand, turning around to hide the blush that he could see all down the backs of her arms and her slim neck. She was, he believed, the most stunning female he had ever seen. Her shirt was sweat-soaked and he now saw clearly the lines of the simple bindings she had worn to cinch up her breasts. He was intrigued by the glistening sweat running in lines down the side of her sharply angled cheekbone. He came up behind her, wrapped his arms about her waist and tasted the salty rivulets trailing down her skin. "You taste like the English Channel."

Although they were both sweaty, she snuggled close. "That's an unusual analogy. How so?"

"Home. Freedom. Victory. Life. You taste like life, Kathryn. You are simply magnificent."

She reached down to grip his huge thighs while he began a regular pattern of licking her cheek, ear, neck, cheek, ear, neck. She was becoming weak with desire. "You are doing it again…you will…owe me."

"What I will do to you right here and now is part of no debt or wager." He moved his fingers into position at her breast and the apex of her thighs and matched their rhythm to that of his tongue. Kathryn's knees gave under his onslaught, his arms having no trouble holding her and she began thrusting into his hand. He felt the pressure between her thighs building to a crescendo. He kept at her relentlessly until she shattered in his arms, moaning his name. He felt her waves of pleasure course through her, and she slumped fully into his embrace.

Without disturbing her shuddering, Michael lifted Kathryn into his arms, turning on his heel back toward his house. She let her head fall against his chest but held onto him loosely. He removed her arms from his waist instead choosing to carry her dead weight. He wanted her like this. At his mercy. Dependent.

Weak, just for a few minutes.

Completely sated and fragile.

His.

Chapter Nine

They had been out for hours and it was well past tea time. He reluctantly allowed her to walk when he realized that the household had probably begun to worry and someone perceptive would most likely be watching for them. They were sorely at risk for being late for dinner.

Hallthorpe opened the grand doors and turned his face so Michael could not see his startled expression at their appearances. They must look quite shocking with the sweat and dirt of the race and the ground. "You have a message from Lord Weatherford that is waiting on your desk, sir," Hallthorpe whispered after Kathryn had taken a few steps and was just out of earshot.

Asterleigh
We have found some distressing evidence. Meet at Worley at 10:00 p.m. Do not ride alone or unarmed. Weatherford

That sounded more than distressing, he thought after getting the message. He was grateful that the meeting had been arranged already however, as he would have had to do so himself after the events of the afternoon. Michael was now convinced that there was a plot against Kathryn's life and for the life of him, he could not figure out why. She had not acted like there was anyone after her. She was too honest in her expressions and she was so far away from home he could not countenance that someone from her past or her present harboring the kinds of resentments to kill her had followed her this far. Who around here would want her dead unless…

Michael pushed the thought to the back of his mind but it found its way forward again. Julian's words came back… "Is she more than just a houseguest…it could explain things…" such as if she is the Duchess presumptive and then if she was carrying an heir someone with designs on the Duchy could be targeting them. *What if someone was trying to end his line and they were starting with Kathryn?*

Michael didn't invite Kathryn for late evening entertainments after dinner. He watched her reluctantly retire to her room, and he hoped she would spend the time reflecting positively on all of the happenings in the last twenty-four hours. Kathryn had mentioned visiting with Cassandra, but his sister had seemed distracted and busy and even Agatha had not come down for dinner. He did see Kathryn had taken a book up to bed. He hoped if she wasn't going to be thinking about him that the book would put her to asleep, before half nine.

As soon as his small band of horses were assembled in the forecourt, Michael knew that Kathryn would hear the crunching of horse's hooves and come to the window. He felt her gaze on his back and forced himself not to acknowledge her. If he did so, later he would have to answer her inevitable questions as to where he went. He hoped she would not admit to spying on him so he could avoid it altogether. Mounted on Fury, Michael whistled to his grooms Thrasher on Thunder and Marsh on Lightening. They departed in a blast of speed for Worley.

Michael's feelings were decidedly mixed as he headed off in the direction he had run with Kathryn that afternoon. The hair on the back of his neck prickled as he approached the spot where the assassin's bullet had whizzed past her ear, just wide of her thankfully still-beating heart. Being stalked by a shadowy assassin was unnerving but not altogether unfamiliar. He had many times known the fear of being hunted. Michael's battlefield skill and his known position as one of Wellington's favorites made him a regular target of French agents bent on eliminating Wellington's best men. Killing a battlefield commander did more damage to troop morale often than the loss of dozens of men so to them, it was like the beheading of a serpent to Boney's minions. Only now, why was he still a target? The only explanation could be the succession.

As the three of them approached Worley, a cold, sick dread began to take root in Michael's mind that the person who stood to gain the most from the demise of his intended and then from his death was his heir presumptive, his cousin Harold Stafford. The same man who had been with Charles when he died after falling from his horse.

* * * *

"Your Grace." The elderly housekeeper greeted Michael with a deep bow.

"Mrs. Soggs."

"They are in the Master's study." She indicated the direction.

"Is everyone here who is expected?"

"Yes, Your Grace."

"Thank you, Soggs." She bowed then melted into the dim hallway. Michael knew his way but he reflected ruefully that even so, a woman did not announce visitors. But soon enough Matthew would have a proper butler. Soon.

"Worley, Weatherford, Hamilton. I see I am last to arrive. What have I missed?" Michael announced, striding into the midst of the somber gathering.

"Actually, we have been here for some time. We summoned you to join us at this hour on purpose so that you could come alone, under cover of dark. We have grave news," Matthew said while reaching for Michael's outstretched hand and indicating a seat near the fire.

"It sounded serious. You perceive me all ears and I, too, have news," Michael reported.

"We found a woman, dressed as a maid, in a shallow grave on the Eastern border of Worley and Hawthorne," Matthew Drake, Baron of Worley, reported. "Colin had brought the dogs and we were investigating my property as there have been some strange occurrences here over the last few weeks and we chanced upon the freshly turned mound."

"I assume since you are reporting the woman was dressed as a maid, that you removed her from the grave?" Michael asked.

"Yes, we wanted to get a look at her face to see if we recognized her from the households or the village. We knew that was unlikely and we were hoping to discover the manner of death." Matthew paused, then continued. "Manner seems easy enough to identify. She was strangled. There is a fresh thin line around her neck from a cord and her eyes were grossly protruded. While neither of us was a particular expert, it seemed quite obvious," Matthew finished, while blanching at the retelling.

"Her assailant…could you tell anything else?" Michael asked.

"If she had fought or had other damage? No, there was none. It was as if she had been fine one moment and strangled the next. She didn't even have abrasions on her hands from a struggle to pull the cord from her neck," Julian added.

"She knew him." It was not a question. Michael noted that the others agreed with him.

"Aye," Colin Hamilton confirmed.

"My news is just as ominous. Kathryn and I were shot at today as we ran along the path connecting Hawthorne and Worley."

"*Shot at*. Are you sure?" Colin asked for all of them.

"Quite. It was a long barreled pistol, I'd wager Fury on it," Michael exhorted. "We had been stopped on the bridle path and just as we started running again, the shot cracked and whizzed past her ear."

"I know this is off the point, but did you say you were running?" Julian asked, twisting his lips into an almost Byronic grin.

"Yes, Kathryn has this ridiculous notion of running for exercise. As you can imagine, I am not going to allow her to do it alone, so therefore I have to go and to challenge her to footraces to appear to enjoy it. It was all very unmanning to then actually lose," he admitted to the group, each of whom had silly grins in their own particular styles on their aristocratic faces. His silly grin was for another reason altogether! Losing in the fashion he had had been entirely pleasurable.

These men had been his best friends and closest confidantes since they were boys. Each had saved the other's life on at least one occasion and they had all served their country on the Continent in some capacity over the last ten years. Julian as a spy behind the lines in France because of his uncanny resemblance to the native population and command of their tongue, Matthew the youngest, as a much-celebrated Cavalry officer, Michael as a battlefield commander and trusted confidante of Wellington himself and Colin who had been an emissary attached to the consulate and who on many occasions had run messages from Wellington to agents of Prinny himself. Michael trusted each of them with his life and more importantly with that of his bride-to-be. They needed to know the full extent of his thoughts, about just what was going on.

"I think my cousin, Harold Stafford, is behind all of this," Michael informed the group that at that moment was still mulling his announcement that he and his proposed fiancée' had spent the afternoon running around his property. He thought it might be the fact that he'd had an altogether too cat-with-the-cream look on his face that had actually gotten their attention.

"The succession?" Colin asked.

"Exactly. Make sure to eliminate any possible posthumous heir or shall we say, the chance of one and then kill me."

"When I asked you…" Julian began.

"You were absolutely right. I was too stubborn to admit you had the right of things. I had only known her for one demmed day and have only really just admitted to myself that she is going to be the Duchess." He gave a sheepish half-smile that had Julian smirking again. His friend knew only too well that Michael had been hedging and was clearly besotted with his intended long before his admission to this group. "So Kathryn has to be eliminated even before we can get married so that she's just a dead *visitor*. If we made our wedding or even our betrothal official, she'd be a dead *Duchess*." He winced as he said it and the other men looked gravely forward knowing he was right, no matter how callous it sounded.

"Because once you're married, both of you dying are too suspicious. As long as she's an unknown traveler who you really haven't introduced to anyone yet, no one is likely to hear of her death in London, so your demise is not nearly as suspicious," Matthew voiced for the group.

"I know Harold's your heir, but why suspect him?" Colin asked not because none of them knew the answer but more because they needed to hear the answer said aloud.

"He is the only one. All other potential heirs are far away and have no reason to think I might not take up the reins. He was probably planning this since Charles…" he stopped in mid-sentence and he was not the only one who realized where his thoughts were leading. Charles had been with Harold Stafford when he died or more to the point, Harold had been with Charles when he died.

"He probably had a hand in it then and realized while I was off at war…"

"And possibly wouldn't return…" Julian observed, not particularly helpfully.

"That with both of you gone and your father's dissolute behavior…" Colin added.

"He was as good as the Duke in short order," Matthew finished for all of them.

"Thank you all for the Shakesperean rendition of reading your lines. I can take it from here, as I know damn it all to bloody hell that my family's behavior is what got us here. Now, how do we catch him?" An emotionally spent and now altogether shaken Michael slumped into the nearest chair. "I need a brandy."

Colin crossed to the decanter and poured three fingers, then handed the glass to Michael.

"We'll have to draw him out in the open, catch him in the act of trying again. A trap," Julian proposed.

"A trap is all well and good, but I am sure I'm not going to like the suggestion of bait. Can we think of something else?" Michael asked wearily.

They debated and schemed and strategized until Michael's head was ready to explode with all the myriad ways his conniving cousin could kill his bride-to-be and then take him with her. "I need to be getting back. All these clandestine meetings will be noticed. Jules, she saw you the other night and she asked me about it but I am just not ready to scare her yet, mainly because I'll have to tell her why she's a target."

"Haven't gotten around to the proposal yet?" Colin chuckled.

"I don't think anyone but the staff is ready for it, least of all Kathryn," Michael admitted.

"So, you haven't really told us much about her. What has made you sure this is the one?" Matthew steepled his fingers and leaned back in the chair, waiting for an answer Michael was not completely ready to divulge. He was not ready to discuss why she was indeed right for the job. But they were going to help him save her and catch a murderer. They deserved the truth.

"She is the perfect candidate…smart, generous, capable and before you ask, she is quite comely for those of you have not seen her face."

"Comely how?" Julian seemed to be interested in the lady's looks, capability and generosity be damned, in the face of a pretty face.

"Kathryn is the woman you would create if you wanted to mold the earth, the sun, kindness, happiness, freedom, health and intelligence into one package. She is quite literally every color of the earth—bronze, honey, gold and brown with a touch of green in her eyes married with the intelligence and heart of the goddesses—the strength of Diana and the sense of Artemis. For sheer physical charms, she is a blatantly, frighteningly, brilliant Aphrodite."

No one said another word for a very long time.

Chapter Ten

The next morning after breakfast, Kathryn decided it was time to take matters into her own hands regarding underwear. She needed some badly. She would ask Ellie to make her some panties. Washing or rather rinsing in soapy water the same panties over and over again had made them rather ripe and wearing none was just too freaky for her. Going commando was for guys and she just couldn't take it anymore. In the meantime, there might not be any women's underwear in this house but there darn sure were some man's boxer style drawers.

Well I know one way to find out about a man's underwear she thought determinedly and turned toward the stairs to corner her prey.

~ * ~

"Your Grace!" Mrs. Luverna Pembroke effused, reaching for Michael's hands. He took hers, bowing over them and getting a dreadful nose full of her fragrance. If Kathryn was essence of America, Luverna Pembroke was essence of boudoir! She smelled as overdone as she was dressed, too many flounces and feathers and odors. His study would need to be aired out after she left and he was already getting lightheaded.

"We, the committee and I, want to talk with you about the fall harvest festival. Now that you are here and established, it is high time we got back into the swing of things. We've missed it the last two years." She penitently bowed her head to him he thought to show respect for his family's losses.

"Mrs. Pembroke, it is my intention to reinstate the festival. I have invited my Aunt Agatha Adger to come serve as a hostess in my house and my sister Lady Cassandra is recuperating. They will both need a little time to…"

"Yes, yes, they will want to jump right in but no fear, we will have it all under control…the committee and I."

"Mrs. Pembroke, I will have Lady Agatha call on you and the Committee once she has settled in." His tone had become more firm and only a slow top would have missed the steely edge.

"Well, we will need to get started soon…should plan on having…"

"Mrs. Pembroke!"

She finally stopped and looked into his face and realized too late that he was taking charge of the conversation.

"I have just returned from eight years overseas and my Aunt has just taken up residence. We will call on you when we are ready." His icy stare had her cheeks flushing and she looked like she might have just realized she had angered him. He wouldn't tell her that she had come on the worst possible day. Fear for someone's life had made him absolutely foul.

"Yes, well…just so…" she stammered.

"Just so. I appreciate your interest and we will certainly be glad for your assistance and that of the committee when we are ready to proceed. I will have Hallthorpe show you out." The erstwhile butler was at the door, ready to remove the malodorous matron.

First of all, Michael did not want her there when Kathryn next bounded down the stairs. It wasn't that he was in any way embarrassed by Kathryn, he just didn't want her cornered by the gargoyle and forced to answer personal questions. He certainly didn't want any matrimonial speculations poking Kathryn. Michael shuddered to think that Kathryn might truly go running if faced with the possibility of being stuck out here in the wilds of English back country with the likes of that woman, whose scent, by the way, had made him completely nauseous.

Second and most importantly he could not think about opening Hawthorne to a festival when there was a would-be murderer on the loose. *Women!*

"My Lord?" The door to his study eased open and Kathryn peeked in.

"Come." He set down the report he had picked up, absently thrumming and regarded her. The maid had piled her hair once again and loosened one tendril to brush her shoulder. He rather liked the way this

102

maid was able to make her look almost proper, coiffed and dressed as she was. She was still wearing the clothes from the morning but she seemed to have freshened up.

Something about seeing her brightened his mood. She was sunny and well-disposed and he thought a bit nervous. He watched as she turned to shut the door and hesitated. Then the minx reached for the key and slowly turned the lock until it fell into place. She slipped the key from its hole and glanced down for any pocket. In the swishing skirts, he watched as, finding no pockets, turning to Michael, she dropped the key into the valley between her breasts. Michael stiffened. "I was wondering…well…what men wear under their clothes…"

One dark brow rose in question. "Under our clothes?"

"You know, underwear…you call them smallclothes?"

"I believe you got a sense of what I wear under my clothes yesterday." She blushed coyly at him. He hoped it was for the memory of his lips on the fabric that he had licked.

Struggling not to show his smug satisfaction for how thoroughly he knew he had pleasured her, he forced himself to remain passive. She was going to have to say exactly what she had come for, what she wanted of him, if she wanted his compliance or participation. Michael wasn't about to let the woman out as she struggled with her motives and he was enthralled by the flush that continued to blossom on her cheeks. What did his little minx want to know of *his* smallclothes? "Yes, don't you call those shorts you wear under breeches 'smallclothes'?"

"Yes, what about them?"

"I'd like to know if you wear them." She seemed to now have herself fully in hand despite the warmth in her face.

His rod pulsed at her question so Michael shifted in his seat to release the pressure building in his groin. His guest took a deep breath and stood up straighter while taking another step toward him.

"I haven't noticed lines in your breeches suggesting maybe you don't wear them," Kathryn questioned.

"Lines in my breeches?" Michael lifted a brow.

"You know, panty lines, where the underwear shows on your backside."

"Panty lines? On my backside?" He lifted the other brow to join the first.

"Yes, your *bottom*," she exclaimed impatiently. "I am convinced you know exactly what I'm asking and are being particularly…what would you English say, *obtuse* on purpose!"

He allowed her to see his smile as her frustration with his intentional thickness rose.

"Yes, I am teasing…it's just that this is a most…improper conversation. You are a lady in my…" *shouldn't say "care" to this lady, especially after so much highly improper behavior of late.* "You are a guest in my home and it is highly improper for me to discuss smallclothes with you." *Can't you tell I am already just holding to some small degree of self- control?*

"I know this is highly improper but it's… just…well…I am…" Kathryn stammered.

Michael regarded Kathryn's perfectly blushing cheeks and longed to feel the heat. His palms itched to touch the swells of her breasts that were peeking once again from the scoop of the modest gown and almost as peachy as her gorgeous cheeks. He remembered how she had enticed him the other night with the masterful working of her supple hands over his rigid flesh. Then he saw the same tendril of hair dancing seductively that had come to tease him. She was moving closer.

"Would you mind …showing me?" Kathryn asked in a warm purr.

"Showing you?" He allowed the shock to register in his face.

"I know…I know…it's highly improper. Am I embarrassing you?" Her drawl had become even more sultry than usual and had dropped an octave in pitch.

"No," he lied.

"Well, *I* am a little embarrassed but I'd still like to see." He rose slowly hoping not to embarrass her even more with his tightly tented pants. He had never stood thus before a woman, proudly displaying his erection. He was as he had admitted to himself earlier, a prude, and unused to becoming aroused by his acquaintance. Their previous interludes had not changed that part of his nature. She seemed unfazed but wide-eyed, almost satisfied, and continued moving closer.

"You're…" she breathed.

"Yes," he whispered.

"Oh." She shuddered.

"I told you this conversation was highly improper," his tone low, gravelly. Kathryn flushed deeper but closed the distance until she was within arm's reach. He reached down to his waistband to slip a button, slowly, seductively moving his fingers in front of her. When he reached for the next one, Kathryn stayed his hands. She took his right hand and rested it on her shoulder. Her skin flickered under his grasp and he moved one finger on her glowing skin. She took his left hand in hers, placed it on the other shoulder, and reached her hands to his flap.

Kathryn's touch knocked the wind from Michael's chest and his grasp on her shoulders tightened in response. She moved slowly over each of the remaining buttons until she had them all released. For a moment, she hesitated, then pressed on, focusing on a point down the length of his leg clearly avoiding staring at his protruding length.

Michael's breathing was shallow and he struggled to hold the reins of his desire as Kathryn knelt before him, her posture almost...reverent. When the temptress reached for his boot, he closed his eyes and gripped her shoulder tightly, instinctively lifting his foot. The gentle tug loosened and the boot dropped to the floor.

Kathryn released his leg after holding him fractionally longer than necessary. He took a deep breath and she grasped his remaining boot. Kathryn's hand followed the boot down his leg and then stroked all the way down the rock hard calf she had revealed. His stockings were no impediment to her progress and she pulled gently on the fabric of his pants. The fabric on the leg gave slowly as the pants were tightly fitted to the solid thighs at her eye level.

With two hands, she guided the pants past his hips, over his knees and down to his ankles.

Michael's instincts were to pounce on this woman, devour her. She sat before him like a prize catch but there was something so touching, so worshipful in her movements that he shackled his desires and waited for her next move. Sirenlike, she was controlling the game.

Kathryn was giddy. She had never seen such legs. She had already grown accustomed to Michael's beautiful face and his form but now, with her hands on his thighs, she discovered his legs were s like steel with muscles rippling at every touch. His skin was alive and her fingers were tingling at the tips where she met his hair-dusted flesh.

Taking a deep cleansing breath, Kathryn reached for a foot and slipped the puddle of pants from his ankles. She repeated the action until the garment was free, laying his pants carefully aside and reached for his underwear. "What do you call these?"

"Drawers," he hissed just as her hands reached the waistband.

Using both hands, she slid the lightweight fabric down the expanse of his thighs in one swift motion. She could not continue to remain this close to him without making a much more direct move on him. Drawing a deep breath, Kathryn forced herself to shackle her rampaging desires.

With the underwear at his ankles, she took the opportunity to seek out his eyes but as her gaze rose, it stopped at his erection. Stunned and wide-eyed Kathryn was riveted to his groin, on the thatch of heavy curls that were as a mane for his huge manhood. She ducked her head but curiosity got the best of her and Kathryn could only marvel at the sculptured god she had uncovered. Allowing a faint smile to cross her face, Kathryn turned her chin to him and whispered, "You are beautiful." His strong fingers gripped her shoulders in answer.

She moved quickly to remove the shorts from his ankles, picking them up while straightening to her full height. Then, she organized the shorts in both hands, leaned over and slipped one foot into them. His arms fell from her shoulders and he watched in stunned appreciation as she guided the shorts up her devastatingly shaped legs under her swishing skirts. As the fabric rose and disappeared from view, his skin remembered her touch and it felt the slide on skin as if he was actually joining with her.

Lifting her lids slowly, Kathryn graced him with a most angelic smile. Michael raised a questioning brow for he could not imagine what she would do next.

When she bent to gather his breeches, Michael beamed over her head, realization dawning that she was going to put his clothes back on! His mind struggled with indecision. He ached to touch her, pull the pins from her hair, strip the fabric from her breasts, recover his stolen smalls, penetrate, possess…but she was in his study. And he had lost his control so easily yesterday afternoon and last night.

If he took such a risk, by having her here in daylight for anyone to discover them, he could ruin what he wanted from her forever…

As her hands moved the fabric up his legs, his control quaked and he doubled as if in pain. She gasped and stopped, then he grabbed his waistband and tugged the final inches. Kathryn retrieved one boot and eased his foot into it. When he was sure she was determined to see all of his clothes righted, he reached for the other boot and slipped it on for himself, stomped it into place then straightened and worked his shirt back into his waistband.

Kathryn stood again grasped her hands in front of her and locked his gaze. "Thank you. I am much more comfortable now." Michael's eyes flared with desire. She drifted dreamily into the deep black pools and had to blink to be sure that she was not mistaking his stance. *He wanted her. Now.*

She could not help herself then from the piece-de-resistance for this magnificent moment. Keeping her gaze locked with his, she trailed her own eyes to the valley of her breasts where the key lay safely hidden, and retrieved it ever so slowly. While he did not release her gaze, she still caught the flex of his hips and pulse of his erection.

She handed him the warm key a brand in his palm from her body heat and he greedily folded his long fingers around the fiery metal. "No, thank *you*," he whispered. "I am greatly relieved to be rid of the offending garment." He smiled teasingly at her and she could not help grinning back.

The man's sharp mind was as sexy as his incredible body. Kathryn knew why women loved to read historical romances—why *she* loved them. These guys were out of this world. On the thought, she turned to the door and started her exit slowly, swaying her hips and sighing like a cat with her cream.

When she reached the knob, Kathryn realized her error, but she was not to worry, he had prowled behind her like a tiger slinking through the jungle. He reached around her to slip the key into place and she shuddered as his arms brushed the sides of her breasts, enclosing her in steel bands, her nose inches from the panels. He edged her back into his massive chest as he eased open the door.

Removing one arm with a gentle sweeping gesture, he showed her the hall. She felt him inhale at the nape of her neck, sending shivers down her spine. If she turned to look at him, she could not trust herself not to kiss him. Again. So she slipped wordlessly into the hall.

Michael sank back into the chair and closed his eyes. Just four days ago, he had been dreading returning and claiming his place among the Dukes of Asterleigh. Now an improper American for-the-love-of-Pete minx had brought him to life and made this house feel warm and welcoming, his body awakened to a desire he could never have fathomed, while a murderer threatened to strip it all away from him. His tenants already loved this Kathryn, his staff surely did, and he could not imagine his dining room or his study, nay his staircase, or his stables without her.

Even in Catherine's and Cassandra's borrowed clothes, she was entirely unique and special. The desolation and emptiness that had kept him away through the winter had been replaced with anticipation and longing. *Desire*. Kathryn was just what he needed. Getting his hands on her permanently would take a well-executed battle plan and he was just the person to help bring her to heel.

"Hallthorpe…"

~ * ~

Kathryn couldn't catch her breath. That last sensation was still roiling through her body. His skin touching the sides of her breasts, they burned, itched even through the layers of that ridiculous bustier. Or was it a corset? Nonetheless, she felt him even through all of that. She took the stairs two at a time until she realized the staff would not approve, but think she was uncouth. Maybe that wasn't the word but improper certainly served as a description for a woman running at breakneck speed up the stairs of a fine mansion such as this. It was all a bit of an effort to contain herself after such an unbelievable interlude.

But she did have her much desired smalls!

Kathryn waited until she regained her breath before pulling the cord for Ellie.

"Yes, miss?" the efficient maid said before Kathryn could expect her even though she was beginning to learn how this servant situation worked.

"I need you to sew something for me…" Her words trailed off and she imagined just then what Michael might think of her undergarments. "These are panties," she announced rather more stridently that she meant to.

Ellie stared wide-eyed at the small triangle of royal blue satin Kathryn was holding. Freshly washed in the basin and still barely damp, the panties had an almost human smell and Kathryn could tell Ellie had never seen anything like them. "Whatever are they for?" Her curiosity had won out over propriety and Ellie just had to know the answer.

"They're drawers, women's smalls."

"They *are* small, miss."

"Yes, I guess they are and tight too. They fit snug so all your private parts stay close, no looseness bagging between your legs and chapping."

Ellie reached for the satin. "Miss, you want me to make more of these?"

"Yes, please. They are getting a bit ripe and I can't go on without something.

"Ripe, miss?"

"Overly pungent...needing a good scalding clean."

"Ah, yes, I shall see to that too. When do you need these smalls? We'll probably have to send for the satin."

"I umm...borrowed a pair of the Captain's and well, they're good, but these are better."

If she thought Ellie's eyes had bugged out at the thought of making a pair of low-rise bikinis, it was the added comment that she had borrowed and was most likely right now wearing men's drawers that had the usually unflappable Ellie stunned to silence.

"You can make yourself some too if you like. I think you could probably be very frugal with the fabric. I was thinking that they could tie on the sides if elastic was not available."

Ellie had stowed the panties in her apron and was holding her lips very tightly shut listening to her mistress's words and working her brain as fast as it would go. She liked this job and she really liked this lady, but she greatly feared bringing these things into the servant's quarters. She could only imagine what they would think of her mistress. She would have to figure out how to work on them somewhere private.

Chapter Eleven

After a fitful and all-too-brief rest to get her swirling wits back together, Kathryn pulled the bell once again. The interlude with the drawers had left her needy and although she had put on a brave face with Ellie, she was aroused to the point of pain. The pressure between her legs had mounted to a throbbing ache as she played over and over the erotic sensation of stripping him, of his face savoring her every touch, of his breath on her nape at the door. Shuddering again, she braced for Ellie's return.

~ * ~

"Miss, I have another dress. This one's for dinner." She held in front of her the most gorgeous gown Kathryn had ever seen. It was royal blue silk, maybe a shade darker, with a low, wide neckline that would show her shoulders, and tiny sleeves. The color looked exactly like something that Cassandra would wear with her striking Snow White coloring, but Kathryn looked pretty good in blue as well. Maybe she would be a little dazzling.

"Wow, it's gorgeous. What did you have to do to make it fit me?"

"You're a bit shorter than the Lady so I moved the seams in the bodice a bit lower."

"So you mean I'll be showing a bit more of my breasts?" Ellie had the sense to blush a little. "Has anyone ever told you that you are amazing?"

Ellie stopped, looked down at her hands, and then straightened to her full five feet. "No miss, no one's ever said that to me."

"Well, you are. This sewing and hair and all the things you can do with your hands. You are a very talented woman," Kathryn declared.

110

"Thank you, miss." Ellie returned to the buttons she was undoing down the back of Kathryn's dress, her sweet face blushing thoroughly.

"Ellie, I want you to promise me something?"

"Yes, miss?"

"Promise me that after I leave and you return home, you will take up sewing or something like it and make a profitable life for yourself."

Her mistress's tone had become wistful and Ellie did not care for it at all. She'd been here less than a week, but this life, this mistress and this house were what Ellie wanted, not a "profitable life" in the village. She loved the other servants, the comfort of her quarters, having her sisters come and work with her, sending money home with them, and the extra fabric her mistress gave her. And she had made friends and dared she hoped, even a beau. Leaving here was the last thing she wanted. How to make her mistress understand? "Miss, you aren't leaving, are you?" She hoped her tone did not belie her cold disappointment.

"Ellie, I don't belong here. This isn't my home. These people have been so kind to me, taken me in when I literally had nothing... but this is their life and not mine. I feel wrong imposing, more I feel like an imposter."

Chest thrumming, Ellie forced herself not to pull the red-gold hair too tightly...her hands trembling, she had never contradicted gentry before, but this was going to be a first. She saw how the master appreciated the mistress; the look in his eyes was the same one that she saw when she looked into Thrasher's. She also knew what Hallthorpe had told her. This would be hard and take all their efforts to convince her to stay. It was her duty here and now to try.

"Miss, I don't know exactly how to say this, but I think you belong here. You are kind to the staff, all of them love you, say they've never had a real mistress before, least not one who smiled and was happy. You like the gardens and riding horses and you look great in the dresses. Then there's Lady Cassandra..." Her words trailed off and she willed the tears not to fall.

"Oh Ellie, I'm sorry. I didn't even think how my leaving would affect you. Would you allow me to ask Michael if you can stay, maybe there are other needs you can serve? I can't believe that they would let you go."

Trying mightily to stifle the next sob, Ellie turned her back to Kathryn

111

and wiped her face on her apron. "Miss, it's not all just about me. You *belong* here, I am telling you."

"Ellie, you know I am different, right?"

"Yes," she answered warily now the tone had become even more desperate.

"I told you I'm not from here, right."

"Yes."

"I am not English but more than that I…I…" She could not say *that*. She just could not say when she was from. There had to be other words. "I have a sister far away and she and I are all each other have. I just don't know how to get back to her and I have to try. I'll be leaving soon but I promise, I will ask Michael to keep you on. It might…work for you to stay and serve the woman he marries. I am sure he'll have to find someone soon for this big old house." Her half-laugh wouldn't fool Ellie one bit.

"Miss, I beg pardon, I really do but don't you see? *You* are the one we want to be mistress here. *You*. You belong here. This is your place. Your home."

Kathryn sat silently facing Ellie, let her eyelids fall, then reached her arms for her maid. Ellie came forward and Kathryn stood to embrace her. The hug was a relief for both of them for the pent up frustrations. Ellie let tears stream and Kathryn gave vent to days of frustration over her own helpless situation.

Kathryn did love it here. She loved Ellie and Hallthorpe and Cassandra, all in that platonic wonderful way you feel about friends. She was devastatingly attracted to Michael but he was far away on the social scale and arrogant and because she would never be a presentable public companion for him, she thought he treated her probably like he would a mistress. If she really knew how anyone treated a mistress. They were wonderfully comfortable in the privacy of his house or in his own meadow but in public, he would probably not even know her. She knew enough about how gentlemen treated their mistresses that the kindness could be very real and affectionate behind closed doors, even more so than with their wives in most cases, but it was a false security that only existed inside her home. There was no publicly acceptable acknowledgement of her presence forthcoming. The tenant visits had been the only indication he might not see her as a totally unworthy distraction …but that was the tenants. Who knew what Michael thought the tenants thought of him and whether he even cared.

Kathryn had never fooled herself into believing that Michael saw her as a wife candidate and she had had pleasure and companionship from her time with him. Recalling the visit of the neighbor lady yesterday that she had overheard from the stair landing, Kathryn replayed Michael's assurances to the woman that his Aunt and Sister would work with her on the festival. His respectable family. Not her, not Kathryn. Even without this confirmation, she had no question about their relationship and she accepted it for what it was. Indeed, she knew who she was and no man had ever looked down on her. Kathryn and her mother and sister had long ago made their own way in the world and needing a man's approval had never been part of her vocabulary.

Pulling a few inches away from Ellie, she looked at the young woman's now mottled face. "I am going to ask him and I am going to try to make it right. You belong here." Ellie looked at the floor, wiped her face again on her apron and resumed the task of dressing Kathryn's hair.

From deep in the house the dinner gong rang and Kathryn straightened to see Ellie's handiwork. The person in the mirror was becoming more familiar but this incarnation was so much more fabulous than she had ever felt before. The blue dress was like the deep of the Gulf of Mexico miles from shore where the bottom fishing was the best. Its lace hem floated and bounced teasing the floor like the ocean waves. The scooped low neckline showed her tan lines at her breasts and was so low that her white flesh was on display. Ellie had woven green, blue and gold ribbons throughout Kathryn's hair and even through the dangling strands so that instead of bouncing ringlets, she had slender braids down her neck.

Kathryn felt like a princess.

~ * ~

Michael snapped to attention as the parlor door opened but the woman who entered knocked him back a step causing him to bump the low table nearby, and scratch the floor behind him. Reining in his swirling emotions, Michael strode to Kathryn's side, placed her suddenly trembling hand on his sleeve and brought her with him deeper into the room toward the chaise nearest the fire. He seated her before he spoke but he could only manage a breathy whisper. "You, madam, are exquisite."

She smiled at him beatifically and his heart stopped in his chest for one fraught moment. Michael was saved from embarrassing himself further by the arrival of Cassandra in company of her footman. "Oh, my, Kathryn, look at you. That dress has never looked better…certainly didn't do me that kind of justice," Cassandra declared as she swept in.

"Wow, between the two of you my head's going to swell like a pumpkin. Thank you. I do feel rather splendid. Isn't that a British expression?"

"Splendid, Michael, would you agree?" Cassandra dared him.

Michael turned his attention to his sister. "Yes, my darling I do believe Miss Ragland is splendid but I had actually said exquisite. But I would be remiss if I didn't compliment you also on your radiance. What a treat to be in the company of such exquisite radiant splendor. I shall endeavor to be able to eat without spilling my food and stumbling over my conversation."

"You are such a tease, brother. However did we get along all those years without your quick tongue?"

"In your case, you didn't get along all that well."

"Touché." Cassandra surprised herself at how well she took that little comment. She glanced at Jem whose eyes were wide as saucers. He had never heard Michael mention her illness in any but the most reverent ways. This must be good. She was glad to see Jem react. He sure did have the most lovely jaw line and she hesitated just a second more than she should have in regarding him.

Agatha came bustling in. "Oh dears, I am so sorry. My maid was feeling poorly and I tried to get my hair by myself but I finally had to call on Kathryn's maid to help me." Immediately Kathryn realized she had the perfect opening to ask Michael about Ellie.

"Lady Agatha, didn't you think she was just the most wonderful help?" There were always people getting sick. She could be a fill in for either Cassandra's or Agatha's maids.

"Yes, she is a strong, capable girl. Got everything done in such a quick fashion. I can see why you like her."

"Oh yes, she's been a godsend. You know that all these trappings are a little beyond me. She's guided me through it."

"So gel, how has your stay with us been so far?" Agatha turned her full attention on Kathryn.

"This has been such a wonderful adventure. I'll never forget it," she answered wistfully.

"Forget it?" Michael asked. She heard the suspicion in his tone. All the ladies turned toward him, for he had not spoken in several minutes.

"Yes, when...uhh...I am no longer here. When I am...home."

This was not a conversation Michael was going to have in front of his sister and his aunt. He was tired of the repeated threats of departure. She wasn't leaving and she needed to get it through her head but this was not the time or the place. He could be a good host and change the subject. He would right now. "Cassandra, I noticed your easel had been brought out of the attics."

"Oh yes, I dug out paints and brushes. Well, actually Jem dug them out and then we went through them all to see what worked. Most were dried and shriveled. I've made a list of what I would need to get started painting again. Will you place an order for me?"

"First thing in the morning if you desire, just mark it for Smithers and he will handle it. Are you also going to teach Miss Ragland to paint? I know you two have been working on the rose bushes."

"Roses yes, paints no," Kathryn declared. "Not much I do with my hands ever looks like it's supposed to. In fact, I was just complimenting Ellie on her handiwork such as this hair and her sewing and it reminded me that there is not where my talents lie."

"Miss Ragland, where do your talents lie?" asked Agatha in a rather more pointed tone.

Michael shot her a reproving look.

"Well, My Lady, I am really good with people. It sounds trite but if I told you what I did for a living, you'd probably be a little shocked."

"Nothing can shock me, gel, as long as you don't say something provocative like you're a courtesan." She laughed and the others followed but it wasn't really all that funny or appropriate.

"No, not that. I'm a counselor. I work with women and children in crisis."

"Crisis?" It was Cassandra's turn to sound surprised. "What kinds of crisis?"

115

"Abuse, homelessness, poverty, unemployment, mental illness, anything that would cause them a tremendous amount of stress. I work at an agency where we help women get back to being productive members of society, or get away from abusive husbands or simply get training for new careers."

All three of the mouths of the gentry were gaping as were Jem's and Hallthorpes' who had returned just as she had begun speaking. "You're all staring at me."

"You are right and we have all lost our manners, terribly uncouth of us. Do tell us what kinds of help you provide," Michael said, looking at her as if for the first time all over again and trying to recover some of his usual élan. What she had said had shocked him to the core. She was someone who worked with poor and downtrodden women to help them improve their lives. Wouldn't that be just what he'd expect of her? What an intriguing, beguiling, good woman he had found.

"One example is recently a woman came in with a baby and she didn't have a job but she couldn't afford childcare to go job hunting. She was in the proverbial catch-22. How to get out? We set her up for a few days with our resident day care that allows people to job search, got her some clothes from our thrift closet, and identified some job leads. After four interviews over eight days, she got a job at a day care. She takes her daughter with her and makes enough money to keep her own apartment. A storybook ending I'd say."

"Sounds like it. Do you believe in story book endings, Miss Ragland?" Cassandra asked skeptically.

"Not for me. But for some."

"Miss Ragland," Michael intoned in the soothing voice he used when he spoke to her. "Why should *you* not have a story book ending?"

"I am too much of a realist. I've seen too much in my life, but don't get me wrong," she said, her tone lightening the mood. "I absolutely believe in Sleeping Beauty and fairy tales and romance and love."

"Kathryn, I'll bet you could teach us all about love. You seem to be a very giving person."

"Thank you, Cassandra. Don't know for sure that I am a love guru but I do think I know how to make people recognize happiness or at least reach for it."

"You made me want to reach for it. I think you have a gift. Doesn't she, Michael?"

"Yes. Let's drink to gifts." And he winked at his glowing baby sister.

~ * ~

The dinner conversation with Agatha and Cassandra and Kathryn had finally lightened and become animated. *A houseful of women*. How had he come to that? But these women... he cherished them each one. His years of being responsible for hundreds of men was now exchanged for the responsibility of a stable full of intriguing, amazing, stubborn, difficult, women. As odd as it seemed, Michael believed he could get used to this.

Since he was the only gentleman, he took his port in the drawing room with the ladies even though it was not really socially acceptable to drink in front of them. The awkward moment came when the tea tray was delivered and Hallthorpe hesitated a fraction of second in deciding who to place the tray in front of. Kathryn would someday be the lady of the house but she wasn't yet. Agatha was the senior lady but Cassandra lived here all the time. Thorpe's quick thinking placed the tray by Agatha and she smoothly began the pour. No one questioned his judgment.

~ * ~

The next morning, Michael was attempting once again to catch up on his neglected business. "My Lord?"

"Yes, Thrasher, what is it?" Michael waved him into the room.

"One of the lads said as he saw a midnight black hunter stabled over to the woodsman's cottage on the Hamilton property. He was coming back from visiting his mother over to Badlinton and was cutting through. Figured there shouldn't be anyone in residence when he heard the horse."

"Did he see anyone about?"

"No but it did look like fresh activity. Hoof prints were churned by the door. Said he wanted to see the horse. It was a beauty, the man announced.

"Thank you. We'll need to put a watch on the place. Can you tell me which grooms we can spare from the stable?"

"Aye, My Lord and..."

"Yes, Thrasher?"

Olivia Ritch

"I...we...want to help you lay the blackguard low, sir."

"Thank you, Thrasher." Watching the groom's retreating back, he realized there had been much more in Thrasher's offer than simple loyalty. He suspected Thrasher and indeed all of his servants had been affected by the warmth of his home that had bloomed from the moment *she* had arrived.

It wasn't just Kathryn's dazzling smile or her quick wit, her earthy beauty or her mesmerizing voice...it was her radiant *joi de vivre*. She just lived so fully, like when she took the stairs two at a time, or caught the hem of her gown hopelessly in the rose bushes and laughed at herself until she tore it beyond repair, or when her smell of vanilla and warm woman filled any room she entered. The reactions of his servants, the males especially, were not surprising. Kathryn Ragland was the most delicious female he had ever met. Ever. And she would be his for the rest of his life, once he 'laid low' the villain trying to take her from him.

Her knock interrupted his musings. "Come."

"There you are. Working hard or hardly working?"

"Kathryn, you have my measure, I was woolgathering. What can I do for you?'

"I need another run."

Immediately his imagination conjured a vision of her passion drunk, sweating and sated from their previous run. But the assassin had targeted them as well. He still had not told her she was being targeted by an assassin who could strike from anywhere at any time so how could he discourage a run. "Was our last run not just a bit too eventful?"

"As I told you at the time, it was great. I am hoping you might *indulge* me again."

"You, minx, are absolutely mischievous. How could I possibly refuse that invitation? We will however choose another route."

"What, too many vivid memories of the last time?"

"Ahhh, I...don't always know what to say to you, My Lady."

"Say you will race me and that'll be enough for now."

~ * ~

Michael had chosen the path through the woods away from Worley and Hamilton, deeper into his own property. Maybe the villain—if it was

Harold Stafford or another—would avoid coming too far into Hawthorne's park and they would be safer. He could not countenance any other outcome.

They set a slow pace on the well-trodden bridle path. She spoke first while he was contemplating their safety. "I wanted to ask about your wife. You have never really mentioned her and well, as I am getting to know about you, that's one area of your life I know nothing about." She turned and glanced at him. "That is if you are comfortable talking with me about it."

"You know, Kathryn, I never thought I would feel as comfortable with a woman as I do you. My mother was sad and fragile. My sister has been a veritable recluse for the last years and Agatha is a formidable matron. You are much like a...friend."

"Thanks, that's a compliment. So what was she like?"

"Catherine was a Baron's daughter. Her family spent the Season in London, and she met and I believe fell in love with my cousin who...dishonored her."

"By that I take it you mean, they had an affair?" She looked at him without the judgment he expected to see in her face. His family, even his sister had thought he had been mistaken to take Catherine to wife. Why he felt that Kathryn Ragland would understand his decision, he did not know but unburdening himself felt somehow comfortable. He had held this anger in for too long.

"Yes, she was with child and he might have married her but he dallied and did not ask her and she was afraid her condition would out while she waited on him to make the arrangements. I don't think she would have come to me of her own volition but I happened upon them talking privately in the gardens at a soiree' and I could tell she was trying to bring him to some point, and he was being particularly evasive. When they separated, she began to cry and I showed myself. The words just rushed out of her. When she realized she had told me enough to guess that she was with child, she looked as if she would die right there. I took pity on her and offered for her."

"Just like that, a woman pregnant by another man?"

He regarded her river moss eyes and saw an altogether unexpected emotion... admiration.

"I know marrying her yourself was certainly chivalrous but why not encourage your cousin to marry her?"

"I had made the offer and I just somehow knew that if he had been so lost as to have bedded a virgin and then not immediately married her, he probably wasn't going to. He had a certain reputation—all of the men in my family do."

"Except you?"

"Except me."

"Michael Stafford, you are a truly amazing man."

She thought again about telling him of the portrait that had brought her to him but decided to let his admission sink in before throwing that at him. They had been out for what she estimated to be twenty minutes or so and it was as good a time as any to suggest they turn back. It would be about a four mile run at this rate.

She hesitated and he asked, "Is something amiss?"

"No, I think…it's time we turned around."

More than grateful to be heading back to the house and hopeful that they had not been followed, he stepped out in front of her and led the way back to the house. He sensed the danger as they crested a small rise that gave onto wide views of the park. There was an arriving carriage. *Visitors.* And Michael and Kathryn dressed in breeches, sweaty and breathing heavy. This was very bad.

Hoping to have secured her agreement for staying with him permanently before greeting any guests, Michael was aware what would happen if the two of them were discovered as they were, not betrothed. A betrothal would allow for a lot more flexibility in their movements and for now, his presence with her like this would compromise her reputation. He had no choice but to tell her their problem. "Kathryn, please slow down for a moment."

"What's wrong, you look worried."

"Visitors. They really should not find us like this. I mean alone together and dressed scandalously."

"All right, okay, so what do we do?"

"Servant's entrance I think. I can towel off and greet them and you can slip upstairs and call for your maid."

"Lead the way, Captain." There was a tone in her voice he did not

120

recognize and he regarded her face for any sign of that elusive niggling doubt that said something was amiss.

They parted just outside of the kitchen and she made her way toward her room. Michael regarded her retreating back and could not help but sense something was wrong. There had been no dazzling smile, not so much as a word. But she had done exactly as he had asked and disappeared without alerting their guests to her presence. What had he said or done to cause her hesitation?

~ * ~

The click of the door was louder than she had meant it to be and she hoped it did not draw any attention. She wasn't brooding. She wasn't. It didn't hurt that he wanted to keep her secret from visitors. Maybe, actually, it did hurt a little. If she really thought about it, it made her feel cheap and dirty to be thought of as a sex partner, playmate, even friend, but not one he would publicly acknowledge. That was it…dirty. She had never let anyone make her feel dirty and as nice as he had been, he made no secret of his wish to keep her from polite society.

It was as good a time as any to begin contemplating her next move, actions she had let fall to the back burner because she had been enjoying her visit with the Stafford family. Tonight would be as good as any to have dinner in her room so she could plan in quiet.

Chapter Twelve

Dispensing with the Stogwells had been even more difficult than ridding himself of the matron Pembroke days earlier because the Stogwells were actually decent and pleasant. He just couldn't focus on what they were saying while he was distracted with Kathryn's withdrawal at the end of their run. He wanted to talk to her to dispel the unpleasant tightness that had settled in his chest. She had looked…hurt. *Surely not over their conversation about his deceased wife*. Something he had said or done had caused it and he needed to fix it. "Vicar, I know my aunt would like to learn more about the Flower Committee. I will encourage her to seek you out to discuss it."

"Wonderful, Your Grace. Your presence here is so…so… stabilizing. The village has needed leadership. I trust that we will see a renewed spirit what with the festival and…"

"I intend to take my place of leadership," Michael declared to dispel any notions the Vicar may be harboring.

"With that, we will leave you Your Grace," Stogwell demurred.

Michael turned to find his frighteningly efficient butler at his service. "Hallthrope. There you are. Will you order…"

"The Vicar's carriage is waiting, My Lord."

He waited for the unmistakable crunch of gravel before asking of Hallthrope. "Miss Ragland?"

"She has ordered a bath and dinner to be served in her room, My Lord."

Damn.

Michael hoped that Hallthrope might have an idea what was troubling

Kathryn. "Did she give any reason for not coming down to dinner? I don't think she's ever skipped a family meal before?"

"No." Michael recognized the unmistakable flicker of indecision in his man's expression.

"You're hesitating. You've realized something just now. Out with it man."

"It occurs to me that you have had several visitors and she has not been introduced to any of them, Hallthorpe offered.

"Why would that…" but his words trailed off as he realized exactly what she must be thinking. He had sent her in the servant's entrance no less and she had accepted that gracefully, without her usual warmth but nonetheless she had allowed him to treat her like his private playmate to be hurried off into the shadows when proper company arrives. "You think she thinks I am keeping her secret, don't you?"

"There is that, yes."

"Damn!"

"As you say, My Lord."

Michael paced his study until late in the night, the recognition that he had hurt her, albeit unintentionally, settling in his gut to pull and ache. He wanted to secure her hand so she would know, absolutely, that he was not ashamed of her, indeed that she would be his Duchess, his partner. He had just been giving her time, nothing more. Michael was in fact exceedingly proud that Kathryn would be his wife and could not wait to tell her so. Morning could not some soon enough for him.

~ * ~

Kathryn had spent a fretful night alone in her room, having been determined to not do or say something she would regret after Michael's apparent embarrassment over her presence in his home. "Miss Ragland, there you are."

"Well, you did arrange this appointment. So formal."

"What I wish to discuss with you is rather serious. Please sit down."

Almost reflexively, her brow shot up and she realized in just a few short days—had it been ten?—that she had taken on one of the household's most artfully executed expressions. "Oh?" She arranged herself in the chair before the fire fully expecting him to take the chair

123

across from her. Instead, he sat on the edge of the desk and dangled a booted foot over the side toward her.

"Yes. I am a rather direct and practical man so I shall ask you without further delay. I would like to make you my wife. Will you accept me?"

Marriage? Kathryn had not at all expected this meeting to begin with a proposal of marriage. She thought she had made it clear to Michael that their affair was informal and that she could not abandon her plans to get home. She also thought pointedly back to his rejection of her the day before. How had he come to a marriage proposal when he could not introduce her to the Vicar? She wondered momentarily if it had been the presence of the Vicar that had made him determine he needed to make her respectable.

She allowed the silence to stretch because frankly, she just couldn't answer him. When she remained quiet, he continued.

"You would be the mistress of this house. All the decisions regarding the household would be yours." He waved his arm to indicate her surroundings as if she didn't know what he meant. "You could determine to live here, in London, or on one of my other estates." He paused and when she continued regarding him stoically, he went on. "I will need an heir. It will be expected of our station. Additional children would be appropriate as well. You would be the Duchess of Asterleigh."

After collecting her thoughts Kathryn felt she could speak. She took a very deep breath. "It sounds like you've given this request a lot of thought and I do appreciate that, however…I can't commit to marry you now."

"What exactly does that mean," Michael asked with that thinly veiled menace she had heard in his voice before.

"You know I am committed to getting home."

"You can go home any time we can arrange it," Michael waved off her concern.

"You don't even believe me about my home." She was becoming frustrated. "You can't make a promise to take me somewhere you do not believe exists."

"Kathryn, I know very well you have a home." He glared at her. "I just don't believe how you got here."

"And that is as good a reason as any that we do not need to marry each other."

This time *he* allowed the silence to stretch and she saw the muscle in his jaw twitch. She could tell he was trying very hard not to reach his hand up to rub his forehead. He thought he was making her the offer of a life time but being married to someone who was going to let her live anywhere and who did not love her, did not even believe her, probably was worried about introducing her to his neighbors was not Kathryn's idea of a proposal.

Oh, she knew well enough that it was the way of nineteenth century autocrats to order women to marriage but she was just not one to be cowed.

"My Lord?"

"Michael."

"Michael, I want from marriage a partnership."

Yes.

"Someone who wants to spend time with me more than anyone else on this earth."

Yes.

"Laughing, joke telling, making love until noon…"

Yes. Yes and Yes.

"Someone who wants to have babies with me so much he thinks of baby names in his dreams.

Yes.

"And someone who will never have a mistress, not only won't have one in the future but never had one. That it is only me and with a commitment to make our marriage be something to be proud of. Simply… someone who loves me."

Yes.

Oh, hell. Did he love her? The thought had come unbidden in Michael's head. But had she just said she didn't love him, didn't feel any of those things? Hadn't she? Michael could not recall in all of her scathing diatribe if she had rejected his heart.

"And for me, I want to be school-girl crush, heart-racing, weepy-eyed in lust kind of in love." She paused and he did not interrupt her. "I want *it*, that magical relationship that makes you whole. You are not offering me that."

She did not move. She was finally quiet, and it was his turn but what was he supposed to say after she so artfully threw his precisely worded proposal of marriage back in his face? Was he supposed to declare undying love for her, infatuation of her grace and charms, throw himself at her feet? As she watched him outwardly calm, Michael realized that was indeed what she expected. She should not hold her breath. "Kathryn, what you are asking is not a conventional marriage. I am making you a very lucrative offer."

"My Lord, you've only known me a few days so I am trying hard not to be offended but really, do you think I'm someone who would want to choose to live anywhere but with my husband? Do you see me as someone who would prefer London to the country or social events to horseback riding lessons or London balls to visits with the tenants? Do you see me as the type of person who wants to think of having children as the duty to provide an heir? And can you see me as a Duchess? I still prefer pants and men's drawers to big hair and bodices. And, can you possibly see me being someone to accept anything but full and complete fidelity?"

She paused for breath. He did not even twitch.

"I cannot accept your proposal."

At least she had the decency to look down but she didn't seem to be embarrassed. No, she really seemed to be well, content. "Will you excuse me now, My Lord? Umm...Your grace?"

"Yes."

She turned slowly and he thought for one moment he saw regret in her eyes but she shuttered her gaze from him so fast that the fleeting emotion was gone. He heard her taking the stairs two at a time.

Dropping into his chair behind the desk, Michael turned to stare out into the blackness of the garden. For just a moment, he saw Kathryn and his sister laughing and giggling conspiratorially and his heart locked, his breathing sped up and he broke in two the quill he had heedlessly grasped. Closing his eyes, Michael let the nausea roiling in his gut flood him and he wept silently.

~ * ~

Kathryn locked her door dropping back against it. Her heart was racing, underarms sweating. Oh, great, she knew would stink again. She must also be about to start her period because the tension and anger in the

126

aftermath of that absurd experience downstairs were building to unbearable levels and yet, if she examined everything he really said, he had not done anything so bad. For him it was a great offer. Duchess for crying out loud, live anywhere, host parties, be rich beyond words but for what? To have a separate life from a husband? To be subjected to the possibilities of sharing spouses, mistresses, lovers, orgies. Kathryn's parents had had that and it had sucked.

It wasn't like she was in love with him. He had been a great host, perfectly polite, mannerly and sometimes he had even been fun. He had been generous and chivalrous and sexy, but all of those things came with the package he offered her. He'd enjoy sex with her and get her pregnant, but he didn't say he would help her through labor or even get her ice cream in the night. He didn't say he would be with her in the birthing room. He probably wouldn't, but maybe that wouldn't be his fault. Michael would probably care for the child, but he didn't say he was looking forward to taking it fishing or teaching it to ride. His father hadn't done those things for him. This man really didn't seem like the type to cheat, but he also didn't seem like he'd be doting or even affectionate. Everything Michael offered was surface, no feeling, no emotion. Kathryn needed the emotion. She would have the heart of her husband.

Now that she had rejected his marriage offer, especially since it had badly blindsided her, Kathryn had to face the unpleasant reality of what to do with herself. Not accepting Michael's hospitality was a start. She had to look forward. But before she moved on, she had to look back at what now had become so clear. She had thought he was being hospitable, treating her so wonderfully out of the goodness of his heart and because he genuinely enjoyed her company. When all the time it had somehow been part of a plan for him to get a wife and not a mutual relationship that they had been pursuing after all. He had brought her here to marry her. That was cold reality and it made her feel slutty and cheap and…like she had been used. And it was just then that Kathryn realized he had never once offered to help her get home and had never believed her or even been willing to discuss her claims. She wasn't feeling a deep down hurt at these revelations about his motives, not even that he had deceived her in any sort of horrible way, just that he had used her rather more than she would have liked. With that she had made her decision.

~ * ~

"My Lord, will that be all?"

"Yes, Minton, thank you. I will be riding early in the morning."

"Of course." As his valet slipped out the door noiselessly, Michael scanned his room for a place to sit and ponder the question of Miss Kathryn Ragland...*a partnership, laughter, joke telling...horseback lessons in men's breeches...making love until noon...dreams of baby names...I want to be heart-racing, weepy in lust.* In a flash of realization, Michael knew what he wanted. He wanted her to be in that heart racing lust with him.

Sleep did not come.

Dawn was welcome.

All would be better today. It had to be.

The ride helped some. Not much.

The cool morning pre-dawn air gave way to the stickiness of daybreak. Fury was not yet winded but Michael was restless and frustrated, thoughts colliding in his brain. But after an hour of pounding, blistering riding, his thoughts had still not cleared. *Did he love her?* He could not conceive of her with another man. That was sure, set in stone. She would never belong to anyone else. She was his.

Could she come to love him? And did he even want to be in a love relationship with her? And demmit, when the hell had she ever thought he would be unfaithful? Had she so little faith in *him*?

Cassandra. Of course, Kathryn had the example of what happens to trusting women from faithless husbands and blind-eyed society, right here in his home. Surely, Kathryn could not equate him to that lousy, good-for-nothing reprobate Penthoven? But as he said it to himself he knew; Kathryn would never be able to contemplate a marriage without a declaration because she knew it could be just such as Cassandra's. Heartless, hurtful and dangerous. He understood, he thought.

Michael rode neck or nothing back to the house to break his fast and speak with Kathryn over the meal when he met Hallthorpe in the hall. "Miss Ragland has not come down, My Lord." *Is it that obvious?*

"Yes, My Lord."

"I didn't even say that out loud."

"No, My Lord."

"Demmit to hell!"

Michael had long since finished his food and forced down a second cup of coffee in an obvious attempt to delay leaving the dining room so that he would have a legitimate reason for being there when she arrived. At half nine when Kathryn still had not joined him, he rose just as the door was swinging wide. "My Lord, Miss Ragland's room…"

"What? Spit it out."

"She seems to be gone, My Lord."

"Gone? What the hell do you mean gone, Thorpe?" He bellowed at the servant whose worried expression told Michael exactly what he meant. *Gone*.

Chapter Thirteen

"Departed, My Lord. She took two dresses, left the others and she must have only her riding boots. She has some new smalls but everything that was in the room when she moved in is in its rightful place. Her personal effects are gone."

"Bloody hell. Have you asked the staff? Has anyone seen her?"

"Footmen are scouring the grounds now and Mrs. Staggs is questioning the maids."

"Thorpe, do you bloody well know what this means? Someone tried to kill her in my own house and shoot her on the bridle path, and she only lived because she was being watched over. Now she is out there alone!" He fairly roared and because Hallthorpe was so well trained, he took the master's rage with all of the training that had.

"I want two…"

"Yes, My Lord."

"And two…"

"Yes, My Lord."

"And the carriages."

"Yes, My Lord."

"Demmit, Hallthorpe, are you going to let me even finish a sentence?"

"My Lord, two footmen have been armed and dispatched toward the London Road, two to the Wilton Road and the carriages—both of them—are being readied."

"I'll need…"

"Thunder is being saddled."

"Okay then, tell me what I have not thought of."

Hallthorpe finally had the good sense to blush.

"Send for Worley and Weatherford and a note over as far as the Grange. Ask for Hamilton to send some of his footmen, and if they can, bring a hound or two. I don't want Cassandra left unprotected."

"As you say, Sir." For Hallthorpe knew Cassandra's safety was important but he had assured it long ago. His own son James was her personal footman.

Michael clattered out of the forecourt determined to find Kathryn before the villain who had ordered her poisoned and who had tried to put a hole through her, found her. An unholy fear had gripped him from the moment Thorpe had said she was gone. She didn't know she was in danger and while he didn't know why, he did know that her being alone on the roads was tantamount to suicide. He had immediately regretted not telling her of the attempt on her life; it had been arrogance on his part. Knowing the danger might have made her consider…

His fear had driven him to Wilton before he even saw where he was. Catching sight of one of his grooms, he recognized the negative head shake. His other groom was coming from the Inn and he too shook his head. By mutual consent, they converged just out of earshot of the guests coming and going at the front door. "Marsh, head back to the house to inform Hallthorpe and get word to the others that she is more likely on the London Road. Toole, you're with me since you're on Lightening. To the London Road."

With that terse command, they were thundering after Kathryn in a race that reminded him he had done the very same thing just eleven days ago. He was no less frightened and uncertain of her safety today. Indeed, he was probably scared out of his mind if indeed he let himself dwell on it. Someone was trying to kill her. They had come very close already. This time she was alone and totally unprotected.

~ * ~

Julian drew on senses honed by years overseas behind enemy lines to scan for his prey. However, the woman was so distinctive he didn't need his training to spot her. Bronzed earth and sun Michael had said and he had not been far off. She was an Earthy treasure. Sitting on the bench just outside the Laurel, Kathryn Ragland was as Michael had described but right now, she also fairly reeked of desperately-alone-gentlewoman. He watched her, hugging her traveling sack, because that's all it looked like, and rocking ever so slightly back and forth. She was obviously nervous, and he wondered if it was of being spotted by Michael and his posse or did she know the danger she was in from the outsider? As Julian watched her, he also saw easily why Michael was so smitten with her. Indeed, if he had seen her first...

Her odd coloring belied a distinctively English face, high cheekbones, pug nose, cleft chin, pursed lips even with the faint bronze skin color, wildly striped reddish-brownish-blond hair and freckles. He was sure of the tiny dots existence. Her hair flowed like a dazzling mane over her shoulders and he recognized the Viking warrior goddess Michael had unwillingly described. Staid, perfect, upstanding Michael had entangled himself with a minx of such extraordinary features. She was stunning in her look, utterly distracting, not a *tonnish* beauty of pale blond ringlets but of pure, healthy, sensual woman.

Julian steeled himself with the thought that maybe he would meet a sister...

He had to get her off this street and he couldn't just walk up to her. She didn't know who he was and he wouldn't make a scene in front of the Laurel's customers. Pulling his pad from his waistcoat, he penned a short note and spotted an urchin lurking nearby. "See that exquisite titian haired lady? Give this to her." The child eyed the shiny coin sitting on top of the note, grabbed them both and raced for Kathryn. As he approached, she welcomed him openly. When she favored a dazzling smile on the grimy child, Julian all but lost his seat. He was extraordinarily jealous. Her face lit up like the light of a shooting star—vibrant, colorful, and almost elusive. That look was pure Valkyrie. Her brow furrowed as she dropped her hands back into her lap and raised her eyes to scan the riders milling in the street.

When Kathryn's gaze came to rest on the Frenchman, a shudder of frustration gripped her chest and her stomach fluttered. What was he doing here? Too late to run, she took measured steps toward him. "Miss Ragland, I presume? I am Julian Thornton." Yes, there was definitely a faint French accent. She knew she had been right about him.

"You're a friend of Michael Stafford's?"

"Yes, Miss Ragland, I am one of what I believe is a small army of men dispatched to find you and return you to Michael's safe keeping."

"Safe keeping isn't something I am accustomed to, Mr. Thornton. I should ask, are you Mr. or are you My Lord? I understand it makes quite a difference."

"My Lord for my sins."

"That many sins?"

"That many, yes. But …"

"You don't need to lecture me. I know what you are supposed to say about him," Kathryn retorted. She was not thrilled to have been discovered.

"You do?"

She adopted a deep drawl. "My honorable friend…"

Julian cut in. "You obviously do not know me, my dear. I have no intention of pleading his case."

"You're not here to convince me to return with you?"

"No, I am here to take you back."

"I don't like to be taken."

"Miss Ragland, nevertheless, his company surely is an improvement over this." He swept his hand across the bustling street toward the bench that had now been occupied by other less savory characters waiting for the afternoon coach.

"Sir, I can assure you that it's not Michael's company or the lack of it that has me on this road. I have to get home and it's time. He would not have worked with me to move on so I did us both a favor."

"A favor? Is that what you call this?" His French accent coupled with the sarcasm grated on her last nerve and she forced herself not to tell him what she thought about Julian and his arrogant, over-bearing, self-indulgent, unloving friend.

"Yes, a favor. He was exceedingly generous to feed and house me for the last almost two weeks I am embarrassed to admit, but I couldn't stay forever. It was time for me to go so I made a clean break, no messy goodbyes, no need for him to plead with me to stay, not that he would have anyway. Now he can get back to doing whatever he was doing and I'll work to find my way home."

So Michael had botched the proposal? Jules dismounted because arguing with her from this height and in such a public fashion was drawing querying glances and some outright gaping mouths. Assured that she would walk with him if he kept a pace toward their ultimate destination, Jules fell in beside her. "And what do you fancy he was doing before you came into his life?"

"You've got me there. I have absolutely no idea. Not, I'll predict, looking for a bride."

"I believe he was not looking but he did indeed find."

"Is this where I say 'touché?"

"Very good. We'll have you English yet."

"Now my turn. You were at the house several nights ago? You arrived escorted by a guard, worked in his study and left. What was that about?"

So Michael hadn't told her. Seems his sins were adding up. Jules had not really expected it of him but out here now, it seemed she needed to know she was in danger. "He asked me over to discuss a matter of your safety." They had gotten off on an uncertain footing and she was well inclined not to trust him, even more very unlikely to willingly go with him. Julian had made the decision; later consequences be dammed.

"My safety?" He could see that was definitely not the answer she expected.

"Yes, there had been an unknown maid in your room and he inquired of me to assist him in locating her." But since she hadn't mentioned the matter of the gunshot, he didn't have to lie about it.

"He didn't tell me."

Julian could see her simmering rage and he resented being the one to have to take the brunt of what he was sure would be a lot of female outrage. Damn Michael for keeping this from her.

"No, he didn't want to worry you." At least she was still walking the right way…away from the avid listening ears.

"Figures. Fits in with the other things he said last night. He is a rather arrogant man and knows nothing about me. If I am in danger, he should have told me."

Julian was surprised at her clipped but civil tones toward him. He wasn't after all going to be the one to endure her tirade. She regarded him coldly but not so far to show disdain and she seemed to be making an effort to resolve that he had been honest with her and somehow was deserving of respect. He relished the thought of this woman saving and storing her ire for the one who would deserve it but he also felt a little guilty that he had not been completely honest with her. "I hear you saying your plan is to go in search of your family. I think if you had but asked, Michael would have helped you. He's good at finding people."

"I thought it was you who was good at finding people. You found me first."

Not as first as I'd have liked to be. "A sharp wit. I like that. I can see why he chose you."

"*Chose me*. It shouldn't surprise me that you say it like that. No one chooses me. No one says… 'You will be mine.' I choose who I want to be with. It's absurd all of this arranged marriage nonsense. People marry for love or not at all in my world. Period."

"Do you believe in love, Miss Ragland?"

"Absolutely.

"I see in your eyes…"

"What do you think you see in my eyes?" she demanded, rounding on him so fast that she kicked dust onto his polished Hessian boots.

"I think you love him."

He saw a flare in her eyes, either from anger or because his comment hit a nerve of truth. "And did you make this careful observation from anything other than my one comment about love?"

"No. You are running, are you not? You either felt you needed to see him declare himself by chasing after you or something more. You have the idea your feelings are unrequited and you had to get away."

"You know, My Lord, the first moment I saw you, I thought you were a spy. I'm right I know it. Do you get paid a lot of money to dissect the emotions of your victims?"

"What am I supposed to say to that, Miss Ragland?"

A look of contriteness came into her eyes. "I'm sorry. That was way out of line. You've obviously troubled yourself to come from your home to help hunt for me and I've been a horrible bitch. If you'd just leave me to keep going on my own, I'd appreciate it."

She looked up at him, her eyes tired. "You asked if I ever asked for his help. I have pleaded with him to help me get home, but he chooses not to believe my situation. Why would he want to marry me if he thinks I'm lying?"

"I sound redundant but again, what am I supposed to say to that?"

"Nothing. But you do seem to be a good listener with common sense."

"Ah, my lady, what you don't know about me is that I have a small but terribly fierce noble streak that comes out just at the wrong times. Such as now when I cannot possibly say something unkind about a man who saved my life twice, even though his actions do seem a bit daft." She looked at him with those thoughtful eyes, eyes that had suddenly turned gold in the shadows of the tree they were walking under and he felt a sizeable pang of jealousy. *Again.* She was most extraordinarily charming, intelligent, thoughtful and exotic. Yes, call it jealousy or envy; he felt them both.

"Now that we've walked some way and my boots have gained enough dust from the road, can we mount and I will take you to the closest estate which is that of Matthew Drake, Baron of Worley's estate? He and his staff are also part of this grand hunt for the runaway American."

He said it with a slight laugh and her shoulders visibly eased. He saw the very moment she gave up the fight because he had seen that same look one hundred times in the last ten years. She was defeated. She would come with him and go back to Michael. When he realized it, he also saw the hint of the love that he knew he had seen earlier. She was going because somewhere in her heart she knew she belonged even though her head had not acknowledged it yet. He was very glad at that moment for his skill in recognizing people's thoughts in the expressions on their faces and the movements of their limbs.

Julian mounted and reached for Kathryn's hand to pull her up in front of him, not sure his clamoring senses would be able to manage the ride with her so close. He had never coveted another man's woman before—well, never the woman of a *friend*—but this was really testing his control.

"Can I ride behind you? I can't sit on a horse sidesaddle and I know I am not riding in your lap."

He nearly laughed out loud; not at all surprised she would demand to ride behind him. "Put your foot on my boot and swing up." Of course, Michael's minx would be wearing breeches under that dress. Of course!

"So I am not going to put my arms around you since that would feel weird. Can we make it with just me gripping with my legs?"

Ahh, she didn't really just say that, did she? This was torture. Maybe he could call himself even for that one time Michael had so smoothly dealt with the assassin in the tavern outside of Dover.

"I'll keep to a canter and you should be fine." *Not sure about me, however, with the way you smell. Vanilla?*

She was the first to speak. "The first time I met Michael he chased me down this road. I should have known better than to think he would let me go." She sighed. "I figure he told you he asked me to marry him? Isn't that why this 'army' is after me?"

"He didn't tell us he asked you. Am I to assume you refused?" He kept his tone mild, knowing he was going to be on very shaky ground having this discussion with her with his control already stretched to its limits.

"Okay, so he didn't tell you. I guess I should have expected that. He actually made me a bizarre business proposal about running his estates, living in the social whirl and oh yes, birthing a son or two. I felt like property or a well-placed mistress. It was the most humiliated I think I've ever been by a man."

He felt the heat rush through her body and could see her arms flush. Julian could only imagine how embarrassed she must have been at that admission. "I have to admit the way you put it, it does sound rather business like but well, we English are rather staid and Michael is one of the most proper you'll find." And it was a wonderfully good lesson to know that laying your title and riches without your heart in front of a woman of sensibilities such as hers was of no use. He would take that to heart for his own use in future if he ever found a woman he truly loved.

"Lord Thornton, is that your name or can we skip to first names since well, I've already totally humiliated myself in front of you. I'm Kathryn."

"Kathryn, please call me Jules."

"Are you part French?"

"Yes, what gave me away?" He laughed of course because really everything gave him away.

"The night I noticed you I thought immediately you were part French and imagined you had been a spy."

"You imagined me a spy? You do have an imagination." The thought of his years in France brought Julian up short. *Martine.* Could he bring her

137

here? No. It was one thing to set up a poor English girl as a mistress but quite another to import one from France in this day and age. There were boundaries even he would not be able to cross. It was definitely time to dispense with this conversation.

"Kathryn, I know Michael seemed shall we say 'reserved' in his approach but I can assure you, he is not reserved right now. Indeed, the night I met with him to talk about your safety, he was deadly serious and this morning, I daresay from his missive, he was the same. I believe he has a fierce notion about protecting you."

"Oh yeah, I think you distracted me back there. Do tell me about this mystery maid."

He chuckled. She hadn't forgotten and she had changed the subject back to her own designs. Damn clever chit. "She was in your rooms but was no one from the staff. That means there was something very wrong. Right now, we don't know any more about her mission." He didn't have to tell her they had found her body several days ago. There was informing her of the truth and then there was frightening her for not a good enough reason that he would not do.

"Why would someone be in my room?"

To kill you. "We don't know. But we're looking. I have some contacts…" he trailed off. She had wrapped her arms around him and her flesh burned his chest.

Kathryn leaned her cheek on Jules' back; he drew in a quick breath.

"Oh gosh, I am so sorry. I didn't mean to freak you out…by…"

"Touching me? It's okay. I frightened you. While you are an incredibly beautiful and highly intelligent woman, I do not make a habit of lusting after the women to whom my friends have proposed marriage. Keep your head on my back and I will think of other subjects such as the lovely meadows and birds and maybe what I will buy my nieces and nephews for Christmas."

She laughed; it was a fresh, delicate, honest sound. "You're so funny. At home, we say we're going to think of our mama and that works well as a distraction. So, on that subject do you…have someone?"

"Not at present. I am avoiding the *ton* because you see the marriage minded matrons find me especially…how would you Americans say it…?"

"A good catch? Prime target? A hottie? Eligible? That's it. You are a highly eligible bachelor."

"Yes, that's what they say," he sighed knowingly. "You know, Michael is the most eligible of all us with that Asterleigh business. Day after tomorrow was to have been his investiture. I expect he must have now delayed it because of you. Likely, he proposed yesterday so he could take you with him as his betrothed to the ceremony. Your carriage would be on its way to London, almost half of the journey accomplished I daresay this day. He'd never make it if he left even now." Julian surprised himself at being so forward but she needed to know how much his damn lucky but short-sighted friend Michael wanted her and how much she had already cost him.

She gasped. "Day after tomorrow…he was to become a Duke and he is going to miss it because of me?"

"Don't be so surprised. You thought he made you a business proposal but all of his actions have shown a man whose heart is engaged. You do see, don't you?" She sighed and it was all he could do to keep his blood from shooting from his brain to that nether region. Being so damn chivalrous was giving him a monstrous headache and this woman better damn well have a sister.

"Yes. Where I come from it's called actions speaking louder than words. Let's agree, he does feel possessive and he seems to be willing to go to lengths for me but how will I know with someone like him when his heart is engaged?"

"I've known Michael all of my life. We grew up together and then we went to Eton together and then we went into the service together. I believe I've never seen him more engaged in my life." It was true. He knew Michael well and that night in the study, he had seen the paralyzing fear, the determination to protect, and all of the possessiveness that men like him pour into the one they choose. Choosing for them was much the same as loving. It was a life mate, someone they would cherish, revere and maybe even love a little for the whole of their lives. "For Michael, it's also about honor since…"

"His Father didn't exhibit much?"

"I daresay."

~ * ~

Julian had been quiet for a few minutes and Kathryn felt no compulsion to fill in the air with words. He had said Michael's heart was engaged, he was possessive. Was that enough? *No.* He would have to love her first. None of that romantic I'll marry him and make him love me flim flam. Kathryn would require a declaration, and soon, and before any more sexual activity. If none was forthcoming, she'd get back to finding her way home. If he cared enough to be possessive and to send all the countryside after her, then maybe he cared enough to listen.

"I am going to give my horse a rest by sliding off and walking. You are no burden however and Valiant will be happy to continue with you."

"Yeah, just admit it. I put my arms around you and you thought I was making a pass at you. I'm sorry. Please don't think that's what I was doing. I am still not used to horses and I felt like I was going to fall off."

"Scared? No, Kathryn I don't think you made a pass at me. But, you? Afraid? I shall not believe it."

"Thanks. Actually, are you involved? I can think of some friends who…"

"Not you, too?" he bellowed in an imperious tone and then threw his head back and laughed.

"What's so funny?" She felt a little miffed that he was laughing at her.

"Dear Kathryn, I have just realized that I like you very much and I adore your bluntness. If Michael weren't already so tied up in knots about you, I'd try to rein you in myself."

Kathryn released an un-lady like snort. "Thanks. I think."

They moved along companionably. Suddenly, Kathryn looked up. "We seem to have come to a fork in the road. Which way?"

Jules pointed toward the right. "We take this one."

"The fork seems fitting for my situation today," she answered.

"Someone should write about this, then?"

He did, exactly 100 years from now.

I shall be telling this with a sigh
Somewhere ages and ages hence:
Two roads diverged in a wood, and I—

Duke of Her Dreams

I took the one less traveled by,
And that has made all the difference
                    —Robert Frost, 1916

Chapter Fourteen

The house came into view but of course, it was not a house. It was a manor or a mansion or what? It was a beautiful, English manor home of stacked stone foundation and glorious windows, myriad gables and rooflines. It was exquisite. The yard was simple, not as elegant or imposing or perfectly well-tended as Michael's but with amazing potential to be lush and overflowing with flowers.

Kathryn could see the garden, much smaller and on the side of the house. There were not the same rioting rose bushes. Something about the house looked almost ...bare.

"I believe I will ride. No need to look as if I was so heroic as to walk the entire way."

"And I promise not to freak you out again." She cleared her throat. "Julian..."

"Yes, Kathryn?"

"Thank you. You've been very honest with me and given me a lot to think about. I can tell you, or maybe assure you, that I will consider all you've said. And if Michael asks me again, I will have a well thought out answer."

"I am glad to hear it." After a moment's hesitation, he decided she deserved to know what he thought of her. "Michael is a very good man. He deserves someone like you."

"That's kind of you. Thank you."

It was all they said until they reached the house. No boy came running for the horse but the lights were burning and the doors were opened by a slight, elderly woman. "Ahh, Mrs. Soggs, you can see I have accomplished our mission. Worley?"

"Still out, My Lord."

"I thought you said to call you Julian or was it Jules?" she asked him in all seriousness.

"You yes, but the servants would not do so. Now we're back to civilization, they would expect it of you too." His cerulean blue eyes twinkled and she tweaked his arm. "Ow, you little termagant are going to deserve the tongue-lashing you get from Asterleigh when he arrives."

Mrs. Soggs had stood gaping at them. She had surely never laid eyes on anyone like Kathryn and the familiarity with which they addressed each other must have been a shock for her. Servants were very conservative about address. "If you will wait in the study, I will fetch tea."

"Thank you Soggs. I believe Miss Ragland would appreciate a chance to freshen up. Would you first show her to a room?"

"Yes, My Lord. This way, miss."

"Oh, and Kathryn. I have business and must leave you. I am sending notes to the others. I do hope to have the pleasure of your company again soon."

"Julian, I don't know for sure if I should thank you for dragging me back but I definitely appreciate your taking time to explain things to me."

"Good day, Kathryn." And as she nodded her head in that regal way some women do, Jules thought she would make a fine Duchess.

Kathryn looked in the mirror and almost shrieked at her disheveled appearance. Her hair was virtually plastered to her head and limp, her clothes were dusty and even her face was red and splotchy. She looked awful. There was a rag and water, but no brush so she combed through her hair with her fingers. Having no makeup available, she was eternally grateful for the tan that kept her from being hideous. She changed into the yellow muslin dress, the only one she had taken from the house that had not been hers. Her list of debts to Michael included the cost of a new dress so she wasn't stealing it and she had been determined she would pay him back every penny.

Mrs. Soggs was waiting in the bedroom for her because she realized that she would not be expected to make her way back downstairs on her own. While she had been focused on making herself look remotely presentable, Kathryn had not taken in her surroundings. Once she did, she noticed the contrasts with Michael's home. There was no young maid hovering to cater to her every whim. In fact, there had been no servants anywhere she could recall except for this woman who must surely be the housekeeper.

The room was clean but not perfectly so. Dust motes floated in the streaks of sun from the half-drawn curtains and the furniture sported not recently polished surfaces, aging bed covers and a lack of pillows. This room looked acceptable but nothing more. As they descended the stairs, she noticed that the walls were barer than Michael's, no tapestries, certainly no imposing suits of armor or swords or knickknacks in corners. There were fewer candelabras and almost no wall sconces. The inside of the house was much like the outside, bare.

Kathryn wondered if Michael knew that his friend Matthew was hard up because this house looked like it had been stripped of anything of value and had not been redone in some time. She had a lot of experience recognizing the signs of poverty and she would have to tell Michael about his situation.

"The Master's study, miss. You can wait in there. I'll bring tea."

"Thank you, Mrs. Soggs. You really don't need to trouble with tea. I'm not a hot tea drinker." That earned her, she saw, another censorious glare.

"Very well, miss."

Kathryn stepped into the room and immediately realized why she had been brought in here. This room was generously furnished and spotlessly clean. This must be the room in which Matthew Drake, Baron of Worley received guests to keep up the appearances of a wealthy country gentleman. The deep leather chair behind his huge, elegant desk was one for a commanding figure and his blotter was meticulously ordered, a lovely silver inkstand among the implements on its surface. Candlesticks on the mantle were polished to a high shine, leather-bound books lined the shelves that were also interspersed with small valuable trinkets and as she continued to scan the room, she saw *it*.

Far down the wall from where she stood, sitting in a picture holder on one of the bookshelves, was the painting of the cavalry officer. Heart racing, palms moistening, and her mind running a mile a minute, she made her way to the small portrait of Matthew Drake. She knew it had to be him because Michael had mentioned to her that Matthew had been a cavalry officer.

Kathryn reached for the painting, carefully lifting it from its resting place. She knew she had only moments before someone would show up and take away her chance to leave Christine some sort of note. At this moment, she was so grateful she had not chosen the cavalry officer's portrait to purchase because it would be the first one to draw Christy's attention when she finally made her way to the little shop while looking for her big sister. Quickly Kathryn found a quill on the desk, dipped it in the inkwell and wrote as small and neatly as she could in the corner on the paper backing of the wooden frame.

> *Christy,*
> *I'm safe. I ♥ U!*
> *KitKat, 1816*

She blew on the ink to dry as she had seen Michael do before and replaced the painting. She didn't know how to get rid of the evidence of the ink so she lifted her skirt and wiped it on the inside of her hem, replaced the pen and the inkwell's lid and stepped away from the desk. It would not occur to her until much later that the cavalry officer's portrait frame had not been papered when she had seen it in the shop at home.

Just then, the study door slammed open and Michael almost stumbled in. His features relaxed and then hardened and then softened again all in the space of seconds. He was trailed by...the cavalry officer. "Kathryn! Where the devil have you been? Do you know what you have done?"

"What? No hello, darling?"

He had determined to choose his words carefully to not dress her down in front of Matthew Drake or the servants but the force of seeing her safe, standing there looking perfectly innocent, gorgeously disheveled, safe—beautiful and safe—completely undermined his best intentions. Cautioning himself as her chin lifted and he saw the hardening of her stare, he reminded himself that he would wait, until he was home, his home, to tell her what a foolish and spiteful thing she had done. For now, he would relish the sight of her, even if it was a less than well-appointed appearance she made.

"Michael."

"Miss Ragland, may I present Matthew Drake, Baron of Worley," he said, acknowledging Matthew who had come fully into the room. He used the opportunity to school his features and contain his giddiness at the sight of her.

"It's nice to meet you, My Lord," she said with the slightest quaver in her voice Michael noticed.

"Miss Ragland, it is my pleasure." He took her hand and bowed over it.

She curtsied better, Michael thought, then usual. She must have been practicing, probably under Cassie's tutelage.

"As it is mine to meet you," she responded coolly.

One word answers and short phrases were not her usual. She must be angry but she had no right to be angry with him, Michael thought. She had scared him half of out his mind and he had sent the entire landed gentlemen in the county after her. She should be damn grateful. "Kathryn, I know you must be tired and hungry. I have the carriage. We can go home."

"I assume, you are *asking* me to come to your home." Her tone was not icy, but cool. She was not entirely pleased with his rescue.

Michael forced himself to maintain calm, but his façade would not hold long in the face of her indifference. "I am."

She turned to Michael's companion. "It was kind of you to allow me to rest in your home, Lord Worley. I expect we will see one another again soon." She didn't ask it in question form. She knew she wasn't leaving the area today, or not even tomorrow, and she would have no more chance to bolt. For a while, she'd have to play out Michael's scenario. She had never been one to do another's bidding but she was stuck. This time, she had no choice but she didn't have to like it.

"It was my pleasure as I said, Miss Ragland. Michael has invited me to dinner tomorrow night to get to know you and re-establish my acquaintance with Lady Cassandra. I shall see you then."

"Well, then I will look forward to it." He noted she at least acted civilly to Matthew. That was something.

Michael also recognized her comment did not register in her eyes. She was indeed being only just barely polite. He would have to speak with her about that too. He took her arm tightly and she pulled back from him presumably with the excuse of picking up her things. She did not return her hand for his sleeve and he shut his lips against the reprimand rising in his throat.

John Coachman dropped the steps and Kathryn pulled herself up into the carriage before he could assist her. Everything she was doing was severely trying Michael's patience and as if to pique his foul mood further, she spoke not a word for the entire drive back to Hawthorne.

"Will you join me in the study, Miss Ragland?"

"Yes."

Wonderful. "I am truly glad you're back but I'd like an explanation."

Her body language suggested she was going to be terse but then she relaxed and looked him in the eye. "I told you I wasn't from here and that I needed to get home. I long overstayed my welcome and then you offered me a business-like marriage proposal. I felt, under the circumstances—those being you wanted to marry me for some odd reason but didn't believe who I was—that it was time I made my own way home since you weren't likely to help me. I left you a note in the desk and a list of the things I owe you money for. I didn't intend to leave England without repaying you and I expected to send some sort of good-bye letter with the funds."

If she had announced her intention to join a band of pirates and sail the oceans, she could not have shocked him more. "Where do you suggest I start in addressing all of the concerns you have raised in one such eloquent and well-rehearsed speech?" he asked bitterly. He was not a passionate or intemperate man but this day and now this bizarre pronouncement—or series of pronouncements—had about undone the last of his fragile control.

"Michael, what do you want from me? I have told you and I thought I had showed you. I've always made my own way and I'm not much one for male dominance. I thought I was doing you a favor. You were too much of a gentleman to turn me out but surely you would not want me here after you proposed marriage and I turned you down."

His nostrils flared. "You don't know what I want."

"No, I guess I don't," she said, her voice rising in pitch as well. "You've never told me. You only said things like I could marry you and go live somewhere else and have my own social life and breed your kids.

Tell me what you want."

"I want you!"

Shaking and a little scared of the violence of his response, she took one step toward him. His expression softened and he reached a hand toward her. "Kathryn, I want you," he whispered.

"I...I'm so sorry...I didn't know."

"Have I not showed you? Have I not done what I should?"

She felt herself soften toward him. "You have been kind. I didn't realize that was how you were showing me...affection. I just thought you were being gentlemanly and that we were having a great deal of fun being sexually daring."

"Kathryn, I...only know one way. My...possessiveness...it's what comes out. When I took Cassandra back, it was by sheer force but I could not put into words what I needed her to know from my heart."

"Are you comparing me to Cassandra? To someone who is in your heart?" she asked tremulously.

"Yes."

"Oh, dear heaven."

No other words were spoken and as he turned from her, she saw the tightness in his expression. That was a huge admission for someone such as him. It wasn't a love declaration but it was good enough for tonight. She slipped out of the room, grabbing her things and took the stairs two at a time to her room.

~ * ~

She had left a note. It was in the desk. But in fact, it was not in the desk but sitting on a salver on his desk now along with another sheet. He glanced at the list. It was an impressive cataloguing of all the funds he had spent on Kathryn, indeed every single solitary pence he had ever spent on her. It was appalling, insulting. He crumbled it and tossed it into the fireplace. The fire consumed the paper in seconds.

The other was a folded note, presumably to maintain some semblance of privacy from the servants.

Dear Michael,
When you find this note, I know you will be at first angry and

then frustrated with me because I'm not here and not explaining to you in my own words why I have gone. I believe you will remember I told you I was not from here. I meant, not from here and now. I was actually born in 1991 in Alabama, one of the southern states in America that gained statehood on December 14, 1819.

I know this is all very unbelievable but now that you have known me for these almost two weeks, surely you can see I am not like the other women who you know. I am used to making my own way, supporting myself, and taking care of my sister. She needs me to come home and I have to try to get to her.

Please tell Cassandra how special she is every day and tell her to follow her dreams. Also, Ellie is very talented. I hope you can find a place for her in your household. Thank Hallthorpe and Aunt Agatha and Jem and everyone who was so kind to me.

Michael, please don't come after me. It is the hardest thing I've ever done to leave here for your own good and mine. I can't be in a house taking advantage of your family's kindnesses, being treated like a princess and not feel that I am mooching. You have been so good to me and I am eternally grateful. I will work to repay you in some way if it's even possible. Some lady of your day and age will be very lucky to marry you as I have no doubt you will be an honorable spouse. I told you in spoken words what I need from marriage—nothing but love. I hope you find your right mate and I intend to look for someone with many of your qualities.

The time I have spent with you has truly been extraordinary. You are still the hottest guy I have ever had the pleasure of being close to, so the bar is set very high for the future Mr. Right. Please try to look for someone you can love. It will be the best thing that ever happened to you.

You deserve it.
Kathryn

Olivia Ritch

Reading the note for the umpteenth time, he had wondered how everything had gone so wrong. Had she not realized that she was the one who had brought his world to life? How could he possibly search for someone else? He could not let her go. Whatever he had to do to be the *Mr. Right* of this letter he would do. Rather than reducing the letter to ashes as he had her ridiculous list, he held it and wept out of sheer relief that he had found her before she got out of his grasp.

Chapter Fifteen

"You're back," Cassandra charged.

Kathryn noticed the tension immediately. "And so I am. It seems that your brother has rescued me now a second time from the London Road."

"I'm hurt, you know. You left without saying good bye." The old Cassandra would have sulked, cried, and not shown herself but clearly the new Cassandra was going to confront her.

"Oh Cassandra, I'm sorry. Really. I never would do anything to hurt you and I did leave a note. I just didn't think about exactly how everyone would take it. I thought about me and my sister who I am sure is frantic and not sleeping and scared out of her mind and your brother and his ridiculous marriage…"

"His what?"

"I said that out loud, didn't I?"

"Yes, you did. He has asked you to marry him?"

"He did. I said no."

"No! Why would you do that? You're perfect for him." She was incredulous.

"But he also has to be perfect for me. I'm not sure he is. I have to be loved."

"Oh, Kathryn, has he not told you how he felt?" Cassandra cajoled.

"Not in so many words, although he did open up a little downstairs just now."

"Can I ask what he said?"

"He admitted grudgingly that I was 'in his heart,'" Kathryn acknowledged.

"Oh, Kathryn, he…I think he must love you. That is a stunning admission for him."

Kathryn had sensed this, too. "I figured it was pretty big. Maybe he does have feelings for me, but I have to have more. I want it all. That kind of heart melting, mind-blowing love that makes you want to get up every day and thank the Lord for your blessings."

"How do you feel about him?"

"I feel…I don't know for sure what, but I am very physically attracted to him. He is sexy and when he touches me, my mind turns to mush. I sense him when he is near, smell him in so many things, hear his voice in my head. I dream of him and wake up wet, frustrated and agitated or oddly sated and I was desperately relieved to see him although I was seething mad that he dragged me back. His voice makes the hair on my neck stand on end and …oh my gosh. You heard how all that sounded, didn't you?"

"Kathryn, you *are* in love with him."

"Yes."

They sat there in silence for several minutes both feeling rather proud of themselves. A sly smile crossed Kathryn's lips and she began "feeling" him and a smug smile was on Cassandra's as she realized her dream of becoming Kathryn's sister was coming true.

After the silence stretched some more, Cassandra tentatively moved toward Kathryn. "I would like to talk with you about something important to me now."

"Yes, absolutely. What?"

"You just described all the feelings I am having."

"Jem?"

"Yes, how did you *know*?" Her shock was palpable.

"I see the way you watch each other, the way he loads your plate just so, holds your chair, lingers. He sometimes wants to touch you and then he grimaces and steps back. I have seen him inhale your hair. He is clearly into you."

Cassandra's eyes were shining. "Oh, you think so? I have loved him for all these many months. You know he has been with me for more than a year and he has so gently and faithfully tended me. I want him, Kathryn. I want to be his."

This was a big deal Kathryn knew, on some level, because rich gentry didn't date servants and having a possessive, protective brother like Michael would be even harder. "Have you spoken with each other?"

"Kathryn, he won't even look me in the eye. He avoids my eyes on purpose. What am I going to do?"

"Okay, first let me ask you in all honesty. What will Michael say if you date Jem? Will he let you? Truly."

"If *you* ask him or tell him how important it is. You can help me I know it. Together we can convince him. It's not like Jem is poor. He's a footman, a rather well educated, incredibly handsome footman. He speaks French, you know?"

"Impressive. I don't speak but a little Spanish. But back to me helping you…I might be persona non grata right now."

"Nonsense. Michael is so grateful you're back. He was like a caged tiger, screaming at the servants, pacing, bellowing, not even getting a sentence out when he was looking for you. He was really quite hysterical. I think he was hanging on by a thread."

"So maybe he is a little relieved. Tell me more about your Jem, though."

"He sings, too. Once I cajoled him into singing for me, convincing him I could only fall asleep with a lullaby. Seeming to be of a fragile mind has some advantages you know." She gave Kathryn a sly smile. "He has a beautiful voice. As soon as I said so, he excused himself. He doesn't think he is worthy of me, I am sure of it."

"Okay, so we have two males to deal with. Jem needs convincing to allow his feelings out and Michael needs to be convinced to allow you to be with Jem. Do you want to marry him?"

"Marry him? Do you think I could?" she effused, an enchanting smile breaking across her delicate face. "I mean I would love to be held by him. His hands are so safe and strong and I want to…to…"

"Make love?"

"Yes," she whispered. "I want to make love with Jem."

"Well, you will start on Jem and I will work on Michael. With the two of us committed, how can we fail?"

Cassandra laughed a little for the first time since giving voice to her feelings for Jem. She had loved him for so long but never had felt like she could even talk to him much less to anyone else about it. Now, she thought that maybe, just maybe she could make her dreams of being his wife, of having children she could love, a house—a small one—of her own, come true.

Kathryn took control. "Here's what I want you to do. First, get dressed in your sexiest, lowest cut dress. Dismiss your maid and tell her you are done for the evening. Then, ask for your tray in your room. Tell Cook to give you an extra serving of dessert, that you are hungry. After you've eaten a little, invite Jem to sit near you and have your second dessert. Keep eye contact with him."

They continued plotting until the plan to seduce Jem had been fully hashed out.

"You are so bold, Kathryn. Can I do it? Will this work?"

"I don't know if it will work, but I know how he looks at you. You've just got to give him the chance to make his move. You do that and I will start on Michael. It'll give me the chance to change the subject from us. Which I daresay he will be grateful for at least for a while."

"You know he postponed his investiture for you?"

"I heard. I don't know exactly what it means, but it sounds really serious."

"I think he wants to be married to you or at least betrothed when he takes his oath, somehow that you are agreeing to the duties along with him. Kathryn, I think he really loves you and values you. You have given him so much these weeks."

"What have I given him? He has everything."

"No. He has never been happy. Not since he was a child. Our father…well, Michael has never laughed and joked and played like he has since you became part of our lives. And then there's what you did for me. He thinks you saved me. He's right." Cassandra reached out and touched Kathryn's hand and at that moment, Kathryn knew, she just knew that this was her family and her place. She still had to find Christine and bring her here, some crazy way, but she would stay and be with these people who obviously loved her very much. Even Aunt Agatha liked her a little.

~ * ~

It was harder than facing her horrible husband, harder than sitting alone for hours with only her thoughts and harder than thinking of one more day without knowing if he cared for her. Planning was one thing but walking into the room with the express purpose of making a cake of herself, throwing herself at Jem Smythe, was altogether the most difficult thing Cassandra had ever done.

He sensed her before she appeared and when she did, his breath involuntarily sucked in. She had never worn that before and she was eating in. *He would have to watch her eat in that!* Why? Why was he being tortured? The most beautiful, fragile, precious woman in the world, whose black eyes and pale skin and very round breasts, were covered in low-riding, flowing gold silk. Her hair was piled more haphazardly that she ever wore it. *What the hell was she about?*

"Jem."

"Lady Cassandra." He was very cautious. *She had a light, was it a light in her eyes? Her cheeks were flushed. Oh, god. There was something wrong. Was she drunk, no maybe laudanum. What to do?*

"Jem?"

"Yes, Lady Cassandra?" *This was bad, very bad. There was something wrong. Was she firing him and this was the lead up? No, that wasn't it, what was it?*

"Jem, will you sit with me? You always tower over me."

"Yes…ma'am?" *Am I allowed to sit? What the hell is she about?*

"How long have you been my footman?"

"Eighteen months, ma'am.

"In all of that time…" she trailed off. She couldn't ask him out right if he had ogled her, if he wanted her. Could she? "Have I been good to you?"

"Ye…ess…ma…am. You have been good to me."

"Have I been difficult?"

"No ma'am, you have not been difficult." He breathed in, but couldn't seem to bring the air into his lungs. He felt dizzy.

"Jem, what would you like me to be?" She looked at him with those black eyes that he had wanted for so long. She stood straight and tall, draped loosely in gold silk that barely covered her generously rounded white breasts. The mounds were heaving from her deep breathing and his gaze was fixed. He couldn't stop watching them. They pulsed and then he saw it. He saw them pebble. He raised his eyes to hers and he saw the

155

blush on her cheeks. His gaze dropped to her bosom and her pebbled nipples did him in. What was he supposed to say to her in the face of that? How was he supposed to continue standing? He had lost his physical control. His rod was firm and erect. Soon, she would notice and he would be fired. He wanted to cover himself but that would draw her attention.

But then, dammit, her eyes began traveling down his chest. *Oh, god, oh god. He couldn't make it stop. Stop, dammit Lady Cassandra, stop. Please don't fire me. I can't leave you.*

"You are sexually aroused by me." She said it in modestly clipped tones but she nevertheless ground it out so that he could tell she seemed to be enjoying his distress.

He tried to speak, but nothing came out. He tried to cover himself but failed, as she glanced at his groin.

"Jem, are you aroused by me?" she asked him as she moved closer.

She was moving closer. He kept slipping backward but he could not hold his ballocks and keep from falling over the furniture at the same time. "Jem, do you desire me? It is a simple question."

"No ma'am…it is not a simple question," he ground out yet again.

Her joy, her absolute satisfaction at seeing his erection tent his pants was horrifying. He wanted her. He desired…*her*! He had an *erection* because of her.

"Jem?"

"Ye-es...ma'am?" His voice choked.

She took two more steps toward him and he froze. He absolutely froze. And then she cupped him. *She cupped him.* "Oh, my god… Cass...oh my…"

"Do you want me? Do you, Jem?"

"Please. Please, Lady …Cassandra…if you make me…"

"What Jem?" Her tiny hands stroked back and forth across his flap.

"If you…do this…he will…"

"No, Jem. Michael will not sack you."

"Whaaat? You are…you are…making me…"

"Jem? Please answer my question. Do you want me? If you do not, this will stop. If you do, I will…"

"Stop, Lady Cassandra. Can you see what will happen? I have watched over you and cared for you for all of these months and if you...you...do this, I will lose you. Please don't make me lose you. Please."

Triumph. It sang in her heart, her bones, blood thrummed through her vessels. He was as affected as she was. He wanted her. He was hard for her. He didn't want to lose her. Now all she had to do was show him how much she wanted him. Doing that would be very hard for she had no experience but what Kathryn had taught her. It made her blush all over again to think about what she was going to do but she would for Jem, for them.

Cassandra touched her stomach and looked him in the eye. She licked her bottom lip and moved her hand up a little to just below her breast. Her own arousal surprised her and the sudden lift of her eyes, moved his gaze from her belly to her face. She had him. He was mesmerized.

Her lips just bumped his.

He froze.

Her lips touched him again.

He instinctively pressed his to hers and she started.

He jumped back and her eyes flew wide and then narrowed and glowed.

Her eyes were glowing for him.

Jem was hard and throbbing for Lady Cassandra. He was responsible for her. She was his...his...he couldn't think.

"Jem?"

"Yes," he hissed.

"I don't know what to do." And she touched his chest, when she did it burned him. He grabbed her hand and held it to him. He couldn't, wouldn't push her away. He wanted to prolong the contact but it, this couldn't happen. He should not let it. She was so fragile and he was so responsible.

"Jem, please. *Please.*"

"Lady Cassandra, I..."

"Cassandra."

"Cassandra, I...I am your footman," he ground out.

He had said it. He was her footman, unworthy of her no matter what she wanted. No one would accept his feelings for her. He watched her face for recognition and when it came, it broke him. He screamed fiercely inside.

"You don't want to hurt me."

"No."

"But yet, you seem to be rejecting me."

"No. Yes. No! Lady Cassandra?"

"Cassandra." She stood toe to toe with him now and realized something she never had in her life. She had power. This man was not going to hurt her or manipulate her. He cared for her and she loved him so much she was going to fight for him like he deserved. He didn't even know how special and important he was.

"Jem, you have been so good to me. You have looked over me and supported me through so many dark days. Now, the days are not dark and I don't need you as a crutch. I need you. As a man. I *want* you."

His breathing was ragged. He had heard every word she said yet still couldn't believe she truly wanted him.

He was rock hard and his head ached. Resisting her was killing him. "Cassandra. Do you know what you just said?"

"Yes. I want you to touch me like you would touch a woman you want, not just a person you are helping down the stairs. I want you to look at me like Kathryn says you do when I don't notice."

"Kathryn?"

Cassandra nodded. "She says you look at me."

"You asked her? Miss Ragland? You talked to her, about me?"

"Yes. She says you look at me with longing. Do you, Jem?"

~ * ~

Lying to her would never work because his eyes, his hands, his entire body would give him away. But she had talked to the mistress about him and surely the Master was coming right now to flog him, shoot him or just pitch him out on his ear. "I do."

She pressed her advantage. "I love you, Jem."

In that moment, Jem felt that his heart stopped. Did it? Surely, the world stopped spinning. Did it? She loved him. "You what?"

"I love you. I have for some time. I told Kathryn earlier and she encouraged me to…to see if you had real feelings for me. I believe…you do."

"I do." His resigned admission felt like victory. It felt sweet and terribly hard fought to get that admission from him, but the battle was not won, not yet.

"We can be together, you and I. I have funds and a small home, and you are strong and capable. I also believe that Michael would accept you— me and you—if he believed you cherished me as much as he does."

She felt triumphant. He had been resisting her because he thought he had to. Now that she had spoken with Kathryn, she was sure he no longer needed to, but he did not even realize it. She had means even if Michael disowned her, but with Kathryn's intervention, she was sure that wouldn't happen. Even so, she had a small house and Jem could work. They could be very comfortable, but if Michael chose to accept it, Jem could be a full member of society since no one would speak against the Duke of Asterleigh's brother-in-law.

"I do cherish you as much as he does. More so, Cassandra. Can't you see it? I watched you melt away for so long and I wanted to pull you out of it, outside, into the world of people and gardens and riding and so much more. Then she came and you bloomed and while I was afraid you might leave me behind, more than anything I wanted you to be whole again. It was all I wanted."

"What do you want now?" she asked as she raised her hand to touch his check. He closed his eyes and turned his lips into her palm. She shuddered and it shattered the remaining shards of his control.

He leaned his head toward hers and his lips skirted her temple, moving with feather-light caresses down her cheek to her ear so he could whisper words that had haunted his dreams for so many months. "I want to possess you, to know that you know you are mine, as you have been in my heart. I want to love you, openly."

"Love me, Jem. Now. Show me." It was a breathless invitation.

~ * ~

Kathryn had sat on the Dowager's bed for more than an hour wondering about all that had happened today. She had left at dawn expecting to break away and this family had pulled her back to them. That Cassandra was in love with Jem and right now trying to explore their mutual feelings was a pleasant surprise. That Michael might love her was a startling surprise. That she might be ready to turn her back on America, Alabama, even finding Christine, was a shock. She was not, however, totally surprised. She loved this family. They were loyal and true and they loved her. She was becoming central to their happiness, she believed. They needed her.

If she was the Duchess, she would have enormous power, enough to see Jem and Cassandra married, maybe? It would take so much of her energy and most likely overcoming Michael's objections would be their worst obstacle. Society would pale compared to him, her huge, imposing, possessive, predatory, arrogant beloved Duke.

She did love him. Making a life with Michael no longer seemed a pipe dream. It seemed imperative, vital… but she still needed, would have, his declaration of love for her, too, before she agreed.

Ellie rushed up to her. "Ooh miss, I am so glad, so glad you are back. I was worried sick, I was."

Kathryn reached for the ecstatic maid, clasping the young girl's hands in hers. "I know you were Ellie. It was wrong of me to leave without telling you. I tried to last night, but I didn't want to be stopped. You know I value you, don't you?"

"Oh miss, yes, I know you had your reasons. I don't want you to leave though. Are you staying?"

"For now. You know, he may not ask me again."

"Ask you? Marriage you mean?"

"Yes. I refused him, and it was very civil."

Ellie pulled away and began straightening the articles on the vanity. "I think he cares for you, miss."

"Yes, he does. Now we will just have to see how much. Do you have a new dress for me?"

~ * ~

Michael paced the back and forth in front of the fireplace, listening as the chime clock struck another hour. Kathryn had been in her room for almost two hours since she had been back and there had been not one word from her. Did she think to spite him more? He couldn't stand this feeling, of being caged and harnessed, waiting, wondering what she was about. Growling low, he let the snarling rage and rampant fear find its home as he continued to move about the room punching the air, flexing his muscles, fighting an invisible foe.

"Michael?"

He hadn't heard the door.

She stood just inside his study door in a gown, if it could be called that, of diaphanous gold gauze. It nestled low on her breasts, tightened at her waist and flowed in waves over her hips. It belonged in a boudoir, not a dinner table. "Kathryn." His voice was pinched. He was staring at her breasts.

"I was wrong…about a lot of things," she began.

He raised one sardonic eyebrow. "*You* are admitting to being *wrong*?"

"Yes. If I apologize for everything all at once will you forgive me and take me to dinner and smile at me again?"

"What are you apologizing for?"

"Leaving without a word, turning you down, and not allowing myself to explore my feelings for you."

"You are being daring Kathryn, telling me of feelings when I have told you not of mine," Michael countered.

"You have shown me, remember? I learned from my mistakes. I believe you care for me more deeply than you are willing to admit in words."

"You are presuming to know my mind without words?" He raised his brows.

"Your actions give you away, *mon Capitaine*," she demurred.

"Parle francais?"

"Un peu. Only enough to say Je t'adore, Michel."

"Moi aussi, ma belle. Moi aussi. Je ta'ime."

Chapter Sixteen

Michael had never felt such satisfaction as he did when he led Kathryn into dinner and seated her beside him at the table in that dress that was barely presentable. He wasn't sure how he would react when Agatha and Cassandra arrived but he would manage, since he had the greatest prize at his right. Kathryn would surely be his now. She had declared herself, albeit in French. It was very nearly a perfect oath.

They had waited until well past the dinner gong for both ladies, he impatient to be sitting with her sharing a glass of wine. Extending his arm to the goddess in gold, he was still expecting to be joined any minute by breathless women rushing in. Somehow, he realized a bit late now that he thought about it that no one should have been expected. The other women in his household could be as managing as the best and occurred belatedly that they had made themselves scarce tonight for his and Kathryn's reunion meal.

He put his hand over hers. "I am so glad you are here tonight, with me at this table, Kathryn. You cannot imagine how I felt when you were gone."

"I can say I'm sorry again and maybe you'll forgive me but you have to understand, I thought I was doing the right thing."

He tilted his head, puzzled by her explanation. "Leaving me was the right thing?"

"Staying was not the right thing. Leaving you was an alternative."

"You will never leave me again?"

Kathryn pulled away slightly. "That's not fair."

"Is it not fair to ask you not to put me through again what I have suffered today?"

"Suffered sounds rather dramatic coming from you."

"No, it is true. You caused me no small amount of fear today. What would I have done if Julian had not caught you before you got on the coach?"

"Michael." She placed her hand over his. "You would have gone on without me. You would have found someone else."

He put his soup spoon on the saucer. "Kathryn, there is no one else. No one. Promise me you will not leave me again."

"I promise I will not leave you like I did this morning." She looked into his serious eyes.

"A grudging and unsatisfactory admission, but I will not press." He smiled then at her. "For now, I will enjoy watching you in that excuse for a gown with your artfully piled hair and rather generous expanse of bosom exposed and be contented that you are gracing my table."

"If I didn't know better, Captain, I'd say there was a batch of compliments in that pronouncement."

"I have noticed, my dear, that none of the other members of my household have joined us for dinner. Is this something you have arranged or are they all artfully occupied of their own volition?"

"I believe the ladies of your household thought I should face you alone during dinner. I take it there was a bit of raging and bellowing today so that everyone is more than happy to let me alone stand in the path of your wrath."

"Quite a speech. What other witticisms do you have planned for me?" His tone was sarcastic but somewhere in it, she knew he was determined not to act terribly angry with her. It might be a good sign. Seducing him to her bed was going to be a challenge because of his injured male pride. Wanting him, though, was a strong incentive.

"I wasn't trying to be ugly," she said softly.

"No, maybe instead to spite me for my highhandedness, for dragging you back, for not listening to your protestations about your home and family... for choosing your clothes, for offering you a Dukedom...and oh yes, for *not loving you*! Have I covered it all, your list of my shortcomings?" His vehemence struck her like a blow and she shrank from the rage in his eyes and the stinging lashes of his words.

Olivia Ritch

"That was totally uncalled for, Michael. Where did that come from? I thought we had just made up a few minutes ago and now, now this. You're shouting at me like you've wanted to all along but didn't because your friends were around. Is that it? You were playing the controlled Captain-Duke-Lord-of-the-manor role for their benefit. Now that we're alone, and I am compliant and sweet, maybe even groveling just a bit, then you start railing at me…"

"*Enough!*"

"That is not enough. I am only just getting warmed up you arrogant, self-centered, egotistical…"

"Kathryn! Please stop." He yelled her down because he saw it all coming out and he knew beyond doubt that if either of them said another word it would go beyond the repairable stage and she would run from him again and his still aching heart would cease to beat.

"Yes, that was uncalled for." He sighed and spoke softly as he gently took hold of her wrist and absently massaged it with his thumb. "I have been high handed and arrogant and I am letting all the pent up fears and frustrations of today make me say and do things I don't mean. So much more than anything, I want to just take you into my arms, pull the pins from your hair, drape it and your body over my chest, and hold you while your heart beats in time with mine." He was not yet ready to tell her of the attempts on her life and how much those had heightened the anxiety for her safety while she was alone and vulnerable today.

Her gaze held both warmth and confusion. "How is it that you can yell at me one minute and say the most romantic thing the next?"

He held her gaze. "Because you vex me like no one ever has and because I was truly terrified of losing you and it was all swirling inside of me. I was not destined to be a Duke. I was destined for command and then for some other type of life. It's an…adjustment to know exactly how to act and what to do and when you showed up and made my life better and my home warm and when you just fit, I was sure you knew it. I did not think I would have to convince you."

"I probably need a little more convincing but that was a very nice speech."

~ * ~

Taking her hand and looking into her hazel eyes, Michael willed himself to say the words that would make her believe he was right for her. "Kathryn Ragland, you are all of the things I never realized I was missing from life—warmth, vitality, compassion and you are the most desirable woman I have ever met. My body aches for yours with a need that is…indescribable. I want you to be my Duchess so that you can be all of those things for the rest of my life and so that we can be lovers …" His words trailed off because he registered the mischievous gleam in her gorgeous eyes.

"We have never made love, Michael," she said. "Do you think we should before you make any life-altering decisions?"

"Are you offering a trial?"

"You can come to bed with me now."

"Yes, I think I will. Go, I'll join you in a few minutes."

~ * ~

While all the family had studiously avoided the dining room to allow them dinner together, no one had retired for the evening and the household was still fully alive. At any moment, someone could come to Kathryn's door. Ringing for and dispensing with Ellie would be a sure way to ensure the maid did not come back tonight or even in the morning before she was needed. "Ellie, can you help me get ready for bed? I am turning in early."

"Aye, miss, sure you're tired after the day you've had. Would you like me to order a bath?"

"No, thank you, I think I'll rinse off and apply some perfume and maybe wear one of the silky gowns that Cassandra gave me."

"Oh yes, the light blue silk is the prettiest. You want me to do something special with your hair?" The gleam in her eye was not lost on Kathryn. So Ellie was expecting there to be an assignation and she was helping. Kathryn bit back a smile. What a little stinker.

"That one is really pretty and you know, I'd like my hair brushed out and wavy, just ease out the pins and the curls."

"Miss?"

"Yes, Ellie?"

"He will, I'm sure of it."

"We'll see, won't we?"

"Aye that we will."

After tonight, he'll have no choice.

Ellie had been gone long enough for her to begin wondering if Michael had changed his mind when there was a light tap on the door. It eased open a fraction, revealing a lounging predatory gentleman in his dark blue dressing gown and loose trousers. In the two weeks she had been here, Michael's lovely dark hair had grown long enough to begin curling, giving him a rakish charm that made him look decidedly more approachable. She turned fully toward him and watched appreciation grow in his gaze. He surely liked her choice of night gown.

Since they had been intimate on several occasions, Michael moved toward her with no inhibitions and as his robe fell open, he allowed it to fall from his shoulders. Kathryn's eyes widened at the expanse of chest it revealed, the rampant erection he sported and the feral smile he directed at her.

He considered talking to her, asking her what she liked and how he might please her but as he could see her nipples already puckered and straining against the satin and her breathing labored, Michael decided that he could take and conquer without restraint. His intended stood her ground and he watched intently as she loosened the ties at the shoulder of her night gown. He reached for her hand and helped her with the second tie, the halves of the gown falling to her hips. He took the fabric in hand at her waist and pulled it gently past her hips, allowing it to pool at her feet. Unbidden, she stepped from it.

"I want you." He spoke to her low and gravelly, dark as he felt. Power surged through him and he pulled her body into the wall of his chest and hips.

He saw her lids drift closed and felt her hands slip around his neck twining in his hair. He kissed her ravenously, claiming her mouth, tasting her resolve.

"I want you. I only...have one...request," she said against his mouth

"Umm...what's that?" he asked her absently as he thrust his tongue deeper into her warm welcome.

"I want you to pull out, so I...don't...get..."

"With child?"

"Pregnant, right."

As with all things, Kathryn got right to the point. He had wondered if she would ask him to do something to prevent conception and had secretly hoped she would not. "No baby...you're right."

"You'll do it? You'll pull out?"

"Umm...hmmm. Let me just taste..." His words trailed off as her hands joined their rhythm inciting his rod to action. She had slipped his pants past his thighs and he was virtually naked in her arms, forcing himself to hold back the welling tide she inspired with her small hands on his length. She had taken him that way once before and this time, he would be inside her before he allowed himself to release his control, while also remembering the promise to withdraw. It was becoming very difficult to contemplate that level of control.

The first time should be memorable. He lifted her still attached to him and eased her onto her bed. He wanted to watch her expression as he filled her, knowing that there would be no pain, only pleasure. Possessing her, seating himself to the hilt in her sheath and claiming her forever as his was the only real thought his swirling senses could comprehend.

The most luscious naked, breathy, gorgeous, sweaty woman laid spread before him as a feast. To enjoy her bounty, he arranged her thighs wide, touched, stroked her core to release her aroma into the room, spread her wild hair over the satin pillows, and lifted her hips, placing another pillow under them. It was not his intention to tease her, but he wanted to watch her writhe, sweat, squirm, ache, throb. He wanted her to need with a deep and frightening desire to be filled by him. He blew a warm breath on her core and she shuddered. Then, he stroked once with strong fingers then again and she convulsed. Two fingers penetrated her and she screamed. "You are...torturing...me," she ground through gritted teeth."

"Yet, you are not sufficiently cowed. You still have a defiant set to your jaw. Give yourself to me, Kathryn. Let me own you."

"I am...equal. I will not..." He had taken up a slow but steady penetration with one finger, not enough to complete her but enough to inflame, incite, threaten, "let...you...control...this." But it was too late for he *had* seized control and urged her agonizingly, slowly, toward the peak. She felt alone and realized that she had already ceded herself to him, to his power, his unwavering possessiveness.

This was how it would be with her and Michael. He would possess and she would yield, but she would not bend, not break. She could be with him and he could rule their loving. She would rule their larger lives. It was a compromise she could live with.

She shuddered around his hand. "Michael…I wanted you inside me."

"I know darling but…" *how to tell her he had needed to control her just for a few moments, to pleasure her in his own way and to watch her melt for him.* "I am fair to bursting. I wanted you to feel pleasure because I might not be able…It has been a long time," he admitted this sheepishly.

"I'll tell you a little secret." She lifted onto an elbow, kissed his firm lips, moving damp kisses across his jaw. She whispered softly into his ear. "I have never had an orgasm during sex."

"While I am quite pleased that the bar is very low for me, I might have done without being reminded you have had previous lovers."

"No one has ever loved me, Michael."

He looked at her askance. "You aren't a virgin, so you have had lovers?"

"I mean the feelings…no one has ever given me their heart and I have never given mine. Surely that means that you and I can…try."

"Feelings are not my specialty." He gazed toward the window.

"Michael, if you truly want me to marry you, you will have to keep opening up to me."

"I want to marry you but right now I want to be inside you more than I want to breathe." He pressed toward her opening and her legs wrapped around his as if they were fit together. He pressed in slowly watching pleasure once again cloud her eyes, melting her glorious face in a passion-blank haze. When he was fully seated in her wonderfully tight sheath, Michael began to move and she moaned, throwing her head back, licking her lips, and pressing her hips into his. His climax threatened long before he was ready to relinquish her body but her moaning and arching and tightening of her legs dragged him to the precipice so that he was forced to ease himself out of the haven of her passage and press into her taut belly long before he had wanted to. She wrapped her arms fiercely around him as he convulsed onto her fine skin.

They had made love in her bed throughout the night. He thought she might indeed describe it as glorious, passionate, heart stopping totally in love, die for your next breath, love and he had reluctantly slipped away at dawn. He had whispered French love words and Spanish and even Portuguese.

Kathryn was grateful he had had enough control to withdraw each of the three times he had been inside her ready to come. She almost kept him there every time because she was sure she was going to marry him but somehow, she still believed the child should come after the ring. She wasn't old fashioned enough to abstain altogether but she was determined not to be pregnant on her wedding day with just a verbal. And really, she didn't even have the verbal any more. She had rejected that. With all her heart, she hoped she'd get another chance.

Chapter Seventeen

"Where is...everyone?" Kathryn asked Hallthorpe as she bounded into the dining room to find it completely empty.

"The Master is working in his study, and Lady Cassandra has not stirred...

I'll bet she hasn't... Kathryn's mind conjured dirty thoughts immediately.

...and Lady Agatha is in the drawing room having already broken her fast."

"The Captain? Is he..."

"He wished you to join him as soon as you have broken your fast. He is going to ride to visit the tenants again."

"And me?"

"To join him of course?"

Her heart leapt and she thought she saw a smug grin on Hallthorpe's face. As hungry as she was from all of the night's aerobic exercise, she didn't want to make Michael wait any longer than necessary so she rushed from the room holding a piece of buttered toast, charging the stairs for her breeches. Someday she figured Ellie and her band of seamstresses that she knew Michael had stashed away somewhere would get around to making a proper riding habit, but as long as she didn't have one, she wore the breeches under her dresses. It took no time to don them and dash back to Michael's study.

"My Lord?"

He turned and graced her with a sly, slightly smug smile. "My Lady. You look radiant. I trust you slept well after your very long day." She caught his gaze, one that challenged her to concoct an appropriate answer in front of the steward Smithers.

"My Lord, it was a long and arduous day. Hitting my sheets was a distinct pleasure." The flash in the obsidian orbs was a sign of triumph. She just loved their verbal skirmishes.

"If you will make yourself comfortable for a few minutes, Smithers and I will be through and you and I will be away."

"As you wish, My Lord," she answered with mock sincerity. He shot her a playful glance that said he knew she was showing off for his steward and not buying the demure miss routine for one minute. She loved doing that to him, too.

~ * ~

Jasmine was saddled and waiting for her alongside Fury and she noticed that the horses seemed to sense the new charged atmosphere. Michael effortlessly lifted Kathryn into the saddle and his hand swiped the side of her breast as he settled her. She smiled seductively at him conjuring images of their night's activities. Thrice had not been enough.

"When we finish checking on the tenants, I thought we would go to the village and I would introduce you. Do you understand what that will mean?"

"A public declaration?"

"Exactly. Are you comfortable with that?"

It suited her purposes to confirm to the world that she was going to be his wife. When she had made the decision to accept him the next time he asked, it had given her such joy and being his wife was fast becoming the most important thing she could comprehend. "I'll answer it this way. If making a public show of squiring me around the village means you'll have to ask me to marry you again, then I am comfortable with it, although I must remind you that there are conditions to my acceptance. It is you who needs to be comfortable with any *declarations*."

He gave her a snappy salute. "Touché."

The path narrowed as they neared the small bridge. She had traveled this way once before with him. The stream fed the tenant's farms, created a larger lake down a few hundred yards and was, she believed, Michael's boyhood fishing spot. Remembering even now how he had once compared her eyes to the mossy rocks of this stream.

As Michael took the lead, carefully guiding Fury onto the planks, a rather loud crack startled Fury who jerked and jumped to the other bank without another step on the split plank. Michael dismounted and regarded the splintered wood. "Come across. Jasmine should avoid the fracture on her own."

"Do horses know to avoid danger?" she asked him casually as she guided Jasmine onto the narrow bridge."

"They are very sensitive."

The next cracking of the boards was so loud it sent Jasmine into a terror. She jibbed, stepping harder on the plank and the board gave way. Jasmine just avoided pushing her leg through the jagged maw but did not avoid jostling Kathryn when she surged forward. Kathryn was unprepared for her horses' burst of speed. "Michael!" she screamed as she lost her seat and landed hard on her back on the railing. It then gave way under the pressure of the agitated horse, tumbling the entire section of the bridge into the rushing stream with Kathryn tangled in skirts and splintered boards.

He watched in horror as she was tossed like a rag doll onto the unforgiving planks and plunged into the water on her back and neck, her head immediately disappearing under the rushing current that swiftly dragged her downstream. *"Kath-ryn!"* Michael tore at his coat and waistcoat and boots plunging into the icy stream just seconds later, then plowing through the waist deep current catching his feet on rocks, knocking his knees on jutting boulders while fighting churning planks trying to grab at the waterlogged fabric. Her head was still under water when he finally had a firm grip on some part of her clothing.

Michael kept his hand on the fabric he had snagged and twined it in his fingers when his left foot lodged between rocks. The pain was instantaneous, his capture complete for more precious seconds, but still he continued twining the fabric, dragging her to him with the same determination that had seen him through carrying wounded much larger soldiers from the battlefield. Finding cold skin, he used his other hand to thrash for her head; his desperate thought was to get her head above water. "Kathryn, lift your head," he commanded as if hearing him she could overcome the rushing water.

He found strands of her glorious hair and twined his left hand into it. With her skirts anchored, he focused his considerable energy on getting her head above water. "Kathryn, Kathryn, hear me!" He pulled her into his now soaked body and fought to bring her shoulders to him. She was limp and heavy and lifeless, the chill of her skin terrifying him. Her face broke the surface, very blue and empty. There was nothing. No expression. No breath. Freeing his leg with a skin tearing tug that sent him stumbling forward, dipping her in the current once again, he made for the side as smooth mossy stones threatened to spill him into the water with every step.

"Kathryn love, wake up darling," he crooned and cajoled as he fought every ache and every fear to reach the bank and drag her boneless body with him. "Kathryn love, I need you to wake up now," he spoke as he tilted her on her side and slammed her back to dislodge the water from her lungs. His soothing words diametrically opposed to the brute force he exerted to revive her. The color of her skin began turning from blue to deathly white and there was still nothing. It was only when he was thrashing her once again from her back to her side that he saw the cut. It was deep and eerily blue and just below the pulse point on her neck. She had been ripped by something; probably a shard of the bridge and blood was oozing lazily from the deep wound.

Wounds he could manage. Drowning was not a battlefield problem he had experienced but staunching blood, he could do that. Ripping her skirts, the fabric came away easily. He wadded his first swath and then tore the next strip with his free hand. All the time he kept talking to her as he worked. Tying off her wound required him to run his bandages under her arm but her limp form made moving her difficult. She had showed no signs of life in the few minutes since he had pulled her from the water. "Kathryn love, wake for me. Fight with me, yell at me, hate me, Kathryn, just don't leave me!"

He worked with the now shredded dress to remove it so he could get her more comfortably seated in front of him on the horse but the soaked layers of fabric were heavy and awkward so he finally resorted to tearing the dress. He fought it fiercely pouring his energy into freeing her from the now-freezing mass of sodden rags. Once he had the last vestige of her dress vanquished, he realized anew that many more precious minutes had passed and she had still not stirred.

173

Heart constricting, he allowed the words from his mouth. "You will not die. You will not. You are my duchess, you are my life!" he bellowed into the woods.

~ * ~

Harold Stafford hove just below the ridge and his blood tingled when the anguished roar reached his hiding spot. He might have actually managed to kill her. He had done it! The faux duchess was as good as dead and there would be no heir. Michael would crumble into himself into a pious prison of guilt and recriminations, faulting himself unmercifully for her death and then he would welcome the taking of his life. It would be a blessing for him to die. It had all been so easy. Cracking two boards was all it had taken. Soon, there would be no one to prevent him from taking Asterleigh.

The lovely maid had been more difficult to dispense with. Having to dig that deep hole had taken hours. Splitting the wood that had sent the Duchess to her death had pleasured him much more than the others. It was becoming fun to be more hands-on.

~ * ~

Michael grabbed madly for his nerve. He was a battle-hardened warrior. Men with mortal wounds, grievous injuries had leaned on him and he had managed to soothe, calm them but Kathryn's injuries were weighing him down with unholy fear. The cold had begun stiffening his muscles and where she had once seemed iced cold, she now began heating. Her face turned paler if that was possible. The freckles faded and her eyelids glued to her cheeks. If she never woke up, he would die inside. He had found love. Her life was everything.

And he had been too stubborn to tell her when he knew that was all she had ever wanted from him.

Fury responded to his call and he straightened with her in his arms. She slumped lifeless as a sack across his saddle and he slung himself over the horse's side. "*Jasmine.*" It was a plaintive cry, not meant to call a horse but to call a life.

Kathryn did not wake on the journey back to the house.

He carried his beloved up the steps, kicked at the door, and, without waiting for a response, flung it open with a free hand. Thorpe looked at him, nearly apoplectic.

"Thorpe, blankets, warm water. Think for me. What do I do?" Hallthorpe's Master was cold, soaked, and terrified and losing his ever so steely nerve.

"My Lord. We are bringing blankets. Your study is warm. Set her on the daybed and we will see to her." Michael staggered a few more steps and the two footmen who had ridden with him to find her on the London Road, who were now hovering in the hall, steadied him. Then his mind awhirl, he stumbled and forgot.

~ * ~

Cassandra stepped cautiously to Kathryn's side, pressing her lips together to prevent them from quivering. Oh, should anything happen to her, Cassandra knew a part of her would die with her. She sat in a chair beside the daybed. "Kathryn," she whispered, "your plan worked. He loves me. We made love or almost made love. It was the most wonderful experience of my life. I am going to tell you everything and I want you to promise not to blush." Cassandra bit back a nervous laugh because Kathryn would not be blushing. She had not responded at all to the heat. She was still gone but not dead, somewhere between life and death.

"I pushed and I pushed and finally told him I loved him and he declared himself. It was so beautiful. Then he kissed me, Kathryn, my knees buckled and his strong arm came around my waist and he held me there against his hips. I felt his need against me and it gave me such a sense of power." Cassandra paused to take a breath. It was so easy to tell her like this when there would be no judgment. Only quiet awaited her words.

"Kathryn, the feel of his hands on my skin. I didn't know. I had no idea. When he touched me privately, I went flying away. He…he seemed to receive the same joy from doing that to me. Kathryn, when you wake up, you will be so happy for me. We will talk about the future."

"Jem is going to talk to Michael. He says we owe you our happiness and he is going to talk to Michael in your stead." She took another breath. All of her lovesick ramblings had fallen on Kathryn's distant ears. They were not hearing. "We want to get married in four weeks and we are going to make love again although Jem says there is even a little more we will do after we are married. I remember that part but it was so abhorrent with Edward, I can't imagine it is even the same as with Jem. As soon as you are better, we will be able to make love again. I won't leave your side for now and he won't either. We owe you. We love you so much Kathryn, don't leave us." She found herself babbling but could not stem the tide of words, for her fear for Kathryn was so great.

~ * ~

On the third day, Dr. Bridlesby retrieved his bag from the end of the bed and called Michael into the hall. "She is fighting the battle but her brain has not yet given her leave to come back. She has not yet won or lost."

Michael was caught between bereavement and fury at his helplessness. "Doctor, what else can we do?"

"Talk to her. Call her back, keep her warm. Try to get fluids and nourishment into her. Break through the haze. Make her want to stay."

"Thank you." The words were hollow. His beard was a day old, his clothes disheveled. He slipped his boots off and climbed into bed beside her.

He curled himself around her, pulling her close, drawing in her scent. "You are a saucy little minx, Kathryn Ragland. Wearing breeches and walking to London. You come back to me because you owe me. You *owe* me, minx. You owe me years of your life." His voice grew louder. "You owe me children. You owe me love. I know you have it because it's all in there waiting to burst out. Do you hear me minx…you…owe…me love!" The sobs broke from his chest before he could finish telling her that *he* also owed her love, to say the words that would bind her to him forever. She owed him that, to hear how he loved her. With his heart and soul. She was his life. She must live.

"My Lord," Hallthorpe whispered from the door. "Their Lordships are here."

"Thank you, Thorpe…will you see…"

"Lady Cassandra is waiting to spell you, sir. She has a tale I understand."

~ * ~

They sat in the study, all of them, his friends. His companions.

"The bridge was definitely tampered with. We found two boards with very clean axe blows. They would have been at just the right section of the bridge to cause the horse and rider to falter. The first rider was to cause the bridge to lose integrity. It was the following rider that was meant to fall into the water," Jules finished the speech. But he did not relish it. Twice now he had come to Michael's house to investigate the attempted murder of Kathryn Ragland, future Duchess of Asterleigh. Actually, three if the gunshot was to be counted.

"Michael, we have to accept that someone—we assume Stafford—is trying to kill your…your…what is she, Michael? Are you affianced?"

"No dammit, we are not. I was a stubborn ass to make a proposal to *that* woman without one word of deep affection." The bellow drained what little energy he had mustered for the meeting and he sank into his chair. "She is not my fiancée, but she will be my wife. She is my life," he whispered.

What were they supposed to say to that?

Colin Hamilton had not met her but he had heard from Julian about their talk on the road, from Matthew about Michael's affliction and he heard Michael's pain now. She must be very special. "Michael, there have been two very strategically executed attempts on her life and three total if the gunshot was aimed at her. I think we all agree that someone is definitely targeting Kathryn and that it's probably Harold. We've got to assume he's nearby and going to continue to cause harm, especially now that he can probably sense the growing relationship between the two of you and the chance that any day there might be…"

"She's not…" Michael trailed off. "Not…with child." They needed to know. It might make a difference.

"Are you sure?"

"Yes."

"We should figure out a way to make this clear, consider letting the relationship show signs of strain. Maybe the killer will think there is no future, that she won't be the Duchess," Matthew suggested.

"Or we could say that she is dead." Julian knew that Michael didn't want to hear the words but they had to be said. If the world thought she was dead, maybe Stafford would show himself, go for Michael. It was a trump card they could play.

"I…will not…"

"It's okay. It was just an idea," Colin conceded.

"As long as she breathes, I will not consign her to the shadows, not even to find her attacker. As long as I have breath, he will never harm her again." It was a gallant declaration made with the last energy he could muster.

"None of my people have seen him. Let's concentrate on locating him. He's clearly still operating in the area from some secure base," Julian pointed out. "He must have moved from the woodsman's cottage as soon as he realized your man had spotted his horse. He knows these lands as well as we all do."

The next half hour was spent in identifying the hideaways that might be housing a would-be assassin. Michael excused himself to the other three who had some very good ideas that he could hear in the back of his mind but not truly focus on at this moment. He needed to check on Kathryn, never having left her for more than a few minutes at a time since the accident.

~ * ~

Her head pounded and her eyes burned. Opening them was so…hard. Why could she not make them behave? "Christine? Are you there?" Her voice sounded so odd, so husky.

Cassandra stirred at her soft question. "Kathryn? Is that you?"

"Christy?" she whispered.

"No, it's Cassandra. We are to be sisters. I am here."

Slowly, very slowly, memories trickled back, although her mind was fuzzy and her head still ached. "Cassandra? Oh yes, Jem's lover. I know you…" She had no energy to tease.

"Yes, Jem's lover. It sounds so scandalous and wonderful. Does it not? You helped me you know?"

Kathryn licked her dry lips. "Michael?"

"In his study. They're talking about the bridge and what happened. Kathryn, someone wanted you or Michael dead. Jem and I think you are the target. We know that's what Michael is talking about, but he won't tell me. Oh, Kathryn, I am so glad to talk to you."

Kathryn found speaking so very difficult, but she had to know. "How long? How long has it been?"

"You've been unwell for four days. We've all been so worried."

"I guess I did put a crimp in the social plans." It was almost her usual quality retort, although the voice certainly didn't sound like hers.

"As I am sure you are not surprised, we have not had or missed any social engagements of import. No one, absolutely no one, is hosting anything until word of your recovery is spread.

Chapter Eighteen

"Spread the word, sister. I am back!" Kathryn clasped Cassandra's hands in hers.

"Ellie, please get the Master. Tell him she is awake."

Ellie found Hallthorpe at the base of the stairs just as Michael was opening his study door and he bolted past the two of them for the stairs.

"My Lord, she is awake."

Michael snapped to attention and his heart leapt.

"Thorpe, please tell their Lordships the news." He tossed the words over his shoulder.

Throwing propriety to the wind, he nearly flew to her bedside. "Kathryn? Look at you, lying there in that bed." He grinned at her with the silly delirious expression of a man pardoned from the hangman's noose.

She smiled up at him, stretching like a cat. "Yes, I have been rather lazy. I will need a good run."

Michael rejoiced; she was, indeed, back from the dead. "I will certainly win as you have not trained in so many days." He took her hand and it felt right, not too cold, or hot. She gripped him with strength and he crawled up onto the bed beside her.

"Michael is this acceptable?"

He grinned at her but it was Cassandra who spoke up.

"He slept in your chair the first night, but after that he got up there with you in the bed. There was no rousting you. He would say 'what good is reputation if we don't get her back'? It was all very gallant and wonderfully improper."

"Cassandra and Jem talked to me on the second day of your...er...illness. They said you encouraged them."

"Do I detect a not completely negative tone in your voice?"

"You do."

"They're in love, Michael."

"I know. I have...given them my blessing."

"Oh, Michael, I am so proud of you. I think our big warrior heart is softening." She reached a very weak hand to his stubbled chin.

"It's the minx. She made me do it."

"Someday you English are going to tell me what a minx is. Cassandra, did he rail at you first?" she asked turning her face toward her. Michael's heart was bursting as he watched the two beaming at each other.

"No, I told him it was your idea and he made a horrible face and I think he was determined not to speak ill of you. Your incapacitation was a godsend. We're getting married, sometime soon but we haven't fixed the date yet."

"Cassandra, I am so happy for you."

"Now, my sister, you have told your news. Please let me enjoy Kathryn to myself."

"I'll be back after luncheon and we will talk more, maybe wedding plans?" Cassandra bent down and brushed a kiss on Kathryn's forehead.

"I can't wait."

~ * ~

Once Cassandra had left, Kathryn got right to the point. "Okay, I'm ready for you to come clean on what the heck is going on. Someone sabotaged the bridge to kill one of us, and someone came in my room and was chased off. Surely, you have some theories about what is going on."

"Theories only, nothing really." He winced.

"Just tell me. Don't try to lie or hide it. Surely, you know I can see there's something going on. Don't shut me out. I've been..." She hesitated because she didn't want to make him feel guilty about what had happened since she'd been with him but it was beyond time for him to tell her what the hell was going on. "You owe me an explanation."

"Yes." With a resigned sigh, he told her that he and his associates believed someone was trying to kill her first and then would come for him to take over the Dukedom.

"So who inherits if you die?"

"Harold Stafford, my cousin. The one who was with…"

"Yes?"

"Nothing?

"You've thought of something, tell me."

"He was with my brother who, while he had fallen from his horse, actually probably bled to death. He might have been saved. What if…Harold killed him too?"

"Or he just allowed him to die. Maybe it was a convenient accident."

"That makes sense. Once my brother was dead, there was only me and my sure-to-die-young father between him and the title and as long as I was on the Continent, I could be dead any day. He could bide his time with 'no blood on his hands' literally and figuratively.

She gave him a wicked smile. "Then you came back and got a girlfriend."

He chuckled hollowly. "Yes, and now my girlfriend is a target because…"

"Can you just go ahead and tell me? Because what?"

"You have to be killed while you are an unknown. Your death will fall largely into the category of 'no news.' Ideally, you should die before me so there is no…posthumous…"

"…heir." They said the word at the same time.

"What a conniving, murdering bastard."

"Exactly my sentiments, love. Now we just have to catch him.

"How do we do that?"

"A trap."

Their conversation was overtaxing her and he really wanted to stop talking with her about murderers. "Kathryn, you need to rest. I'll come back in a while and we'll spend time together, then later I will tuck you in for the night."

"Promise you'll stay."

He hesitated. "It's not the done thing really, Kathryn."

"Is there a soul in this house who is going to stop you from staying with me or announcing it in the papers if you do?"

"No love, you are right, no one will stop me. I'll be back then."

~ * ~

"Michael, we've got to draw him out of the shadows," Jules said. Two days later, in Michael's study, the battle over the trap had been raging for fifteen minutes, and Kathryn had listened to this group of headstrong, arrogant and she noticed, incredibly large and gorgeous, men debate until she wanted to scream and yell. It was so simple to her.

She needed to be the bait and she told them so.

"No!" The chorus of male refusal was universal but she plowed ahead nonetheless.

"Look, he is watching me somehow I think, so if it appears I am alone or running away again, maybe that I'm sneaking out or heading home, he will show himself. As it is now, we are sitting ducks because he's hiding and all of your efforts, as I know they have been legion, have not been able to scare him out."

The room was quiet as the men pondered her words.

"London. We need to go to London." Michael began talking distractedly but realized he was doing so out loud and firmed up his tone. "Surely he will follow us…"

"But we'll be in much closer quarters and have a chance of anticipating his moves," Julian added.

"I agree, we will do best in London but Kathryn, that does not mean in any way that I have acceded to your offer to serve as bait. We will find another way."

"Listen, I am the one who was almost poisoned, was shot at, and then dumped in the stream on my head. I am the one with the lovely purple hole in my neck." Michael winced and Colin groaned while Julian made a respectful cough to cover his blanch. "This is as much my decision as yours because even though you're the one he's trying to get at, I am the one he has *gotten*!"

"Maybe we can devise a scheme where we don't put Miss Ragland in danger but rather make it *look* like she's the bait," Colin suggested.

"A disguise. Brilliant, man!" Matthew exclaimed while Michael quickly brightened at the prospect of using someone other than Kathryn as the bait.

"I am going to leave it on that note since you all have at least accepted to some extent that I am part of this thing whether I actually face a killer or not. Suits me fine to not but I will not be left out, Michael. Agreed?"

"Not agreed."

Exasperated, Kathryn said, "Michael, I am not going to threaten you in front of your friends but I can tell you that you will not like me very much if we can't at least have a mutual understanding on something like this. You have to let me be part of my own protection."

"Umm-hmm." Julian coughed again because after his one long ride with Kathryn, he knew of what she was capable. Michael might as well surrender now.

"Kathryn, I will not put you in danger. Period."

"I am already in danger and you can't keep me from it, no offense, mind you. All I ask is to be part of deciding the solution. You must accept it."

"I will agree to include you in consultation. That's as far as I can accept right now."

"Deal."

He looked at her, surprised. "Deal? That easy?"

"Yes." She rose from her position near the fire and left without another hint of argument and she made sure she didn't look mad or petulant or scheming.

"Your proposed fiancée' is impressive, Michael. We should all be so fortunate."

"Thank you, Hamilton. Since she's been in my life now more than a fortnight, I've had as much excitement here at home as I did on the Continent. Is it possible that getting entangled with an intelligent, foreign woman could be any more difficult?"

"Well, it should be some comfort that once we lay hold of Harold, the death threats will end. You'll only have to deal with the other big decisions of life. Imagine how she'll be when she's breeding and you're telling her she can't run." Julian laughed sardonically but he did not look directly at Michael.

"Now I have a headache," Michael groaned. "I can't even think about it."

But after they left, he did think about it and found that the idea of Kathryn pregnant with his child infused his gut with the warmest feeling. He could think about it a lot actually.

Chapter Nineteen

How to dress a lady for an investiture ceremony. Michael was pondering such a question as the Asterleigh carriage pulled out from the drive in front of Asterleigh House in Grosvenor Square. It was his first sojourn from the house as the Duke Presumptive and he had two women in tow, each of whom could be unpredictable, embarrassing and downright vulgar if she so chose. They could also be the two most intelligent, intriguing, damnably enticing women he had ever seen. Lady Cassandra Penthoven was regal, aristocratic, austere, severe, captivating, and challenging. Miss Kathryn Ragland was earthy, beguiling, embarrassing, absurd, exquisite, scintillating, and breathtaking.

The two most important women in his life made Michael look like a veritable bore in his gray and black, someone not to be noticed when they moved together down the street, as colorful and stunning as he was drab. Their presence attracted entirely too much attention. Males gaped, gawked, gasped, and groped for a look, seeking even the slightest indication that the Asterleigh ladies noticed them. Michael was struck with as many parts pride at their presence as outright fear at their attractiveness and the looks they drew. He would need all the resources many years on the battlefield had honed to keep away the rakes, roués and blackguards drawn to the spectacle of two such awe-inspiring, fresh blooded prizes as his sister and his love inspired as they alighted from their carriage on Bond Street.

Michael had plenty of experience with jealous males, cads and jaundiced pretenders but no experience with highly paid, egotistical fake French modistes. He knew one way...he knew how to give a mercenary what he, in this case *she*, wanted. "Madame, we are so glad you could receive us. You see I am accompanied by the two most exquisite creatures in all of England who are to sit at my hands during my ceremonies with his Majesty. They must be clad by you, Madame."

She practically fainted at his words. Prinny and these ladies, and an investiture, and them so stylishly turned out. Who the hell were these English country folks she did not know? Madame knew everybody, damn well everyone. She hadn't spent two years learning French and six months memorizing Debrett's to falter when such an exquisite trio entered her shop.

Which was the mistress and which was the wife? It intrigued her that they would come together. What an enlightened and odd wife. The gorgeous dark haired one looked more like the aristocratic wife but she was obviously affectionate with the honey-colored small one. Was this the famous ménage-a-trois she had heard so much from?

"Madame? If you would be so kind as to allow me to present Lady Cassandra Stafford Penthoven, my most beloved sister, and her companion, Miss Kathryn Ragland."

Ah, so the dark-skinned blonde is the consort then? Interesting.

"My sister knows her taste, but Miss Ragland welcomes a more direct approach. Feel free to suggest what you think will be best on her. She will be in our section, Madame."

Ahhh, so it is to be like that. *Monsieur le duc* does not care what the haut *ton* thinks. He will keep the mistress openly. Well, he will pay well, *very well* for the privilege.

Ceres, goddess of the earth. If there was ever a human incarnation of that deity, it was Kathryn Ragland, soon to be Duchess of Asterleigh, wrapped in dark bronze heavy silk with her streaked golden mane flowing over gently bronzed shoulders with fabric trailing behind as if her body blended with the floor of Madame Filene's modiste salon. His Kathryn smiled and the entire shop lit up with her radiance. The other ladies picking fabrics and talking in low tones for fear of his presence gawked at her and Madame's face was twisted into a joyous and confused contortion. "Mademoiselle, you are…exquisite."

"Oh Kathryn, that is surely the most beautiful fabric for you. Michael will have to fight the assembled throng off with his swordstick when you

187

arrive. You are absolutely breathtaking." With that, Cassandra subsided onto the settee by Michael, who could not take his eyes off his beautiful Kathryn. He had seen her naked and in breeches and in lovely hand-me-down gowns and soaked through to the barest of skin and in a futuristic night rail but he had never seen her swathed in expensive fabric as a goddess. All she needed was a crown fashioned of grain stalks and she would be the goddess of the Earth, Ceres come to life. Or, if he were a student of Greek culture, Demeter. Ceres more directly suited his purposes as *searing* had him perfectly in mind of his heart.

Michael was definitely in charge of the room. "My dear, that fabric seems to suit you. Madame, I would like to make a present to Miss Ragland of a gown fashioned from this fabric for her gallantry in saving my life."

"Saving your life?" several female voices intoned including Kathryn's.

"Yes, there was a bridge collapse and sadly she took the brunt of the collapse, leaving me entirely unharmed. This gown will be my gift and she will wear it to my investiture ceremony in two days time."

"*Two days*," Madame shrieked. "It will be a masterpiece, how will I ever...?"

"You will, Madame, because she will be the main attraction at my investiture in front of Prinny himself. I understand she has been brought to his attention. I expect you will want this commission to take precedence over your others?"

"Ah, your grace, yes...it will...take precedence."

"Thank you, Madame. Ladies, shall we right our clothing and take that surprise I promised you?"

"A surprise? You are turning into a regular...what 'romantic'?"

He gave Kathryn a playful grin as he twined her arm through his.

He also wanted to twine their fingers together so that the men who were even now watching this with keen interest knew she was claimed. Knowing from the first that this would happen—men ogling her—is why he had avoided bringing Kathryn to London at all. His already badly worn patience with Harold Stafford's murdering intentions would no doubt be completely shattered as he fended off the advances of the town's brashest rakes.

The gentlemen of quality who knew him would stay clear but there would be some unconcerned for the look in his eyes and Kathryn's lovely open nature and warm earthy smile would be too enticing for them to resist. It was already giving him another headache. "Yes, Gunter's for ices. Ladies, I must tell you that I am being regarded with such jealousy by the men on the street."

"Oh? How so?" Kathryn had noticed a few looks and wondered that men were so forward with women who were clearly with another man. She was thoroughly curious about Michael's answer.

"You two are by far the most exciting creatures out this morning and, because no one has yet been introduced, they are all wondering where you came from and how to get an introduction. I am not inclined to give them one."

Cassandra chuckled warmly. "Brother, are you jealous that gentlemen are looking at your lovely escort?"

"Yes, I am not too proud to admit that I find it most disconcerting but I knew I would. We have all been rusticating in the country so long most likely because I had been hoping to avoid just such."

"A wonderfully mature admission from you, Michael. I think your association with Kathryn has made you quite pleasant."

"That is not a word I would have ever associated with me but yes, I guess I feel rather pleasant, and ever so slightly disconcerted."

"Kathryn, we should have told you much more of London society before bringing you here. You will note that gentlemen are very open with their amorous intentions, and some will have no qualms about approaching a lady even if she appears to be claimed. It is entirely acceptable for married ladies to have affairs with married men."

"However, although we are not married, I have no intention that you will fall prey to anyone's advances," Michael warned.

"Michael is absolutely right about married ladies and it applies to widows too, but the rules are entirely different for unmarried ladies. Reputation is paramount and it is not acceptable to remain in any gentleman's company for any period of time or to dance more than once with him at a…"

"Cassandra, we do not need to frighten her with the archaic nature of the *ton's* views on unmarried ladies." The hint of steel in his voice caused

189

her to look at him and what she saw brought her lips to a curve. She realized her brother had no intention of leaving Kathryn's side and society be damned. "Kathryn will not be abandoned to the throng, dear."

"I daresay!"

~ * ~

Harold had been watching their progress and noting the men who had ogled, eyed, gaped, and goggled at the faux Duchess. If they only knew she was nothing but an American commoner who dressed scandalously and had been ruined by his priggish cousin, they would not be looking at her so adoringly. What did those men, any man, see in her? She was clearly too small, without the sweet luscious plump curves for grabbing and holding onto. She was not pale enough or conventional looking. She wore bright colors and gowns with longer sleeves and less revealing bosom that the current styles. And her hair? How could anyone possibly have more variety in tone in their hair? It was as if the sun had streaked it and when it was curled around her head, it made maddening swirls.

Well faux Duchess…. Harold thought, *what I have planned for you will wipe all that smugness from your face. Although I might just try a taste of you first, see what it is my uppity cousin finds so irresistible.*

Harold faded into the shadows while his henchman eyed the beauty lasciviously while thinking that it would be a pleasure to capture that delicious morsel.

~ * ~

If she could have been more nervous, Kathryn could not imagine it. Ellie had been working feverishly on her hair, but even her usually competent hands were shaking. "His Majesty, miss. I can't fathom it. You'll be…in... Oh, my…I am so sorry. I just can't seem to keep the tongs moving and hold this all tight. I am afraid I might burn you."

"Ellie, let's try for something simple. Is it possible for me to wear it down?"

"No! Oh miss, I am so sorry. I shouldn't have exclaimed at you, it's just…"

Kathryn reached for Ellie's hands and the woman visibly relaxed. "Let's just pin this top section up and let the rest hang down my back. I am who I am and these big up-dos aren't me. I do think we could put that strand of beads woven through the topknot though. What do you think?"

"That's just the thing, miss. I'll take them," she answered, and slipped the beads from Kathryn's hand and began weaving them through Kathryn's hair creating the lovely illusion of a small wreath. Kathryn was reminded that Michael had called her Ceres, Roman goddess of the earth, mentioning all she needed was a crown fashioned from grain stalks. Well, he would be getting his wish. She did feel rather like a goddess.

~ * ~

The woman descending the stairs toward him was going to cause a scene the likes no one had ever seen. Her shining golden tresses were long and flowing around her shoulders, the curls on top woven with a crown of beads and the dress fashioned more like a Roman drape than a gown was not really short of scandalous. His temples throbbed, jaw ground and his hands burned. They burned with an intensity to claim her, haul her back upstairs and lock himself away with her. No one that saw her would be able to resist.

At that moment, his musings coalesced into one horrified thought; what if she did not choose him?

"You look upset, Michael, is something wrong?" She patted her coiffure and the beatific smile faded.

"No, Kathryn, I am sorry to have looked so perplexed. Forgive me. I was thinking about having to beat others off with my swordstick. It might not be the done thing although I do believe there might have been a duel once before in the Lords."

"I would really like to see you with a sword. Do you fence or is it that fight for your life heavy sword version that you prefer?"

"I have had to fight for my life and I expect today it will be as close-a run as some of those with Boney. You, my dear, will cause a riot." He lifted her hand and turned her palm into his lips with a scorching gaze that burned all the way to her inner core.

"I am taking that as a compliment. Are you okay with my hair? We couldn't get it up." She fussed to relieve the impressive tension.

I've got it up all right and at the moment am using the banister to keep from showing you, he thought ruefully. It was going to be a very long day.

191

"It's lovely, Kathryn. I will be very proud to have you on my arm."

"That was incredibly sweet."

"No one has ever called me sweet."

"Consider it done now. Your reputation is very ruined then because you *are* sweet."

As Michael handed first Cassandra and then Kathryn into the carriage, he thought over his life these last twenty days and felt a profound sense of gratitude for what he had gained and come more to fully realize as a series of unbelievable blessings. He had never been meant to be the Duke but his service to the King, leading men had taught him well. He had Cassandra back in his life and he had a woman whose smile made him quiver with desire and her mind challenged every one of his long held notions about the relationships of men and women. He was going to need all of this good feeling to carry him through this day.

~ * ~

Parliament. The Palace of Westminster, all those Dukes and swords and Prinny himself. The pomp and Michael so regal marching with the other Dukes had taken her breath away, so foreign and beautiful and so totally not of her world. The weight of it crashed in on her as she watched him process from the ceremony and she sat with Cassandra very far away from him. She realized at that moment she could not marry him.

In a box, not far away from Kathryn, royal speculation was rampant. "So he's finally come to town *now* has he?"

"Yes, Majesty. Seems there was some trouble with a girl staying with his sister. An accident. Or maybe it was many accidents?"

"Friends of sisters don't usually persuade Dukes to delay their ceremonies. This must be some girl."

"If the rumors in the Lords are correct she is an 'exotically bronzed Colonial.' She is, I believe, not far away from us. The strawberry blond."

"Exotically bronzed and strawberry blond. From that description and what I can see, she sounds like someone I would like to meet," the Prince Regent mused deliciously.

"While I am in full agreement with you, it appears she is already spoken for."

"Yes, I do believe you are right, Foxworthy. She must be quite something. Isn't the sister the one that tried to kill herself or her father-in-law or someone?"

"Yes, she was thought to be quite insane, but it is said that the Colonial has great sway with her and she is much healed. Rumor is the sister is now affianced to her footman!"

"This story just keeps getting more fun."

"If the rumors are true."

"Yes. And Foxworthy, she would no doubt correct you and say she is an 'American', not a 'Colonial'."

"Quite right, Majesty, quite right."

~ * ~

It was not that she wasn't good enough for him or incapable of learning how to move in these circles but simply that she did not belong here. This was not her place, her time and while she loved his family madly, they were not her family. He still had not truly believed her for all of his conforming to her modern ways and funning with her and becoming more relaxed and flexible, that she was someone totally different from what he thought. She worked, supported herself, tended a few plants, managed her small retirement account, read the paper, ran road races, occasionally dated a man, cooked sometimes, and made a life with her sister. That's who she was, not this girlfriend of a rich English Duke being feted in the most regal of ceremonies.

And, he couldn't really fathom where she had been. What would he make of her driving a car, her car of all things—a red Acura! He would probably approve of her private passion for romance novels but not tanning beds. Mercy, what would he say if he knew she had stripped naked in a box and let it bake her bronze? He just would have no concept. She had to go home and this time, he had to agree. It was really for the best. For him, and for her.

All of this made perfect sense in her head; it still didn't sit well in her heart.

"Lady Penthoven?"

"Lord Marbury, how do you do?" Cassandra replied simply without that warmth in her voice that was so much a part of her when she talked to the family. So this was how it went, Kathryn could read Cassandra's

193

movements, her voice, inflection. This was not someone Cassandra liked.

"I am well, thank you but you, you are also well?"

Kathryn thought he might have had a mocking tone but his face was unreadable.

"I am well. I was not ever unwell, my lord."

"Ah, you have a companion with you today." He bestowed a not successfully hidden feral grin on Kathryn that made her decidedly queasy.

"May I present Miss Kathryn Ragland, my dear friend? This is Lord Marbury."

"Miss Ragland." He bowed over her hand and she curtsied in just the way Cassandra had taught her for anyone she was to call "My Lord."

"It is a distinct pleasure to meet you."

The queasiness grew to outright revulsion as he stroked his fingers over her knuckles. Kathryn sincerely hoped Cassandra knew just how to extricate her because if this man touched her for one second longer, she was going to cause him a very big problem and cause Michael a scene of her making that he would not at all like.

"Miss Ragland." The words were firm and foreboding when Michael spoke from just over her shoulder. She knew he had seen the intent in the creepy man's eyes and the jerk immediately released her hand and took a step back. "Marbury." Yes, it was cold, very cold. She couldn't wait to ask Cassandra later what the real story was.

"I must admire your good taste in escorts, your grace. These lovely ladies seem to be quite the rage."

It was then that Kathryn realized a line had been forming around them or maybe a circle but quite a few of the overly dressed men were pressing closer to them, seemingly waiting for the very same rather too close greeting Lord Marbury had availed himself of. Michael's twitching jaw alerted her to his thoughts that he would prefer to escort them out and to the carriage without another single introduction and ensconce them in Asterleigh House at once.

She could read him so well at that moment her heart fairly broke. He cared so deeply for her, her leaving would be devastating to him. He was a man of order, reason and precision and his life would be bereft without her to loosen him up. "Miss Ragland, are you alright? You look perplexed."

"I think I'm a little overwhelmed. I know it's not okay yet, but can you give me an idea of how much longer we have to stay?"

"Not one more minute my dear, grasp your head and wince. We will use your headache as a wonderful excuse to be released from this crush," and Michael was true to his word to whisk them from the crushing throng.

The fresh air and the carriage ride did little to help. Kathryn needed to get away, to think, to figure out how to tell him she was leaving, having decided that she was going to buy passage on a boat to America and at least get that much closer to reuniting with Christine. Her own headache had become real and sensing her distress, Michael released her to slip up to her room.

Cassandra watched as she took the stairs. "She looks unwell."

"Yes, it's not like her but then we have never forced her into such a crowd. Cassandra, did you see how they looked at her?"

"I did and I was most distressed. When you are married, I can't bear the thought of how many of them will make their way to the house hoping to sneak in behind you," she despaired.

"I will never, never let that happen, but it makes me so tired to think about how hard it will be on her. She expects people to be decent and the rakes are decidedly not. Did you see her practically wilt? I am asking so much of her." Michael stared absently at the spot where Kathryn had stood

"She is so strong, Michael, she can manage. We probably should have prepared her better for that, however. We will limit how much we make her do on this visit. Maybe after you are married…"

"You must not continue to say that out loud. She will think I am assuming too much."

"You are assuming too much. You should ask her again," Cassandra declared.

The blue velvet ring box he slipped from his jacket and handed Cassandra contained a brilliant emerald cut emerald. The tiny diamonds gracing the delicate band winked in the light of his study. "Oh Michael, it is stunning. Where did you get this and when are you going to do it?"

"I had it made for her, nothing else would do. It seems I was determined for her to have an emerald. Soon. Soon, Cassie."

Chapter Twenty

She was not running this time, just going for a walk alone in her breeches so no one would bother her. She needed to think, to plan, to gather her flimsy courage when it came time to tell Michael she was leaving and to scrape the bottom of the barrel by asking him for the money for the passage. That would be a regret—that she had never repaid him—but in her heart, she knew he wouldn't let her anyway.

Suddenly, the feeling of not being alone crept up her neck. Too late, before she could react, everything went black.

~ * ~

Michael woke with thoughts of his dreamy duchess. Her muscled thighs that rode him like he rode his prized Fury. Never again would he want alabaster skin, bronze was his preference. At the thought of Kathryn astride his thighs, Michael's staff rose to attention.

Michael fondly imagined his fiery Kathryn running through his fields. While he knew a proper Duchess would never be able to run in London, at Hawthorne…she would run and race him until her belly was swollen with their child. Then after her confinement, she would run again and regain all of her fluid muscles. The thought of his Duchess huge with the children they would have together warmed him.

This was his first full day as the Duke of Asterleigh and also the day Michael would make Kathryn his Duchess in truth. He was certain of it, but the empty dining room this morning gave Michael the most frightening sense of *déjà vous*.

When Hallthorpe reported what Michael had feared, that Kathryn was indeed gone, his anger was quickly dispelled by the dawning horror that she was in danger. Michael had never really believed Kathryn's tale of time travel. He had not only treated her condescendingly, but actively fought any of her efforts to explain how she had been from another time or place. He could have so easily just trusted her; he had not.

But she had promised, *promised* not to leave him again like before and Michael wondered if Kathryn had lied or not. Maybe she had tried to tell him and he had not listened. So she had left, gone home, where he could not follow. Those fateful thoughts told him the truth he had always denied. She was *not* from his time. She was going forward, away from him where his wealth and power held no sway. Blackness threatened.

"Your Grace?"

"Yes, Thorpe?"

"Thrasher has something to report."

"Send him in." Michael said resignedly. He did not think that he could just head down to the docks and ask every ship's captain if they had a stowaway. Thinking of this outlandish idea…he did have enough staff…

"Come, Thrasher. What is it?"

"Well, your grace, it's…well Miss Primble told me as how Miss Ragland never called for her last night and she was puzzled. We were talking about it and it reminded me I had thought I had seen her walking in the garden. She didn't have a bag with her and she was dressed in her lad clothes. She was just walking but then she never came back in. It made me think hard this morning when Ellie…uhh…Miss Primble said she hadn't come in."

"What are you suggesting?" Michael was beginning to experience another fear altogether, one he had not considered in all of the agony of her running away. "That she was just walking and not running away?"

"Yes, that maybe she didn't go off on her own."

Oh, god, Kathryn!

~ * ~

"I heard them blokes say they was looking for a lad…a lost stable lad." The tough Harold had hired reported that the Asterleigh household no knew their precious little faux Duchess was missing.

"Motley, you're a genius." *Flatter the fool.* They are obviously

197

looking for a lady dressed as a stable lad and as we have her that means they will be coming for her," Harold gloated to his henchman.

Kathryn woke with her head groggy. It did not feel or smell like home or like any place of Michael's either. This place smelled dank and stale like an old bar after a long weekend and she gagged at the putrid odor that wafted in through the broken window above her head.

"Well, sleepy faux Duchess..." He looked like Michael but his voice was weaker, slurrier...and when her eyes adjusted to the slip of light streaming in she saw he was not anything like Michael. Where Michael's face was angular with that broad forehead and slightly chiseled jaw, this one had saggy jowls. Too much brandy each night. His legs were long but not lean. Instead of ripples, there were bulges and his stomach not flat and hard but slightly flopped over his waistband. Thanks to the bands holding her wrists, she knew he was certainly not a welcoming party sent by Michael.

"You're awake, Duchess?"

"Who are you and why are you calling me Duchess?" The strangely familiar man jeered at her.

"Ah yes, I am also Stafford...Harold. Because you are to be the Duchess...oh, excuse me...*were* to be the Duchess. When Michael comes to save you, he will die and thus you will not become a Duchess. We will have no use for you but those slavers in the harbor will...you will fetch them a pretty penny and they will pay me well for you. Even if you are ruined. Your odd looks and sassy tongue will make you a favorite in some foreigner's boudoir."

Though she felt a cold, chilling fear, Kathryn forced herself to act calm. "I am not a Duchess. I'm an American and am leaving here. Neither you nor anyone named Michael will have any use for me."

"Michael has every use for you. He is right now hunting all over London for you. You must be a feisty little whore to bring him to heel...or maybe you are with child and his demmed honor is forcing him. For some reason, he wants you back." Harold licked his lips and she forced herself not to react to the suggestion.

"I know no one here, certainly no one who would be seeking me, and I ask you nicely to release me so I can go home," Kathryn declared in her most authoritative voice. It had not even quavered.

"No. You are my bait. You see, Michael has something I want. If you had not been so demmed difficult I would have had you dead days ago and he would not have become the Duke. I would be Duke of Asterleigh but today, when he finds you, he will also meet his fate and I will become the Duke."

The full weight of his words and who this man was sunk in on Kathryn. Kathryn's vast romance novel collection boasted many stories of jealous heirs trying to kill or trick rightful Dukes and Earls out of their fortunes and titles. But actually hearing Harold Stafford talk so callously about killing her and then Michael and thinking he could then just step into the Dukedom...

"You'll be wanting some bread. You've got a long day." Stafford released her wrists so that she could eat. As he continued pontificating, he did not think to re-bind her. "We're setting the trap for Michael and you'll be needing all your strength to play along." Kathryn had not read all those novels for nothing. Thankfully, she knew that there was always an escape route in these waterfront dives and all she had to do was find it and get away from this man and the other gnarly one called Motley. How appropriate!

"Lord Stafford, may I call you that?"

"Yes, *Kitten*. May I call you that?" he slurred more, spittle rising on his lips.

"If you wish." She gagged, the bile coming fast to her throat. Kathryn swallowed and closed her eyes.

"I will call you Kitten because that is what you are...the kitten that lures Tom, then I will be the dog that devours you both. In the meantime, you will be *my* Kitten."

She smelled the stale brandy on his breath and hoped he was not as lucid as she was. If Kathryn could keep Harold talking, learn his plan, then she had a chance to foil it. But, she was no novel heroine. She was regular Kathryn Ragland from Birmingham, Alabama 2010, woman's counselor, part-time road racer, all around nice girl. She did have *one* skill. She knew how to talk to people. That might be just the thing for her in this situation. "So what are your plans for me?"

"So eager—I like that," he purred grossly.

"You see, Michael will hunt you down wherever you are. I just have to put you in a place where he will meet with a most unfortunate accident. Here in this warehouse…"

"My Lord, Stafford. I am still unsure about whom you are speaking. Your plan is based on someone named Michael rescuing me. I don't…"

"Don't think I didn't see you together. You, wearing men's breeches, the two of you running like children, and you riding astride. You, my dear are a veritable hoyden. I know why he found you so irresistible. Even though he spent all those years in the army, women all over the continent, no one was ever good enough for him. No one. You however did something no woman had ever done, held his interest. Now he plans to make you his Duchess and we can't have that. No heirs. That unfortunate problem with the first Catherine, *my Catherine,* and his father's death brought me closer than I expected. Then…" Volume increasing as he spat more and more vilely at her, his eyes wild, then he whirled on her and regained his composure, just like that.

"But he will follow you here and he will die trying to save you. I allowed enough of the dock hands and others about see us drag you into the building so that when he comes asking, someone will tell him. You'll be long gone but the building will be burning and he will come in to save you. He will hunt for you until he is overcome and die in the inferno. A brilliant plan if I may say so myself."

Kathryn couldn't breathe. She needed to think and the only thing she knew for absolute certain what that she had to get away and warn Michael away from this building. Stafford was droning on extolling the virtues of his evil and he seemed distracted. Kathryn thought for a fleeting moment that she might even be able to take him but then what of Motley? And were there others?

No, this was one time when she would outrun them. She knew she could run past them long enough to seek shelter with someone in the outside world. No matter how squalid the buildings, there would be someone to whom she could turn. Kathryn knew she could not run in her slippers but loathed leaving them behind. The ones Michael had given her…one of the gifts from him that she truly felt entitled to keep when she left him. The other, her guinea she would never part with tucked safely into the slit pocket of her skirt.

"Well my dear, you can see how ingenuously I've constructed my plot. There is no use for you to waste either my time or yours with a flimsy escape attempt." The moment Harold tugged his ill-fitting waistcoat at his middle, Harold took his eyes from Kathryn and she knew it was time. Having removed her left shoe in preparation of fleeing, she sucked in a deep breath and kicked her right foot as hard as she could into Stafford's groin. He crumpled in a hysterical fit of coughing and writhing. She pushed past him and discarded her remaining slipper.

No one was at the top of the short staircase and she flew down using the element of surprise to breeze past a dozing Motley. By the time he stirred, the door had banged behind her. Out on the cobbled street, Kathryn chose a path taking her away from the water. Based on Harold Stafford's prediction that she would be sold to slavers, she thought to avoid handing herself over to them just after gaining her freedom. The water was not the direction to turn so she chose the closest lane and put on the speed she would need to keep them far behind. Running at breakneck pace up narrow streets, ignoring the growing soreness of her heels and the disgusting stickiness and grime clinging to her, Kathryn detected a faint smell of stale ale and food signaling a tavern of sorts in the distance. Setting her senses in the lead and her legs and lungs on autopilot, she ploughed through the dingy streets.

The almost dark night was not pierced by streetlight, as was the case she had observed in the fashionable areas. Everywhere the shadows played and teased her frazzled nerves. As the tavern came in to view, she took one glance behind her to see if anyone had followed her and ran straight into a…man.

~ * ~

Michael stepped from the shadows in front of Kathryn as she turned her head and she plunged headlong into his arms. Michael wrapped his arms around her back pressing her face to his cravat. Her chest heaving from exertion, her breath choking as she registered the shock.

His face in her disheveled hair, Michael thought it had only traces of the glorious smell he remembered. Instead, her clothes and hair smelled of mildew and sweat and dirty man. *If that bastard had hurt her*. Her breathing slowed and he eased his hold on her just enough for Kathryn to look up into his face. He watched the numbing fear in her eyes begin to subside and he smiled down at her. Tears formed and began flowing freely down her face filling his heart, and then he heard his name in her muffled sobs. He melted at her outpouring of emotion.

She was in his arms again and he would never let her go.

"Kathryn, my love, you are safe. Please stop crying. Minton is going to be sore at you for ruining my cravat." He held her loosely as she gathered her wits. She found the handkerchief he had slipped into her hand some time earlier and she began cleaning her face. When she took a step back, he released her.

"Michael, I am so relieved...you are not finding me... in an abandoned building." Her breathing was labored. "A man... helped Harold Stafford kidnap me... and they held me for you to find me. He planned to trick you...and catch you... in the burning building." He thought it had been a challenge for her to get that entire speech out with her heart racing and not yet having caught her breath.

He regarded her, knowing she had more to say. Her revelation left him wondering...

"I didn't run away you know. I promised I wouldn't. I had just gone out into the garden to think about how to tell you it was time for me to go. This...interlude has made it easier to form the words. I had planned to say, 'Michael, I cannot stay here...with you'."

"Why ever not?" His heart that had just begun to return to its normal rhythm twisted viciously at this unpleasant practiced pronouncement.

"I don't plan to be your mistress and I know you would not let go now that we have made love and I know you enjoy our pleasuring each other and while you offered to marry me, I can't believe you really meant it or that ours would be the kind of partnership I would have to have. You're a Duke and I'm me, and I have too much pride to watch you with someone else. Then, there's the whole business of you not trusting me and me not belonging here." She paused then laughed shallowly. "You know, Stafford thought *that you really wanted me to be your Duchess.* An actual Duchess for crying out loud. He was crazy, wasn't he?"

"Stafford thought right," Michael interrupted and she looked at him with wide questioning eyes. "He knew I would make you my Duches,s and you would help me fill my nursery with children and he would never get his hands on my title."

She spluttered. "But I cannot be a proper Duchess! You and your aunt have said so. You saw them looking at me at your ceremony. They thought I was your mistress."

"No, thankfully, you will not be a proper Duchess, but you will be a perfect duchess. The love of my life the…"

"The love of your life? Really? You love me?"

"Yes, you daft woman, I love you."

"Are you going to ask me to marry you again?"

"No. I am informing you that today, this afternoon, the wedding of the Duke of Asterleigh to Miss Kathryn Ragland will take place and then you will be my Duchess and we will have no more of this nonsense that I don't love you or want our children or want to teach them to fish or have passion for you, that I will betray you with other women, or that we're not …how did you say it, to-die-for in love?"

"Oh" formed on her lips and she went to protest. "But *I* cannot marry you…"

Stopping her outrageous speech in mid-sentence, he captured her mouth with his and plundered her with the power of the ravenous beast, the animal denied his meal for far too long. Michael's heart soared as he gathered his perfect love into his arms.

When he allowed her tense form to push from him again, she regarded him warily. "I am so grateful he did not get you into that building after me, but …"

"My love, you can see he has not tricked me and I am fine and we are to be wed."

"Ah, but Stafford, you are wrong. I *have* tricked you."

Michael and Kathryn snapped their gazes up into Harold Stafford's wild eyes and found themselves staring into the barrel of a long pistol. Perched on his horse, Harold Stafford let out a long, satisfied cackle.

"Your little lady underestimated me, Stafford. She thought that my plan had only one grand ending but in truth, this was the ending I sought. I knew she would run and you would be waiting and I would have you cornered here. Another messy accident would not sit well with the *ton* and there might be a shadow on my ascendance. No, I need to have you killed here in the Dials, fallen upon by thieves during an assignation with your less-than-worthy American whore."

"Ah, Stafford, a splendidly intricate plan. Now you have me, you can send Kathryn on her way."

"No, you will not…" she demanded.

"Look at the lovebirds. No, Stafford, your Kathryn is just the person I want to be here. Her death will cause you the pain you so richly deserve and I intend on killing her first to torture you."

Michael's hold on Kathryn's elbow stiffened into iron as he contemplated the force he would need to use to push her when the gun discharged. "Surely not even you would shoot a lady, Harold? Isn't that below a man of your stature?"

"A man of my stature? I have no stature since you took what was mine…Catherine. She was *my* love and I believe the child she carried was mine. She tricked you into marrying her because she wanted you. And you took her because of that misguided sense of honor of yours. I saw how little attention you paid her and she groveled at your feet. I felt her death to my bones. The only joy was knowing she had taken the child with her that you seemed to want.

"You rejected her, Harold. She had no one else to turn to for her babe."

"She should have given me a chance if she had really wanted me," Harold spat, his voice rising even higher with his rage.

"You should have married her before you ruined her," Michael declared icily.

"I would have if I had known. It's her fault and your fault. Now, I will take your *new* Kathryn and visit on you the pain you caused me."

With that, Michael saw Harold steel his grip, sight the target and pull the trigger…the sound so loud it echoed off the confining walls of the close buildings. Michael pushed Kathryn with all due force hoping to make a fraction's difference in the bullet's trajectory, then dove for her as she stumbled limply back on the cobbles. Michael caught her arm, at that moment feeling the warm liquid seep through the fabric of her sleeve. In the dark, the widening stain shone black on the borrowed linen shirt. "*Kathryn, no!*" he bellowed.

Falling with her to the street trying to place his body between hers and the unforgiving cobbles, Michael's glare aimed in Stafford's direction where he saw the bastard slip slowly off the saddle, his lifeless form hitting the street in a gangly pile. Stafford's frightened horse bolted leaving him alone, the accompanying pool of dark liquid quickly forming a flowing river of blood.

"Kathryn, Kathryn?" The blood stain on her arm was growing steadily, dripping over her shoulder and the pressure of his hand was not enough to stanch it. He tore at her shirttails for bandages and whispered to her to keep her with him while sweat stung his eyes and tears dripped on her ashen face. He found the opening in her fine skin just below her shoulder under the torn sleeve of her arm and placed a bundle of cloth into the wound. Then he wound more strips from her now shredded clothing around her body as a bandage. It was again a terrible sense of *déjà vous*.

"Michael, how is she?" a familiar voice asked from behind him. Matthew Drake was leaning over Harold Stafford, two pistols in hand.

"Matthew, is he…"

"Yes, but how is Kathryn?"

"She's hit, bleeding heavily but breathing. Help me get her to the carriage."

Michael sent Worley ahead on horseback to warn the staff of Kathryn's injury. His coachman drove like the devil was chasing them and thankfully, when they gained the mews, two footmen were waiting to meet him and help her into the house flooded with light. Hallthorpe admitted them through the rear, the look of fear in place of his usual elegant façade.

~ * ~

Kathryn's lids lifted slowly. Her head and arm ached…why her arm was throbbing, she couldn't remember…but it was. She drank in the glorious surroundings. Vivid colors—oranges and lavenders, blues and greens met her eyes. She felt silk sheets sliding under her caress, smelled a soft hint of perfume, something expensive and for her, wonderfully subtle. Saw a beautiful oval mirror, tiny glass bottles on the dresser. Beside her, a delicate silver candelabra glowed gently, and in the chair by her bed, Michael's slumped, disheveled form.

She regarded him for some minutes, with his short midnight curls drooping over his forehead and black lashes resting on his high cheekbones. His breathing was strong but his color was…pale. He had probably been sleeping in the chair for…*ow*…she moved her left arm and a stabbing pain so real it stole her breath, ripped through her shoulder. She sucked in another breath and with her sudden movement, Michael roused.

"Kathryn, you're awake." She had been unconscious for hours, maybe days, he could no longer tell day from night for his vigil at her bed had been his only concern, so he infused each word with the relief he felt. The Doctor had feared her loss of blood might prevent her from ever waking but her strength had surprised them all. When that first morning had dawned and she was still with him, Michael knew somehow, she would survive and he would not lose her. He *could not* lose her after all they had been though and how deeply she was a part of him. "You gave Hallthorpe a terrible fright and Mrs. Staggs has been an absolute tyrant over you. I am surprised she allowed me to sleep here last night."

Kathryn gave him her bravest smile. "You slept here last night? In that chair? It seems we've played this scene before, haven't we?"

"So we have. Well, actually I read for a while and talked to you and only once I determined that I had most assuredly won our latest argument, I drifted off."

"Harold...is he..." She was afraid of the answer. If he was still out there, Michael was still in grave danger.

"Yes, Matthew Drake was with me. You didn't think I'd let an idiot like Harold Stafford outflank me, did you?"

"Well, I doubt this was in your plan." She raised her arm and winced. Teasing him at her own expense. Well, there wasn't much point.

Suddenly serious, Michael said, "No. You getting shot was not in my plan. His getting shot *was* in my plan. The part that truly was not in my plan was your disappearance. I thought you had tried to leave me." He said it softly, plaintively.

"I thought it was time but now I realize I might have been wrong."

"You *were* wrong. This is your home now."

As if he had asked her a question with that last statement, she fixed a playful grin on her face and said, "I remember something about marriage...?" her words trailed off.

"Yes, well about that. There was the little matter of your injury and the disposing of the crimes against Harold and well, we had to postpone the wedding."

Her heart sank into her stomach and she held the pasted on smile as best she could. "I understand." She bowed her head.

"Do you?" He grinned at her, then winked.

"I—I…don't guess I do, actually." All of this teasing was making her exceedingly tired.

"My love, your bravery is all the *ton* is talking about and as I am the newest Duke and together we rolled up one of London's most notorious criminals to boot. Everyone wants to attend our wedding. We are to be wed in four weeks, once you are well, at St. George's."

"St. George's Cathedral?" Her eyes grew wide. "Me, a wedding in …I can't think. What will I wear? How will I ever plan that kind of a wedding?"

"Darling, that will be entirely the pleasure of my aunt, sister and various relations who have been chomping at the bit for you to rouse so they could get started. It is making Agatha and Cassandra the absolute most sought after party guests you know. Telling our story. It's been declared more romantic than Mr. Shakespeare's *Romeo and Juliet*!"

She assembled every last bit of her energy and blessed him with her most loving smile and she saw that he recognized it for what it was. He dropped a whispered kiss on her lips, the sensation sending shivers through her and she pulled him to her, pressing her lips to his ear. "Well, since they have all the details handled, I guess you'll just have to keep me entertained." And then *she* winked at *him*.

Michael knew that at any minute he might be shuffled from her room by Mrs. Staggs but could not resist the urge to slide between the sheets with her. "How do you like your room? I did it like this because you said you liked bright colors."

"My room? This is my room? Where are we?"

"We're back in Asterleigh House of course, on Grosvenor Square. Our home."

"And this is my room? I had always stayed in the Dowager's room." She was genuinely surprised.

"Well, this is the room where your clothes will hang and your maid will attend your hair, but our Chamber lies through there. You will sleep with me."

"But for right now, you are in *my* bed." Her naughty whisper prickled his skin and he slid his fingers gently over the wound to test the security of her bandages.

"My dear, are you up to showing me your appreciation for this room?"

"Yes, Michael. The bullet hole is in my arm I believe. However, you will have to do more of the heavy lifting." He set to work doing his best to show her the benefits of silk sheets and she showed him just how much she appreciated them.

Epilogue

The music trilled and they began the slow procession back down the aisle waving to the few people she did know and smiling for all of the others. She had waited for this moment to break the news, knowing it would be a most triumphant impropriety.

"Michael, darling?"

He regarded her with an eyebrow raised and kept his smiling eyes trained down the line of guests. "Yes, my love?"

"What is the proper name given to the...the *heir* to the Asterleigh Dukedom?"

"Hawthorne. My heir is the Marquess of Hawthorne. Why do you want...?" He looked at her with his big baby browns and when she winked, his mouth dropped open.

"You're gawking, darling. Close your mouth and smile," she teased.

"Do you know for sure?'

"Oh, very sure. I do believe he will be here in time for Easter."

"Well Duchess, that is very improper...what will the matrons say when they realize we anticipated our wedding?" he returned sheepishly.

"They will probably say, *about demmed time* he got on with his nursery."

They reached the nave and he turned to kiss her right there with every eye in the great cathedral trained on them. "I love you my most perfect Duchess. You are the woman of my dreams."

"And you are the man of mine, love."

Kathryn refused to allow sadness to creep into her joyous wedding day but she could not help but miss that her sister was not at her wedding as the maid of honor.

While the Duke and Duchess strolled into their future together, Kathryn's sister, Christine, would soon be finding herself in a hayloft far, far from home. Her dream would soon be coming to life.

About the Author

Olivia lives in Birmingham, Alabama with her handy husband Henry, two children, cats, and a dog. When she is not writing, or reading romance, Olivia works full time in non-profit fundraising and squeezes in an occasional three- or even six-mile run.

https://www.facebook.com/oliviaritchromances/?hc_ref=SEARCH&fref=nf

www.ingramcontent.com/pod-product-compliance
Lightning Source LLC
Chambersburg PA
CBHW030451250626
47154CB00003BA/1226